Robert G. Barrett  where he worked ... years he moved to ... New South Wales. R... ... a number of films and TV commercials but prefers to concentrate on a career as a writer. He is the author of fifteen books, including *So What Do You Reckon?*, a collection of his columns for *People* magazine, and *Mud Crab Boogie*, his previous novel published by HarperCollins.

Visit Bob's official web site
and the home of Team Norton at:
http://www.robertgbarrett.com.au

GOODOO GOODOO

GOODOO GOODOO

ROBERT G. BARRETT

HarperCollins*Publishers*

HarperCollins*Publishers*

First published in Australia in 1998
by HarperCollins*Publishers* Pty Limited
ACN 009 913 517
A member of the HarperCollins*Publishers* (Australia) Pty Limited Group
http://www.harpercollins.com.au

Copyright © Robert G. Barrett 1998

This book is copyright.
Apart from any fair dealing for the purposes of private study, research,
criticism or review, as permitted under the Copyright Act, no part may be
reproduced by any process without written permission.
Inquiries should be addressed to the publishers.

HarperCollins*Publishers*
25 Ryde Road, Pymble, Sydney, NSW 2073, Australia
31 View Road, Glenfield, Auckland 10, New Zealand
77–85 Fulham Palace Road, London, W6 8JB, United Kingdom
Hazelton Lanes, 55 Avenue Road, Suite 2900, Toronto, Ontario M5R 3L2
and 1995 Markham Road, Scarborough, Ontario M1B 5M8, Canada
10 East 53rd Street, New York NY 10032, USA

National Library of Australia Cataloguing-in-Publication data:

Barrett, Robert G.
    Goodoo goodoo.
    ISBN 0 7322 6737 4
    1. Norton, Les (Fictitious character) – Fiction.
    I.Title
A823.3

Cover illustration by Brad Quinn
Printed in Australia by Griffin Press Pty Ltd, Adelaide
on 50gsm Ensobulky

5 4 3 2 1
02 01 00 99 98

A MESSAGE FROM THE AUTHOR

Actually, there ain't no real message. Things are back to normal and the books should be coming out around November again. To all those people good enough to write, I'm up to my neck in letters at the moment and you'll have to bear with me, but I'm doing my best to answer them all. I also want to thank all those people who come along to the book signings. I truly appreciate the way you queue up so patiently and I do my best to press the flesh, smile for the snapshots and sign everything that's put in front of me. The possum lady said *Goodoo Goodoo* T-shirts are now available. She also said to thank everyone for buying the T-shirts. She's been able to get her broken nose straightened and the ear she had half chewed off in another fight surgically reconstructed. If you want to see the result, check her out on the web site.

In fact you should check out the web site when you get the chance. HarperCollins are running some easy competitions and you can win all sorts of good prizes. The wombat people also said to say thanks for the donations. They've moved house so they can be closer to the action and save more of this endangered species. In their words, it's 'wombat heaven'.

For any readers interested in the off-beat music that appears in my books, Festival are bringing out a twenty track CD called Les Norton's King Hits. Check it out at your nearest music shop. I think you'll be pleasantly surprised.

In the meantime, I'm off to Long Bay Gaol to meet and greet the house guests. So if I get out of there in one piece, I'll either see you at the next book signing, on the web site, or Les will see you in his next adventure.

All the best.

Robert G. Barrett

A percentage from the royalties of this book is being donated to The Wombat Rescue and Research Project. Lot 4. Will-O-Wyn Valley. Murrays Run. NSW. 2325. Any other donations will be gratefully accepted.

DEDICATION

This book is dedicated to Gold Medallist Heather Turland. If what she accomplished and how she accomplished it isn't an inspiration to all Australians, nothing is.

As far as Norton was concerned, life was definitely worth living. You just took the good with the bad, the yin with the yang, and you couldn't go wrong. Yes, the big, red-headed Queenslander smiled to himself as he took another mouthful of orange juice, wriggled his backside around on his lounge and gazed across at the TV flickering away on the other side of the room. You wouldn't be dead for quids would you. You wouldn't be Elvis or Aristotle Onassis for all their money.

It was a cool Tuesday evening at the start of another winter in Sydney. The sun had tucked itself into bed about an hour previous and outside it was cloudy with one of the many, brisk, sou'westers to come, whipping across the roofs, along the streets then over the white sands of famous Bondi Beach and out to sea. Norton was seated comfortably in his loungeroom wearing an old blue tracksuit, watching the early news on TV, and not worrying all that much about the chilly weather outside. In the morning he was jetting off to sunny Cairns to go whitewater rafting, but in about an hour's time he was going down the beachfront to try his hand at something completely different. Norton smiled to himself again as a raft of commercials appeared on the screen — yes, all you have to do is roll with the punches and take the good with the bad. He raised his glass of OJ and winked up at the sky outside. And if it's okay with you boss, I'll take good over bad anytime.

Les was still seeing Tae-kwon-do Kate on a fairly regular basis, although she always seemed to keep him just a little at arms-length. However, her two big, ugly brothers still gave Norton the impression they'd like to have him dangling on a length of rope. Katherine genuinely liked Les and she knew Norton's feelings for her, but somehow between Norton's unsavoury employment background and the tie-in with Nizegy, who was subsequently busted huge time, she had put two and two together and had half convinced herself that Les might have been involved.

And speaking of Neville Nizegy, somehow it appeared the rotten swine had allegedly escaped. He was allegedly well and truly in the hands of the constabulary one minute, the next minute he allegedly wasn't. It made great headlines and the media had a field day with it. He was alleged to have gotten away in a helicopter. Alleged to have dug a tunnel out of Long Bay in record time. Been kidnapped by allegedly crooked prison warders and corrupt police who allegedly tortured him to try and find out where the rest of the loot was. The mail Norton and the team at the Kelly Club got was a little different. Evidently there was a huge blow-up between the Federal Police, the NSW Police and everybody else involved. They all swooped on the garage in Coogee at once and were all forced to count the loot in front of each other. So no one could get any of it. There was no shortage of allegations and nasty words flying around between the parties involved and somehow, in between the allegations and nasty words, Nizegy allegedly vanished.

In the course of their inquiries, two detectives called in to have a word with Les late one afternoon. Their timing couldn't have been better. Kathy happened to have called in earlier as well and it was the first time she'd ever seen two NSW detectives in full attack mode; guns on hips, notebooks at the ready. As well as giving Les the third degree they even asked Kathy her name and address and where she was at the time. But what could Les tell them? Only the truth. If they didn't believe him, they could check the hotel register in Wagga Wagga and watch the grand final replay on TV. The tape was there with the others. However, he had absolutely nothing to do with the big Russian getting poisoned. The cops had left reasonably satisfied, and Kathy had left reasonably unsatisfied. So even though Les had fluked himself a nice little earner when he accidently found the Kruggerands in Nizegy's other garage, he reckoned it might not be such a good idea to go cashing them in around town for the time being. So he had left them buried in the backyard with the rest of the loot. There was no doubt it was as good as money in the bank, and who knew what the price of gold might be a year or so down the track.

He had also finally got his precious rock pool finished. The tiles he ended up buying were that close to matching it didn't matter — so if he came across the Irish scaffolder again he could tell him to stick the original ones, if he ever found them, fair up his sweet Rosie O'Grady. His old mate with the monster boobs, Evelyn, was still keen and she was right about the ABC. Evelyn was now back nursing at a private hospital in Chatswood. So between her shiftwork and Norton's shiftwork and Kathy keeping him shifted to the side a bit, Les was getting enough KFC — kind female companions — to keep him more than happy. And despite Kathy not quite flinging herself down in front of Les, ripping off her knickers and screaming out her undying love for him, she'd still split the bill sometimes if they went out for dinner or do him a favour now and again. For instance, of late — and for a lousy hundred dollars — she had got Les two days at a nice resort in Cairns, bumped up to business class in the plane and a day's whitewater rafting thrown in. Kathy was going to some travel agents convention on the Gold Coast and part of the contra deal for the agency was a spare ticket. She told Les that if he was interested it was his for a hundred simoleans. Les made Kathy repeat with her hand across her heart that this was all strictly honest and there was definitely no shenanigans involved. She had said yes and so he took it. Kathy had already been gone three days and

Les had taken the whole week off from work, getting Big Danny to stand in for him.

But in the meantime Les had scored a gig as a guest disc jockey on a small FM radio station that had opened up in Bondi, working out of the Bondi Hotel. The station was run on a shoestring budget and on a good day the band reached across Curlewis Street and to the second line of breakers off the beach. Somehow it worked its way up to Cox Avenue where Warren picked it up first and now they both listened to it. Mainly because it had catchy jingles, bugger all ads and didn't play any of that horrible baby boomer music the other FM stations like to soak you with. 99FM was also starting to get quite a cult following around the eastern suburbs; and if there was one thing both Les and Warren liked, it was having a cult to follow. For a bit of a promotion the station ran a quiz, idea being you rang up and if you were the first to answer you won the gig plus ten bucks and a T-shirt. The question was: Who was John Simon Ritchie and what band did he play in? Les knew that. Sid Vicious and the band was the Sex Pistols. Les rang up and next thing he knew, he'd won a 99FM T-shirt, his cheque was in the mail and he was going on air the following Tuesday — which was today — at seven. This suited Norton admirably. He had to be up around six to get to the airport with plenty of time to catch his flight, so he could be home, have a mug of Ovaltine and be in bed with his teddy bear by eleven at the latest. He smiled across at the flickering TV again. Les Norton

Disc Jockey. He liked the sound of that. Or what about — Les Norton, radio announcer? That was even better. Or — The Les Norton Show on 99FM. No, he had a better idea — Wolfman Les. Yeah, that was it. He finished his orange juice and reached across for the remote. Whatever I call myself, I'd better get my finger out, he thought. Warren'll be home from the Acme house for the mentally deficient shortly and by the time I get my shit together it'll be showtime. He zapped the TV set then got up, strolled out to the kitchen and rinsed his glass.

Before long Les was showered, had the CDs picked out for his gig and everything packed for his two days in Cairns, with time left over for a cup of coffee. He was sitting in the kitchen wearing his comfiest jeans, a white FM Stereo 107.1 T-shirt the Mud Crabs had sent him from Wagga Wagga, and the East German navy jacket he had conned off the big Russian when Warren arrived home and walked into the kitchen.

'Well, well, well,' said Norton, glancing up from his coffee. Warren was sporting a double-breasted, char-grey suit, a purple shirt, a purple and yellow tie and a pair of grey suede cowboy boots. 'If it isn't Bryan Ferry himself. How's it going Bryan? Still got the shits cause Jerry left you for ol' rubber lips?'

'Get fucked, Les,' replied Warren. 'You don't have to go to meetings with clients, who are ... Italian. And fuckin' cunts as well.' He looked across at the Kelvinator. 'Any piss left in the fridge?'

'Yeah, heaps. Get into it.'

Warren went to open the fridge then changed his mind. 'No, fuck piss. I need something stronger. A vodka.'

'Stollys' sweetie,' purred Les. 'Or wouldn't a hot shot advertising executive like you prefer a martini at this time of the day?'

'No. I'll have a schooner of fuckin' paint stripper with a pubic hair in it, you fuckin' hillbilly.'

'Suit yourself.'

Les settled back with his coffee while Warren got a bottle of Russian Ultraa from the loungeroom, splashed some into a tall glass, rattled a few lumps of ice and red grapefruit juice in it then took a healthy slurp.

'Ohh yeah ... that's better.' Warren took another sip then sat down at the kitchen table opposite Les. He took another sip then looked at Norton over his glass. 'Hey, aren't you going disc jockeying or something tonight?'

'That's right,' nodded Les. 'A rick-a-poodly-and-a-fannnng-doodly. This is Wolfman Les. So sit back at ease, or get down on your knees. Cause I got the CDs that please. Ow, ow, ow!'

Warren nodded enthusiastically. 'Yeah. That's it, Les. Why don't you go on air just like that? Do it baby.'

'You'd like me to, wouldn't you, Woz? Go on the station and make a complete wally of myself.'

'You're going to anyway. In fact, what are they paying you? Ten bucks?' Warren pulled a twenty from his pocket. 'I'll give you another twenty if you'll say that then play "Heaven Is A Place On Earth" by Belinda Carlisle and "Sugar Baby Love" by the Rubettes. Back to back.'

Norton looked impassively at Warren for a moment. 'I'll tell you what I might play, smart arse,' he said. 'How about The Rent Man Blues. If you can afford to throw twenty dollar bills around, you can afford to weigh in more at the end of the week. I'm putting the rent up.'

'What?' Warren slumped back in his chair horrified. 'No, Les, you can't. I'm in enough shit as it is. It'd break me.'

'Are you fair dinkum?' Norton matched Warren's look of horror with one of controlled outrage. 'Christ! When was the last time I put the rent up? They still had horse drawn trams going up and down George Street.'

'You can't, Les. You just can't.' Warren shook his head sadly, took another drink and quickly changed the subject. 'Would you believe I have to get up at three-thirty tomorrow morning?'

'Shit! I haven't forced you into doing burglaries, have I?'

'We're driving up to the Blue Mountains in a Holden. To find a location to shoot an ad for a fuckin' Volvo.'

'This time of the year?' Norton shivered. 'I'm glad it's you and not me.'

'Yeah. What about you, you cunt. You want to make life a misery for me. And you're going to Cairns in the morning. How's your form?'

Les nodded. 'Yep. Fun in the sun for Uncle Les.' Norton rose from the kitchen table and buttoned up his jacket. 'But no matter where I'm going tomorrow, right now I've got to go deejaying.' He rinsed his coffee cup and put it next to the sink. 'I'll discuss the rent issue with you when I return.'

'Yeah, do that,' replied Warren. 'I'll be in bed asleep.'

'Okay. Well, there's a cassette in the stereo. Will you tape this for me so I can have a listen when I get home?'

'Righto.'

'Thanks, Woz.' Les gave his flatmate a smile. 'If I don't see you before, I'll see you when I get back from Cairns.'

'Go get 'em, Wolfman. Have a good trip.'

Les picked up his bag of CDs and went out the front door closing it quietly behind him.

It took Les about ten minutes to walk down to the Bondi Hotel. It was still early on this cool Tuesday night and there weren't many people around. Les walked straight in the Campbell Parade entrance through the old wooden doors with the shiny brass fittings, glanced at the girl behind the desk in the lobby, who didn't seem to notice him, then stopped in front of the lift doors and pressed the button. There was no movement, and there was still no movement about three minutes later. Les gave the lift a brief once up and down. It looked like something out of an old black-and-white movie; any minute Les expected the doors to open and Sydney

Greenstreet would walk out followed by Peter Lorre or Humphrey Bogart carrying the Maltese Falcon. There was a carpeted set of stairs with freshly painted, light green walls on his left. Les gave the lift another minute then started climbing. In next to no time he was on the third floor landing.

There were rooms on either side of the landing and there was a balcony ahead. Les walked out and had a look around. Campbell Parade was on the left, there were buildings in front of him and where the hotel angled out from the balcony on his right, Les saw a red neon sign saying ON AIR. The sign was blinking on and off above a window facing Campbell Parade. I'd say that's it, he smiled to himself. He walked over and knocked on a door with a shiny brass 99 on the front. It was opened a few seconds later by a happy-faced bloke, a bit shorter than Les, with dark hair and dark eyes. He was wearing jeans, a blue jacket and a black and green 99FM T-shirt.

'Hey. You must be Les,' he smiled, and offered his hand.

'That's right,' replied Norton.

'I'm Ron. Come on in, mate.'

Les shook Ron's hand and followed him inside as he closed the door behind them.

Ron noticed Norton's overnight bag. 'Did you bring some CDs with you?'

'Yeah,' answered Les. 'A bit of this. And a bit of that.'

'That's good. I want you to play your own music.'

They went down a short corridor past a room on the right with a whiteboard on one wall. At the end was a door to a Gents with a cymbal hung above it; the studio was on the left and on the right another door to some kind of office. Les followed Ron inside. The office was a jumble of rock posters and photos of bands and singers, along with other rock'n'roll bric-a-brac. There was a small bar fridge in one corner, a rack full of CDs against one wall and a half open window with mottled blue curtains. A fax machine sat next to a CD-ROM on one table and on another small table was a computer with the 99FM logo spinning around on the screen. Standing next to the window was a tall young bloke wearing a black shirt, black jeans and a pair of Bono-type glasses with black frames and orange lenses.

'Les. This is Max,' said Ron. 'Max'll be your panel operator.'

'Hello, Max. Nice to meet you.'

'Yeah. You too, Les.'

Les gave Max's hand a quick shake as a coloured man in a white cardigan and blue jeans came from the studio. A pair of rimless glasses sat on a lean face under a shaved head and Les thought he was an American, but when he spoke he had a fairly broad, North England accent.

'Well, that's it for me, man. I'm splitting. I have to be at Leichhardt by seven-thirty.'

'Righto, Kaz. I'll see you tomorrow,' said Ron.

'See you fellas.' Kaz gave Les a quick wink then left.

Ron pointed a finger at Les. 'Okay, big guy. You're on.'

'Follow me, Les,' said Max, moving away from the window.

The studio had high ceilings, blue walls and was about as big as the spare room at Chez Norton. The panel faced the wall on the right as you walked in and sat next to another window with blue curtains, only this one overlooked the darkened beach and park outside. A microphone jutted out from amongst the buttons, lights and sliders on the panel with a CD stacker sitting on top. Above this was a silent TV set flickering on a swivel arm in the corner and a case of CDs stood against the wall as you walked in. Max pointed Les to a swivel chair in front of the CD case with another microphone on a stand between Les and the panel then sat down on another swivel chair in front of the controls. He adjusted a set of headphones over his ears then handed Les another set as Norton unzipped his overnight bag and had a quick rummage through his CDs.

'How do you want to do this?' Max asked and suggested at the same time. 'I'll introduce you, then you can say, "Hello I'm Les" or whatever. Then we'll play your music and you can say what tracks they are, and so on.'

'Sounds good to me,' replied Les, adjusting his own headphones.

'I'll just get a quick sound level.'

Les spoke a few words into the mike then handed

Max two CDs. 'Track five on that one. And track eight on the other.'

'No worries.' Max placed the two CDs in the stacker above him as the track playing cut out. There was a blurb for the station then Max pushed another button and one of the sliders. 'It's just after seven o'clock at 99FM, Bondi. I'm Max, and with me in the studio is Les Norton, the winner of our 99FM quiz. Good evening to you, Les.'

'Hello, Max. It's nice to be here.' Norton was a little taken aback at first hearing his own voice coming through the speakers, then thought, well, I'm here. Why not have some fun and get Warren's twenty bucks at the same time. 'And hello out there in radioland. Yes this is me. Wolfman Les. Ow, ow, ow! I'm here for an hour or so on a cold night in Bondi, before I jet off to sunny Cairns in North Queensland tomorrow morning. And first up is a request for Warren Edwards of Bondi. Who just jetted in from Bangkok after spending ten years in gaol for smuggling heroin. Here's your two songs, Warren.'

Max gave Les a quick double blink followed by a bemused smile then pushed a button and 'Rattle Snake Highway' by John Fogerty pumped out over the airwaves followed by 'Gettin' Gone' by Lee Kernaghan. The two tracks cut out, Les back announced them then continued over his microphone.

'Like I said, those two were a request for Warren Edwards, late of the Bangkok Hilton. Now ... one for all the girls out there.'

Max pushed the same buttons and 'Trouble Is A Woman' from Gina Jeffries graced the 99FM airwaves followed by 'Just Like A Woman' by Johnny Winter then Shanley Dell's 'Full Time Job'.

After that Les slotted into his DJ gig like an old pro; to him it wasn't much different to standing outside the Kelly Club and waffling on to the various punters as they came inside. Max didn't say much. He just slotted in the jingles and the station blurbs while Les nattered away over the airwaves announcing what tracks he'd just played or was about to play. Les thought how much fun he was having and as he looked at the cold blackness framed in the window behind Max, how good it was going to be in Cairns the next day.

'Yes listeners,' said Les. 'It sure looks cold outside. But I'll bet it's warm in Cairns. One thing I do know — it's getting very funky in here. Too funky.'

Max pushed the slider and 'Too Funky In Here' by James Brown started boog-a-looing across Bondi followed by The Stranglers' 'Sweet Smell Of Success' plus more jingles and blurbs.

'Ow, ow, ow! This is Wolfman Les on 99FM picking you up out of the rut and putting you down in the groove. We had operation NOAH last week. Or operation dob in your neighbour, as some folks call it. So here's a couple for operation NOAH. Dash Rip Rock and "Let's All Smoke Some Pot". And one of my favourites: "I like Marijuana" by Mojo Nixon. Ow, ow, ow!'

They finished and Les gazed past Max at the window again.

'I'm telling you, listeners. It looks cold enough outside to freeze the balls off an Eskimo's pool table. But not where I'm going up in sunny Cairns. And I sure won't need my hot pants up there.'

Max hit the controls and 'Hot Pants' by the B52s filled the studio. Les handed Max some more CDs, played some more tracks and before he knew it his hour and ten minutes of fame was about over, finishing off the night with 'For Today' — Netherworld Dancing Toys — and one for any parrot heads that might have been listening — 'Barometer Soup' by Jimmy Buffet. That ended and Max handed Les his last CD, then got one ready from amongst the others in the stacker.

'Well, thankyou, Les Norton. Our guest DJ for the night. And I think you'll all agree, that was pretty good.'

'Thankyou, listeners,' replied Norton. 'And thankyou 99FM. Goodnight everybody.'

Max pushed another button, there was a quick jingle then some funky blues track started up and he slipped off his headphones as Les did the same.

'Hey, that was good, Les,' said Max. 'You're a natural.'

'Yeah,' answered Les, draping his headphones over the swivel end of his microphone. 'For a one hour wonder. I think it'd be a bit different if I had to work all those buttons and dials.'

'There's not that much to it.'

Ron came in the door with a big smile on his face. 'Hey, Les. You were great, man.'

'Thanks, Ron. I gave it my best shot,' replied Les.

'I liked the bit about the hot pants too.'

Norton zipped the last CD into his overnight bag and stood up. 'Not quite John Laws. But not bad value for ten bucks and a T-shirt.'

'I might give you a ring and maybe you can come in and do it again, Les?'

'Don't ring me. I'll ring you,' smiled Les. 'That's real showbiz talk, Ron. I like it. The same rate of pay I imagine?'

Ron smiled back and made a gesture with one hand. 'Think of it more as paying your dues, Les.'

'We'll see what happens.'

'Hey. There were a couple of messages for you too.'

'There were?'

Les followed Ron back into the office where he handed Les two small pieces of yellow paper.

'Look at that. You're only on the station one night and already the fan mail's pouring in.'

'Yeah,' answered Les. 'I might have to start a fan club.'

Ron led Norton back to the front door. He was being polite and friendly enough, but it was obvious he had work to do and not a great deal of time for idle chit chat with his new DJ.

'I'll give you a ring when you get back from Cairns, Les. Have a good trip and thanks again for coming in.'

'Yeah, thanks Ron. I'll hear from you then.' Les shook the station owner's hand again and stepped out onto the balcony as the door closed behind him.

It was too dark to read anything standing there; Les walked over to the landing and looked at the two pieces of yellow paper by the light at the top of the stairs. The first one said, 'Hi. You sound like a spunky Capricorn. I'm a sexy Gemini into body chocolate and Origami. Why not drop me a line.' There was a post box number in Bondi Road and the name 'Galaxina Starbuckle'. Yeah, righto Gal baby, mused Les, I'll write as soon as I get home. The other piece of paper, however, stopped Les in his tracks. 'Hi, Les. Remember me? BB. You said if ever I needed a favour to call you. I need a favour. I'll wait for you at Redwoods.' Les looked at the piece of paper again then folded it and put it in his jacket pocket. BB? Norton's eyebrows knitted. Shit! Who was that? Les stared into space for a moment and picked lightly at his chin. It sounds like my old mate Beryl Biscayne. Les slowly started walking down the stairs. By the time he'd reached the bottom everything had started to come back to him.

It was around the time Les first arrived in Sydney from Dirranbandi. He was at the Maroubra Seals Club one Friday night and Beryl was there celebrating her divorce. She was a brunette, older than Les, with big round boobs and a backside that was starting to go the same way. She had a nice smile and a pleasant nature and lovely, soft violet eyes emphasised by the slow, lazy way she batted her eyelids. She was wealthy and if Les remembered right her ex-husband was a surgeon. They started dancing and singing and Les finished up back at Beryl's house in Bellevue Hill throwing her up in the air. They'd just started getting into it, however, when the bed collapsed all around them. It wasn't so much from the lust and passion or Norton being some great super stud. When he checked under the bed, Beryl's ex had sawn it almost through before she turfed him out, probably hoping Beryl's first after the divorce would be her last.

Beryl and Les had a liaison for a little while and Les nicknamed her Bouncing Beryl over the way she bounced off the mattress straight back on top of him when the bed fell apart. Les was just about stone broke at the time and living in a shitbox at Bondi Junction which he had to get out of as it was being demolished. Beryl had a rich girlfriend who was going to Europe for a few months and she arranged for Les to stay at her friend's place rent free. All he had to do was look after it. So Les finished up in a big house near Dover Heights for the best part of a year, back on his feet, with a job and all sorts of other good things. They went their separate ways and remained good friends. But Les always appreciated what Beryl did for him and told her he owed her a big one and if she ever needed a favour not to hesitate and look him up. Les couldn't remember the last time he'd seen her, but by the tone of Beryl's short message, this must be it.

He stepped out of the warm hotel foyer into the

cold Bondi night. Redwoods was on the way home. A man would be a cad, a bounder and a complete and utter dropkick if he didn't come to the aid of an old friend in their hour of need ... especially Bouncing Beryl. Les smiled to himself, gripped his overnight bag full of CDs and strode along Campbell Parade towards Redwoods.

It seemed like a quiet night at the restaurant-bar when Les walked in. Staff looked thin on the ground. There was a couple having a meal near the front, a few more down the back, and another couple at the bar — a man standing and a woman seated. The man was tall and fit-looking with dark hair, dressed much the same as Les. Although it had been a while, the woman was definitely Beryl Biscayne. She'd spread a bit more, had her hair styled shorter and her face looked a little aged, even hardened. But there was no mistaking the way she moved those violet eyes. She'd squeezed herself into a pair of green, denim jeans and a matching denim shirt with a knee-length, brown suede jacket across her shoulders, opened down the front. On her feet were a pair of shiny silver Sergio Rossi boots.

Les walked over and smiled down at her. 'Hello BB. How's things? I got your message and came as soon as I could.'

'You're still a sweetheart, Les, aren't you?' Beryl stood up, put her arms around Les and gave him a cuddle and a peck on the cheek. Les cuddled Beryl back and gave her a quick peck on the lips amidst a whiff of expensive perfume and the rattle and shine of expensive jewellery. Beryl took her arm away from Les and turned to the man next to her. 'Les, this is Raymond. Raymond is my driver.'

'Hello, Ray,' said Les. 'Nice to meet you.'

'Yes. You too, Les.' Raymond shook Norton's hand then turned to Beryl. 'I might go down the back and have coffee so you can talk alone.'

'That would be good, Raymond. Les is a dear friend.'

'Yes. We're certainly friends all right. Aren't we, Bouncing Beryl?'

Raymond left, Beryl gave Les a half-smile then sat down and caught the barman's eye. 'Anyway, let me buy you a drink, Les. What will you have?'

'Just a light thanks, BB. A three point three'll do.'

Les put his bag on the floor and eased himself onto the stool next to Beryl. His drink arrived, he toasted Beryl's Frangelico and ice then they got into some small talk. He still worked for Price, he still lived in Bondi, the deejaying was just a one-off thing. Beryl still had the home at Bellevue Hill, she'd been married and divorced again, but times were good. She owned a unit at Rose Bay and she'd recently bought another one in Lamrock Avenue that she was thinking of doing something with. She was round at the Bondi unit with some people who were staying there who happened to be listening to 99FM when Les came on.

Norton couldn't help himself. 'So what did you think of me as a DJ, Beryl?' he asked, taking a sip of beer. 'Grouse or what?'

An odd, half-smile seemed to flit across Beryl's face for a moment. 'No. You were good Wolfman,' she said. 'I imagine some of those tracks you played banged a few tambourines round the old neighbourhood.'

'Thanks,' answered Les, raising his bottle. 'I'd like to think I shook the dust off a few speakers out there in radioland.' Les looked at Beryl for a moment then put his beer on the bar and took the piece of yellow paper from his pocket and read it to her. 'So what's the favour, Beryl?' he asked, putting the piece of paper away. 'What can I do to help you?' He glanced across at Raymond. 'Though you seem like you're in capable hands over there.'

'No, it's nothing like that.' Beryl's face dropped and Les wasn't sure but he could sense some kind of a tear coming on. 'It's just that I heard you say on the radio that you were going up to Cairns in North Queensland.'

'That's right. For a couple of days. I'm going whitewater rafting.'

'Well ...' The tear brimmed up in the corner of Beryl's eye as if it was waiting for its cue to roll down her puffy cheek. 'While you're up there ... could you do me a favour?'

'Sure. What is it?'

'Do you think ... you could see if you could find my daughter, Jade, for me?'

'Daughter?' Norton was genuinely surprised. 'Shit! You kept that quiet Beryl. I never even knew you had one.'

'She was taken from me when I was very young.'

'Kind of like the stolen generation, Beryl. Only white.'

'Exactly, Les.' The tear drop took its cue and rolled down Beryl's cheek onto her double chin. She batted her eyes at Les and put her hand on his as another got ready to roll down the opposite cheek. 'But it's not only my daughter, Les. It's my granddaughter.'

'You've got a granddaughter too?'

'Yes. My little Amy.' Beryl batted her eyes again and two lines of tears started glistening. 'She's the one I'm mainly worried about, Les. Poor little thing.'

Les offered Beryl a hanky. She thanked him, wiped her eyes and gave her nose a delicate blowing. Les gave her as sympathetic a look as he could muster under the circumstances.

'Is your daughter in some kind of trouble, Beryl?'

'No. Nothing like that.' Beryl took an envelope from her handbag, opened it and handed Les a colour snapshot. 'That's a photo of Amy's mother.'

The photo was taken on the back of a dive boat. Scattered round the deck were scuba tanks and other diving equipment with the sea in the background. On the left was a super fit-looking brunette with a sixpack stomach and a build like a lightweight boxer only with perfectly round breasts in an orange bikini. She was wearing sunglasses, but they couldn't hide a pretty, chiselled face and perfect white teeth. Les put her age at around twenty. On the right was a dark-haired man in a pair of white shorts and sunglasses with a neatly trimmed, pepper and salt beard. He looked about thirty or a fit forty, but the girl was a complete stunner.

'So that's your daughter Jade, eh?' Beryl nodded and mopped her nose again. 'Who's the bloke?'

'That's her boyfriend. Hordern Genting. He's Amy's father.'

Les looked at the photo again then gave a double, then triple blink. 'Hey wait a minute Beryl. I know these two. They were in the paper. They're those two scuba divers that went missing off Cairns. He was a scientist or something.'

'A geneticist,' nodded Beryl.

'There was a rumour they faked their own deaths and came back on another boat. They found a message or something.'

Beryl nodded again as the tears started to dry up. 'Yes. It was in all the papers. About a year ago.'

Les looked at the photo in a different light. 'So one of those missing scuba divers is your daughter Jade?'

'That's right, Les. And I think she's still alive.'

Norton slowly shook his head. 'Christ Beryl. The army, the air force and half the bloody Queensland water police searched the area. And they couldn't find hide nor hair of them.'

'Yes. But I'm sure some people in Queensland have definitely seen Jade since then.'

Les looked at his old friend Beryl as if she was either desperate for information or just plain stupid. 'All right,' he shrugged. 'I'll ask around for them in

Cairns. But fair dinkum. I'm only going there for two days. And I'm definitely going whitewater rafting on one of the days.'

'I'm not talking about Cairns, Les,' replied Beryl.

'You're not?'

'No.' Beryl gave her head a shake. 'I want you to go to Cooktown.'

'Cooktown? Shit! That is the end of the line. I've never been there. But it's a bloody long way away.'

'It's not that far from Cairns, Les.' Beryl looked at Les as if she expected him to say something. But he didn't bother. 'How about I hire you a four-wheel drive. Arrange two, maybe three night's accommodation in Cooktown. And you take a look around up there for me. And if you come back with any worthwhile information, I'll give you twenty-five thousand dollars.'

Les breathed in a whistle. 'Twenty-five grand. That's a lot of chops, BB. You must want your daughter bad?'

'I told you, Les,' sniffed Beryl. 'It's my granddaughter.'

'Yeah, Amy.' Les took a sip of beer. 'All right. I'll take a run up to Cooktown for you and have a look around. But shit, Beryl, don't expect too much. I mean, I'm not from the missing persons bureau. And I sure ain't no private eye.'

'I know that, Les.' Beryl smiled softly. 'But you're a guy that gets around. And you're very friendly. You never know,' she added with a slight shrug of her shoulders.

'What's your granddaughter look like? Have you got another photo?'

Beryl shook her head. 'I haven't seen her for a long time.' She looked at Norton for a moment. 'But I'm sure you'll recognise Amy when you see her.'

'All right if I keep this photo?'

'Sure. It's the original, but I've got a copy.'

Les stared at the stunning-looking woman in the photo again then absently turned it over. On the back were three neat lines of script written in black biro; they appeared to be poetry. 'Hey, what's this?' he asked.

'Where there's no tune,
through spiders and snakes,
in the big cat.'

Les looked quizically at Beryl. 'What's that supposed to mean?'

Beryl took a sip of Frangelico and shrugged her shoulders. 'I wouldn't have a clue. Jade used to write a lot of poetry. At school,' she added.

Les read the three lines again then shook his head. 'Yeah. Allen Ginsberg eat your heart out.'

'While you're up there, Les, I'd like you to drive out to a place called Cedar Bay, it's not far from Cooktown. She was supposed to have been sighted near there.'

'Okay.' Norton placed the photo back in the envelope. 'Anything else you can tell me?'

'Jade had a girlfriend in Cairns. A chef. Sherry Waldren. She left Cairns about the same time Jade and Hordern disappeared. There's a chance she might be in Cooktown somewhere. She could know something.'

Terrific, Beryl, thought Les. That's a real help. 'Have you been up there yourself?' he asked.

Beryl shook her head. 'No thankyou. Surfers Paradise is far enough into Queensland for me. I'm a Sydney girl.'

'Fair enough,' smiled Les. 'Well, why don't you write down that girl's name, and anything else you think I should know. And I'll ... see what I can do for you.'

Beryl took a notebook and a thin biro from her handbag. She wrote down the girl's name, where Les'd be staying in Cooktown, phone numbers and so on. All Les had to do was find the Avis office in Cairns and buy a map. She also took out a cheque book and made Les out a cheque for five hundred dollars for expenses. Les didn't think it would be doing the right thing accepting money from a grieving mother and was about to knock it back, but then thought how it wasn't actually Beryl's money he was taking; it was only what she'd fleeced from her ex-husbands. He put the cheque in his pocket along with the rest.

'You will tell me when you get back, if you saw either Jade or my granddaughter. Won't you, Les?' said Beryl.

'Of course I will,' replied Les. 'Be nice if I had a photo of Amy though.'

'Don't worry, Les. You'll recognise her when you see her. She'll probably be with her mother.'

'Okay.' Les finished his beer and placed the empty bottle on the bar. 'Well I might leave you to it BB old mate. If for some reason you don't hear from me in Cooktown, I'll see you as soon as I get back. Probably early next week.'

'Thanks, Les,' Beryl smiled. 'You are a sweetheart.' She finished the rest of her Frangelico and picked up her handbag. 'Actually, I was just about to leave myself. Can I offer you a lift?'

'Okay,' shrugged Les. 'Save me walking up the hill in the cold.'

Beryl waved to Raymond who came straight over. 'Could you get the car please Raymond?'

'Sure.'

A minute or two later, headlights shone as a dark green Mercedes pulled up in front of the restaurant; Beryl left some more money on the bar and they walked outside where Raymond had the back door open. Les waited as Beryl got in first, then climbed in after her. Apart from telling Raymond to drop him off at six-ways, not a great deal was said during the short drive up Hall Street. The Mercedes came to a gentle stop near the small park at the end of Cox Avenue and Les got out.

'Okay BB,' he said. 'I'll see what I can find out for you up there. And I'll be in touch.'

'Thanks, Les.' Beryl's violet eyes slowly opened and closed like the shutter doors on a garage. 'You are a sweetheart. And I really appreciate you doing this for me.'

'That's okay. Anytime.'

'Bye, Les.'

Les closed the door and the big car soon disappeared up O'Brien Street. A minute or two later he stepped inside Chez Norton and, knowing Warren was asleep, softly shut the door behind him. After putting his CDs away he changed back into his old blue tracksuit and made a mug of Ovaltine, which he drank quietly in the kitchen with his feet up on the table. He mulled over the night's events: especially his meeting with Beryl.

Well, ain't it funny how things work out, he thought, feeling the warm mug between his hands. One minute I'm going to Cairns for a couple of days whitewater rafting. I open my big mouth on a little radio station for five minutes. And now I'm going to Cooktown. For what? A fuckin' waste of time if you ask me. Still, it could be a bit of fun and I've never been there before ... Les took another thoughtful sip of Ovaltine. There's just a couple of things that seem a little odd though. Beryl said her daughter Jade was taken from her when she was very young. But Bouncing Beryl is definitely no spring chicken. And the girl in that photo is only about twenty. He tapped his fingers on the side of the mug. Knowing my old mate BB though, she's probably laid that on to extract more sympathy while she was squeezing out the tears. Norton had a quiet chuckle to himself.

Then she said she'd never been further north than the Gold Coast. You'd think when her daughter and her boyfriend disappeared she'd be straight up to Cairns to find out what went wrong and if there was any sign of them. Then again, maybe Beryl and her daughter didn't get on. There's a lot of that going on these days. Maybe it is her granddaughter she's worried about. He couldn't say he blamed her if the poor little kid was wandering around on her own up there somewhere, or worse. Les drained the last of his Ovaltine then rinsed the mug and left it on the side of the sink. One thing he did know. Seeing as how his original holiday'd been extended, he'd better throw an extra pair of Reggies and another couple of T-shirts in the swag.

There was nothing much worth watching on TV and he had to be up fairly early the next morning, so after using the bathroom he climbed into bed, switched on the bedlamp and turned to the page of a book he'd been reading. *Underboss: Sammy The Bull Gravano's Story Of Life In The Mafia*. After about twenty minutes or so of Ralph (Ralphie Wigs) Galione, Anthony (Tony Ducks) Corallo, heists, hits and 'Tony don't know nothin' about construction', Norton's eyelids were starting to flicker. He marked the page, turned off the light and seconds later was snoring peacefully.

The first thing Norton thought when he woke up just after six the following morning was how cold it was in the house. Thank Christ I'm getting away for a few days, he muttered to himself as he swung his legs over the bed. When he walked out in the hallway, Les found the main reason it was so cold: when Warren had stumbled out of the house at three-thirty he'd left the front door open. Fuckin' great, Les muttered to himself again as he slammed it shut. A man could have been robbed or raped in his sleep and wouldn't have known. He went to the bathroom then walked into the kitchen and switched on the kettle. There was a note on the table. 'You were shithouse. Wolfman Jack would be rolling over in his grave. The tape is in the stereo and you can get fucked for the twenty dollars.' Les got a biro, wrote PTO on the front then wrote on the back: 'I won't be back till next week. I was great. And the rent goes up twenty bucks.' He pinned it under a fridge magnet on the Kelvinator. He made some coffee and toast then changed into the blue, Sturt University T-shirt the Mud Crabs had sent him and a light crinkly cotton, two-tone blue tracksuit. By the time he'd put some more clothes and things into his carry bag, sorted out all his travel documents, credit cards and whatever in his overnight bag, made a phone call and had another coffee, the taxi was waiting out the front. After making sure the house was secure, the next thing Les knew he was being whisked off to Kingsford Smith Airport.

All he could think about as the driver joined the morning traffic and the cold wind outside blew drizzling rain across the windscreen, was whitewater rafting and how warm it would be in Cairns. He'd worry about Beryl's situation when and if the time came. The traffic was the usual grind, but before long Les had checked in, gone through X-ray and was sitting comfortably in Golden Wing sipping fresh orange juice and nibbling cake. He read the paper as he ate and watched all the suits around him babbling furiously into their mobiles. A second plate of biscuits and cheese was going down well, but unfortunately Norton's plane was ready for boarding. Minutes later he was ensconced in business class in a comfortable seat sipping more orange juice while smiling flight attendants handed him magazines and just about anything else he wanted.

The plane had barely taken off when the in-flight movie came on. Les adjusted his headphones and settled back to watch *The Wedding Singer*. Les wasn't into it long before he was thinking Warren would absolutely love this. It was like watching a corny version of *Seinfeld* the movie. The lead looked like Seinfeld and spoke like Seinfeld and the plot was completely over the top and about absolutely nothing; just like Seinfeld. Norton's meal of a thick, rolled-up sandwich, croissant and coffee arrived, and by the time the wedding singer had sung his last song and Les had eaten the last of his meal they were getting ready to land at Cairns. Oh well, thought Les, as he took off his headphones and the flight attendant removed his tray, I guess it's the great big lumps of nothing that made that movie something. He pushed his overnight bag securely under the seat in front of him, made sure his seat belt was done up and prepared to land.

Apart from an exhilarating feeling at being back in good old Queensland, the first thing Les noticed when he got off the plane was the heat and humidity. Despite a thick band of grey clouds over the low mountains around the city, it felt at least five times hotter than Sydney and Les was already sweating after the short walk to the baggage claim. It wasn't all that crowded and while Norton waited for his travel bag he noticed a woman in a brown and yellow shirt holding a sign saying 'Colony Resort'. Les walked over and told her who he was; she smiled and checked his name on a list just as his bag came round. The woman put it on a trolley, then led Les out to a white shuttle bus from the resort where she stowed his bag underneath; she then ushered him inside. There was a driver wearing the same brown uniform at the wheel and one other person on the bus, a young woman of some description.

She looked to be in her early twenties and quite petite with long, straight blonde hair brushed down either side of a soft, pretty face. Two very inquisitive green eyes, emphasised by two thin circles around the pupils, looked up at Les from above a tiny nose and a tiny pink mouth. She was smiling enough to reveal two rows of tiny, white teeth. The girl was wearing silvery blue boots with silvery pink shoelaces that seemed to change colour with every movement, skin tight harlequin pants in a variety of pastel colours, and a red hangout T-shirt with pyramids, sphinxes, hieroglyphics and a black symbol of Isis on the front. A pink and yellow cotton jacket sewn with gold, silver and black metallic thread and pinned with coloured brooches was over her shoulders, two hologramed circles of red and gold spiders hung from two dainty ears and round her neck was a silver chain holding a pink crystal. This was topped by a sprinkling of glitter through her hair and a turquoise and gold, flame-shaped Bindi stuck on her forehead like a third eye. For her size she had a very full figure and a neat, little behind and seemed to exude an air of gentle, gregarious innocence. Les gave the girl a double blink and mentally nicknamed her the Rainbow Princess then returned her smile and sat down two seats in front of her. The bus took off, there was a delicate aroma of sweet-smelling body oil and the Rainbow Princess moved down to the seat opposite Les.

'Hello,' she said happily. 'How are you?'

Norton couldn't help but give her another double blink before he spoke. 'I'm good thanks,' he answered. 'How's yourself?'

'Terrific.' The girl offered her hand. 'I'm Woody.'

'Hello, Woody. I'm Les.' Although Woody had the tiniest, softest little hand imaginable, it also seemed to have a strange energy that sent a velvety tingle all the way up Norton's huge right arm.

'So, like, what brings you to Cairns, Les?' asked Woody.

'I'm going whitewater rafting,' replied Les. 'Then I'm heading up to Cooktown on Friday.'

Woody's intense green eyes seemed to close in on Norton for a moment. 'You're also looking for something up here too. Aren't you Les?'

Norton didn't quite know how to reply to that. 'Not particularly,' he said, with a smile and slight shake of his head. 'Just a good time. That's all.'

Woody seemed to smile knowingly. 'You're an ace of cups. That's cool.'

Les screwed his face up. 'I'm a what?' he said.

'An ace of cups,' said Woody. 'You've also got a lot of stored up energy. You need to activate your chakras. They're blocked.'

Norton looked at Woody for a moment and decided to change the subject. 'So what about you Rainbow Princess? What are you doing in Cairns?'

'Rainbow Princess.' A tiny laugh tinkled out of Woody's mouth. 'I think I like that.' Then she looked evenly at Les. 'I came to collect some generator crystals. But mainly I'm up here checking out pictograms and magnetic fields.'

Norton screwed up his face again. 'You're what?'

'Crop circles out at Tully. There's some fresh ones this week.' Woody's intense green eyes seemed to beam in on Norton. 'Have you ever had any experiences with UFO's, Les?'

'UFO's? Ohh shit yeah,' answered Les. 'Only the night before last. A little one flew into our kitchen and grabbed a packet of smoked almonds and two mini bottles of Sambuca. I think they were going to a party.' Les looked at Woody for a moment. 'Warren, the bloke I live with, saw them. Not me.'

'Yeah, right.' Woody nodded pensively for a moment. 'They could have been oxygeneric travellers from a different dimension using a non-aligned energy grid.'

Norton pointed a finger at the Rainbow Princess. 'That's exactly what I thought.' Les closed his eyes for second. Christ! Can they find me? Or can they find me?

While Woody prattled on about limitless light, extraterrestrial entities and third density illusions, Les stared through the bus window. Outside, Cairns reminded him briefly of when he was in Honolulu; the lush green, cloud-covered mountains in the background, the old wooden houses, the heat and humidity. Before long the bus drove through the gates of the Colony Resort and pulled up just in front of the main office.

The resort was all shiny glass windows and stout cedar beams, thick wooden poles painted white, angled roofs and polished wooden floors, and was surrounded by healthy pine trees, native shrubs and flower beds. There were bigger buses and cars coming and going in the parking area and across the road from the resort was a football oval. They got off the bus and as soon as Les had a look around he could see why Katherine had tipped him into the Colony Resort. Milling in front of the reception area were groups of fat Japanese, fat pommies and fat Europeans, all looking like barrels of white seal blubber in floral shirts and leather sandals with grey or black socks. The youngest — apart from two hairy legged, female backpackers who could have been extras out of *Tarzan And The Lost City Of The*

Apes — would have been seventy. The resort itself, as well as probably having seen better days, had a tired, unhurried, overly laid-back feel about it and reminded Les of some sort of tropical old folks home. The Rainbow Princess might have been one of the strangest women Les had ever met. But she had a neat little figure, she was no doubt the youngest and best sort in the place and there was something about her kookiness Les kind of liked.

'Hey Woody,' he said, as he opened the door to the reception for her. 'Are you doing anything for dinner tonight?'

Woody seemed to think for a second. 'No, not really,' she replied.

'Well, I have to go into Cairns and pick up a car. If you'd like to give me your room number, it would be my absolute pleasure to call you when I get back, and maybe we could have dinner tonight. Say around ... sevenish?'

'Hey, that sounds really cosmic.' Woody smiled up at Norton. 'But you know what Les ...'

Norton interrupted her. 'You had a feeling this was going to happen.'

'That's right! That's exactly right!'

'So did I, Woody. It must be the cosmic vibrations.'

'Exactly Les. Celestial harmonics and metaphysical realms. They're all around us.'

The reception was bright and air-conditioned, with a carpeted set of stairs in one corner that led up to one of the restaurants. The brown-uniformed girl behind the desk was all smiles and efficiency and in no time they'd checked in, got their swipe cards and exchanged room numbers. After telling Woody he'd ring her around six, Les picked up a map with a layout of the resort on one side and a street map of Cairns on the other and, without waiting for a porter, took his bags and walked off in search of his room.

Map in one hand, Les walked past a large dining area with high ceilings and a verandah round it and surmised it doubled as a restaurant and the place where all the punters scrummed down for breakfast. He strolled on through more landscaped gardens and rock pools, then past a kidney-shaped swimming pool with a bar and a waterfall surrounded by more gardens and rooms and bungalows all built at ground level. He followed a path through one gate then another and his room was along a short, walled path on his left; it was the last one at the end on the right. He swiped the door lock and stepped inside.

Not too bad for a hundred bucks, mused Les. Not too bad at all. The room was spacious and nicely air-conditioned with white walls and green floral furnishings. There was a comfy, queen size bed, a small fridge, a TV, bamboo chairs and tables with a patio at the back. And at least Kathy knows I'll be safe here. Les threw his bags on the bed, took his tracksuit top off then had another look at his map. He decided to check out a bit more of the resort before he went into town.

He strolled along a passageway, through another

gate, and past a set of steps leading up to a fitness centre. There was a laundry and more rooms, then another landscaped area with a larger pool. Les stepped inside and past more barrels of fat; this lot were sitting on banana chairs next to the pool either drinking, eating, reading or smoking cigars. Facing the pool was a covered, outdoor seating area, a bar and another restaurant with indoor or outside eating. It was all brown wicker chairs and tables, tiled floors and had a nice, tropical feel about it. There weren't many people in the restaurant and he thought, while he was there, he may as well book a table for tonight. A smiling waitress in a green uniform wrote his name down and he got a nice table outside for around seven. As he was strolling back through the beer garden, Les noticed a whiteboard: 'Cane toad races tonight. Eight o'clock. Come join the fun. Bet on your favourite toad and get a chance to win a pocketful of cash. Happy hour 6–7.' That's what I'll do, smiled Les to himself. After I've given the Rainbow Princess a giant spoil in the restaurant. I'll take her to the races. Shit! Am I a good bloke or what. Les had another look at his map and decided that was all he needed to know about Colony Resort for the time being. He put it in his pocket and strolled back to his room.

After splashing some cold water over his face, Les changed into a pair of white shorts, got his Bugs Bunny cap and sunglasses out of his carry bag then tossed his driver's licence and whatever else he thought he'd need in town into his overnight bag.

According to his little map, the resort ran a bus into town on the hour and there was one leaving in five minutes. Les was packed and in the parking area with almost two minutes to spare.

This time the bus was a big cruiser. Les climbed aboard and found the last empty seat down the back amongst about fifty wheezing, grumpy, fat tourists, all smelling of B.O. He'd just got his backside between what was probably some old ex-Nazi and a Japanese war criminal when the bus took off. The driver introduced himself over the microphone as Richard and before they'd even cleared the parking area went into this non-stop, droning, nasally spiel about Cairns which he somehow imagined was both funny and entertaining. With a whining voice that never once lowered or raised its pitch, he blathered on about dancing crocodiles, singing cane toads and if it poured rain overnight here in Cairns, the following morning the locals referred to that as just a heavy dew. Richard's highpoint was cascara plants. And how during the second world war the fun loving locals would make them up as chocolates and sell them to the Yank soldiers. Then the locals would all run around Cairns laughing like drains because they were actually strong laxatives. And there'd be American G.I.s doubled up everywhere with stomach cramps wondering why they were shitting their guts out.

As the bus driver rambled on and on most people on the bus were shielding their eyes in embarrassment. Even the ones who couldn't speak

English were looking at each other as if they'd suddenly found themselves on some strange planet. Fortunately the journey into town didn't take all that long, because as the driver pulled the bus up into Orchid Plaza a lynch mob mentality was starting to spread amongst the passengers. Thank Christ I don't have to catch the bloody thing back, thought Les, who was one of the last to file off. Another five minutes and I'd have ripped that microphone out of the dash and shoved it fair up his date. Now, where am I?

Norton glanced at his map and had a quick look around. He was in some kind of mall with a turning area for buses. There were shops full of clothes, souvenirs and other odds and ends, and escalators leading up to other connected malls and restaurants. But Les was neither hungry nor in the market for a Cairns T-shirt. All he wanted was to pick up the car and maybe have a coffee. He had another look at the map and checked it with the note Beryl had given him. Lake and Alpen. Les smiled. About two blocks away: just over there. Les slung his overnight bag across his shoulder and set off through the people and the steady afternoon traffic.

After only a few minutes walk sweat was dripping from Norton's chin and glugging the armpits of his T-shirt. He found the neat, white, Avis car rental building and stepped into the air-conditioned office. After Sydney, Cairns wasn't just hot. It was bloody hot. There were no other customers as Les removed his sunglasses and placed his bag on the counter. He didn't have to wait very long before a smiling girl in a red uniform came over to him.

'Hello,' she said pleasantly. 'Can I help you?'

'Yes. My name is Norton. I'm up from Sydney. And there should be a car here for me — a four-wheel drive.' Les took his wallet and driver's licence out of his overnight bag and placed them on the counter.

'Just one moment, Mr. Norton.'

The girl went away then came back with some papers and a grey-haired man in a white shirt.

'Mr. Norton is it?' said the man.

'That's right,' nodded Les.

'We do have a four-wheel drive waiting for you, Mr. Norton. Are you familiar with these types of vehicles, sir?'

Les nodded again. A little slower this time. 'Yeah. But it's been a while. It might be an idea if you showed me over a few things.'

The man seemed to look a little relieved. 'If you'll just fill in the paperwork, I'll wait for you outside. It's right out the front.'

'Righto.' Fair enough, thought Les as he picked up a biro. He's probably worried about getting some dill up from the city who thinks he's gonna go bush bashing and ends up stranded in some river out in the middle of nowhere for a week. Les filled in the paperwork, checked the insurance was all kosher then went back outside in the heat. The man was standing next to a solid, white Overlander parked nose first to the curb. Les placed his overnight bag on the bonnet.

'You know about reversing the wheel hubs when you want four-wheel drive?' said the man.

'Yeah,' replied Les. 'But you'd better show me anyway.'

The man proceeded to explain how to turn the front wheel hubs, how to work the gear shift and the front and rear windscreen wipers. The car ran on diesel, so you had to wait for the little orange light on the dash to come on before you started the car and so on.

'Okay, mate. Thanks for that,' said Les finally. 'If anything goes wrong or the motor blows up I just ring this number here?'

'That's right.' The man looked at Les. 'Where are you heading to?'

'Cooktown.'

'Are you thinking of taking the Bloomfield?'

Norton shrugged. 'I'm not sure.'

'I wouldn't if I were you. Not this time of year. You'd be better off to go inland.'

Norton shrugged again. 'Okay. Inland it is.'

'Good luck, Mr. Norton. Enjoy your holiday.'

'Yeah, thanks. I'll see you when I get back.' Les got behind the wheel, kicked the motor over then slipped the Overlander into reverse and backed out into the traffic.

For its size and weight the big four by four handled quite easily. There were five on the floor, the power-steering was spot on and the seat was comfortable; the air-conditioning worked fine and so did the radio. Les bumbled into fifth a few times instead of third, but that was nothing. In fact it was a bit of a buzz sitting up above the other cars while slipping through the gear box. Les drove around for a time familiarising himself with the car, while he also checked out the sights of beautiful, downtown Cairns. He went past Reef Casino, Cairns International Pacific Hotel and other high-rise resorts. He cruised alongside the art gallery and came back down The Esplanade with the ocean on his left, the harbour and Pier Market Place in front of him and the low, cloud-covered, Murray Prior Mountain Range behind Trinity Inlet in the short distance. Les liked Cairns.

There seemed to be gardens full of flowers all over the place, not a great deal of high-rise and despite the city's bustling, cosmopolitan appearance it still seemed to have an old, wooden, colonial feel about it. The only thing Les didn't like so much were the traffic lights. For its size, Les was convinced Cairns had more traffic lights per square metre than any other place on earth; and every time he came to one it was red and seemed to take forever to change. After fifteen minutes of lurching from one red light to another he decided to throw in the towel, have a cool drink and buy a road map. He went through another set of lights, then angle parked at a meter in the middle of the road outside the art gallery.

As he dropped a dollar in the parking metre, Les looked up and noticed a cream-coloured building; it was three storeys high with a green railing running round a verandah over the street. Above the verandah a brown and white sign said 'Jimbo's Blues Bar'. That looks kind of interesting, Les thought. He crossed over the road and looked in the plate glass windows near the entrance. There were posters for rock bands everywhere and a sign saying there were bands every night including two the following night; Jimbo's Blues Band and a rock'n'roll outfit called Rock Solid Steve and The Scorchers. I might come down here tomorrow night and have a look, mused Les. I can't tonight because I have to be up around six tomorrow morning. But tomorrow night couldn't be creamier. I might even bring the Rainbow Princess if she wants to join me.

Norton drifted back towards Orchid Plaza and it didn't take him long to find a bookshop where he bought a map covering Cairns to Cooktown. After paying the woman he strolled back down Shields Street past the art gallery onto The Esplanade. He walked up and back about a hundred metres past a McDonald's, a food hall inside the entrance to the night markets, a KFC, various car rentals and shops selling dive trips to the Barrier Reef, and a number of restaurants and takeaways. Across the road was a long strip of green park; it was dotted with evenly spaced trees that moved languidly in the onshore breeze rippling the muddy, green surface of the bay in front of them. To the right was the pier and mountain range Les had seen earlier and to the left a long peninsula of land ran out towards the ocean.

There didn't seem to be many Japanese tourists around; mostly slow moving hippy types and locals or big-titted Scandinavian backpackers wearing shorts, bumbags, cheap dresses and leather sandals or gym boots. It was all very touristy and very laid-back and still very bloody hot. Les found a nice coffee shop at the entrance to the night markets with outdoor seating. He ordered a flat white and a bottle of mineral water then sat down and studied the map he'd just bought.

Beryl was right. Cooktown wasn't far from Cairns if you took the Bloomfield Track past Cape Tribulation. Only ninety-six clicks. But the bloke at Avis had said the Bloomfield was closed. So it looked like three hundred and twenty-three kilometres inland over Mount Carbine and along the Cooktown Developmental Road. Still, mused Les, that could be fun, bouncing along in the big Overlander. He saw Cedar Bay National Park on the map and noticed a stack of other little bays and points where somebody on the run could hide out. Les looked at the map intently for a moment then drummed his fingers on the table. Shit! If I'm fair dinkum at all about finding Beryl's daughter, I know what I should do ... When Norton was driving around earlier he went past a white building with a row of white columns out the front something like an old Southern mansion. It was the office of the Cairns *Advertiser* and not far from where he was seated. He could go up to that newspaper office, check the files and get a copy of what they said about the two missing divers. It was only just round from the art gallery if he remembered right. Les finished his coffee and the last of his mineral water, then walked round to the Cairns *Advertiser*. The young girl in the grey dress was very polite and helpful when Norton told her what he was after. She pointed from behind the front desk to a row of shelves under the window behind Les, piled with bound copies of old newspapers.

'That was only about a year or so ago,' she said. 'So the ones you're after should still be amongst those ones over there.'

'Okay. Thanks,' smiled Les.

'Pick out the ones you want and I'll xerox them for you.'

'All right. Thankyou.'

Les walked over to the stacks of newspapers and started flicking through them. It took him about five minutes to find the first headline he was looking for: LOST AT SEA. DIVERS LEFT ON REEF. There was a photo of a dive boat and two head shots of Jade Biscayne and Hordern Genting. Jade had her mother's lovely eyes and looked even prettier without the sunglasses. Hordern wasn't a bad style either. There were no photos of their daughter. The next headline read: SEARCH ABANDONED. LEAD WEIGHTS FOUND ON REEF. The third headline read: NOTE PUZZLE. DIVER MYSTERY DEEPENS. There were seven pages in all. Les folded them back and took them over to the girl behind the desk who soon had everything photocopied and rolled up with a rubber band. Les paid the girl, thanked her for her trouble and walked back to the car.

After starting the engine Norton sat there for a moment wondering what he should do. Another mineral water would be nice. A beer would be even better. He wiped some sweat from his chin. No. Seeing as I'm having such a prick of a time, everything's going wrong and I got the shits with the world, I know exactly what I'll do. He slipped the Overlander into gear and headed for the resort.

Back in his room, Les climbed out of his clothes and laid them over a chair. Yes, he smiled to himself. I've certainly got the shits all right. I'm staying in a nice resort, I've got a cute little girl to take out for dinner later, the whitewater rafting is still on tomorrow then I'm going bush bashing to another resort in Cooktown. Plus I'm five hundred bucks in front. So seeing as I'm so filthy on the world, there's only one thing to do — drag my miserable, rotten self over to that football oval across the road and run around in the heat for about an hour. Les changed into his old training gear, got his swipe card and strolled towards the resort entrance.

Les had the oval, the heat and a leaden sky that looked like it was going to burst any moment, all to himself. A fence dotted with advertising ran around the oval and behind the entrance was a small white clubhouse with Cairns Panthers Australian Football And Sporting Club on one wall. Les did a few stretches on the entrance gate, checked his watch, adjusted his sweatband and took off.

After four laps he was in a complete lather of sweat. He was going okay, but the humidity was absolutely diabolical. Bloody hell, he muttered to himself as another lap went by, I don't think it was this bad even in Jamaica. He did another four laps and it started to rain. At first the rain was good, washing the sweat from his face and cooling him down a little, then it got heavier and the track round the oval started turning to mud. Les had another look at his watch then glanced up at the blackened sky. All right. I know I'm filthy on myself, but I'm not that filthy. You can stick this in your arse. Norton finished the lap he was doing then vaulted the fence and jogged back across the road to the resort.

He stopped in at the front office and asked the girl behind the desk if it was okay if he took another one of those small maps. The girl smiled and told Les to help himself. He took a map and as she looked away grabbed a handful of thick rubber bands and some paper clips. The resort had a store just across from the office selling T-shirts, magazines, drinks and so on. Les got a large bottle of mineral water, a sixpack of Cairns Draught, some salted cashews and charged them up on his swipe card. Back in his room, he gulped down half the mineral water while he stacked the beers in the fridge. He then took off his trainers and, with his wet shorts and old T-shirt still on, grabbed a towel, walked back out to the nearest pool and fell straight in.

It was still raining and, as with the oval, Les had the pool to himself. After the awful heat from running, the cool water in the pool felt like heaven and Les was almost convinced he could feel his skin sizzling as he lay there just bobbing up and down in the rain spattered water. He took his running gear off, threw it onto the nearest banana chair then swam around just enjoying himself while he cooled down. He finally got out, wrapped a towel round himself and walked back to his room. Fifteen minutes later he was showered, clean-shaven and laying on his bed in a fresh, white T-shirt and his jocks, drinking the rest of his mineral water while he made a couple of phone calls before he went through the photocopies he got from the Cairns *Advertiser*.

First was the front desk: Yes, Mr. Norton. The bus from Rolling Thunder Whitewater Rafting will be out the front at six-thirty a.m. And you'd like a wake up call for five-forty five a.m. No problem, Mr. Norton. Thankyou. Next was the room of the exotic Rainbow Princess.

'Hello.'

'Hello, Woody. It's Les. How's things?'

'Oh hi, Les. I'm fine. How are you?'

'Good thanks, Woody. How was your day?'

'Oh, fairly cosmic, Les. What about yourself?'

'Oh, about medium rare cosmic ... I got the car. Cruised around town. Had a jog and a swim. Loosened up a few chakras.'

'Hey, that's the idea, Les. Cool.'

'Yeah, cool. Now I'm just taking it easy. Reading a book.'

'What are you reading?'

Norton's eyes drifted from the photocopies on the bed across to his overnight bag. 'Ummh. *Underboss*. It's about the mafia in America.'

'Sounds cool. I'm just reading a book too.'

'Yeah? What are you reading, Woody?' Norton asked before thinking, then closed his eyes for a second.

'*The Ra Material*.'

'The what?'

'*The Ra Material*, Les. It's all about the ancient Egyptian astronauts. Why they first came to earth. Why they're coming back. Why they built all the great monuments.'

'Sounds ... really cosmic, Woody.'

'Oh, it is. This guy is out there. I mean, like really out there.'

'Sounds like it. Anyway Woody, do you still want to go ... out there for dinner tonight?'

'Sure. I'd love to.'

'Okay. Well, how about I call round for you at seven?'

'That'd be great. You know where my room is?'

'I'll soon find it.'

'All right. Oh, just one thing, Les.'

'Yeah. What's that Woody?'

'Where we're going ... is it very expensive?'

Les was momentarily puzzled. 'How do you mean?'

'I mean, like are the drinks very expensive?'

'I bloody well hope so, Woody.'

'You do? Why's that?'

'Because I'm paying. I'll see you at seven.'

'Oh. All right then.'

Les hung up and smiled at the phone. Well, what a little sweetheart. You can bet she hasn't got much money. At the back of her mind she was expecting to have to weigh in. Well don't worry Rainbow Princess. When I was running round that oval in the rain, I had a funny feeling you could do all right at the races tonight. You might just crack it at the punt, as they say where I work. Now, where's those photocopies?

The story and photos in the local paper seemed different to what Les vaguely remembered reading in the Sydney papers about the incident with the two missing scuba divers. It was as if the Cairns *Advertiser* was trying to take a balanced view of the unfortunate incident; which, being the local newspaper, he assumed was only natural. Whereas the Sydney papers, if Les remembered correctly, had gone more for the nitty gritty, adding all the shock, horror and innuendo they could find. Besides that, the local paper's story was written around the time it all happened, while what appeared in the Sydney papers had been strung out over a month or more. Les had also come across an article in a magazine about it somewhere or sometime if memory served him right. He went through his photocopies again and this time jotted down a few notes on some stationery the resort had provided with his room.

Although he was Dr. Hordern Genting, geneticist, they were mainly referred to as the missing couple. Genting was thirty. Jade was twenty-five. Dr. Genting had been back in Australia about a year after lecturing on and off for the last five years at the University of Montana in the United States. Jade was his partner and they'd been sharing a flat at Westcourt, a suburb of Cairns, for the last two months. The day they went missing, they'd been diving off Wine Glass Cay on a boat called the *Sea Trek*, run by Sea Trek Dive Service out of Port Douglas. The company had only been going six weeks and the couple had been missing two days before the proprietor reported them lost. The note puzzle was just a postcard found at their home unit that Genting had addressed to a colleague and never sent, saying he was going diving at Wine Glass Cay and didn't know when he'd be back. There were no photos of any grieving parents and none of their daughter Amy. In fact, apart from a fair bit of padding and smoothing over, there wasn't a great deal to go on in all seven pages. The Queensland Minister for Tourism had flown in and said it was an unfortunate incident for the tourism industry and he didn't wish to make any further comments until he had been further briefed by all authorities involved in the investigation. The proprietor of Sea Trek Dive Service had voluntarily halted operations until further investigations by the police, the Maritime Safety Authority and the Division of Workplace Health and Safety had been completed. A local woman, Christine Cain of Edge Hill, said she'd been diving with Sea Trek and had nothing but praise for them and had recommended them to her friends. And that was about it.

However, Norton now found himself hooked. There was something about the whole thing that didn't quite add up and for some weird reason Les suddenly felt his Dick Tracy, super detective streak starting to come out. He went through his notes again, stared at the photocopies and the photos of Dr. Hordern Genting and his partner Jade Biscayne for a moment then the light bulb above his head suddenly switched on. Les smiled to himself and snapped his fingers. I know where I read that bloody article — J.D. Gloves, Australia's most famous fisherman. He had written a one page article about it in his fishing magazine. Billy had it up the club one night. Les glanced across to the phone at the side of the bed. But what was his number? Shit! Telstra'd soon bloody know — Les glanced at his watch as he picked up the receiver — and with a bit of luck he should be home. Les soon had the number from Telstra and a couple of minutes later he could hear Gloves' phone ringing in Sydney.

'Hello. J.D. Gloves.'

'Hello, Gloves. It's Les Norton.'

'Les. Hello, mate. How are you?'

'Good thanks, Gloves. What are you up to?'

'Actually, I was just on my way out the door. I have to meet a couple of blokes at The Four In Hand.'

'Oh.'

'But that's okay. I can always find a couple of minutes for an old mate. What can I do for you, Les?'

'All right. I'm in Cairns having a break and sort of doing a favour for someone. A while back you wrote an article about those two scuba divers who went missing up here. Would you have a copy of it there?'

'Mate! I wrote that about a year ago.' Gloves seemed to think for a moment. 'That'd be down at my office.'

'When are you going into your office?'

'Luckily not for another week. I'm off to the Kimberley first thing tomorrow morning to go helicopter fishing.'

'Oh.'

'But I still might be able to help you, Les. What did you want to know?'

'Well, the sheila who disappeared ... wasn't she supposed to have been spotted round here a couple of times?'

Gloves gave a throaty chuckle over the line. 'Yeah. They've seen her up there more times than Elvis.'

'And wasn't she supposed to have left a message somewhere? The bloke left one in their flat. But I think I remember reading she left one somewhere else. Is that right?'

'Yeah, sort of. This old sheila reckoned she saw her pinning it to one of those community noticeboards outside a coffee shop in Port Douglas. So she grabbed the note when she left and rang the papers.'

'What'd it say?'

'Fuck all. In fact I think I still got the article here in the flat somewhere. I kept it in my file. Hang on a sec ...' Gloves was gone for a minute or so, then came back on the line. 'Yeah, here it is. You got a fax number where you're staying?'

'There should be.' Les got the number off the resort stationery and gave it to Gloves.

'Okey doke. I'll have that there in about five minutes.'

'Good on you, Gloves. I appreciate it.'

'That's all right. So what are you doing in Cairns, Les? Playing private eye or something?'

'Yeah. Something like that,' laughed Norton. 'I'll tell you about it next time I see you. Hey, before you go, Gloves.'

'Yeah?'

'What do you reckon happened to those two divers?'

'What do I reckon? I reckon they're both sliced bread. Especially the bloke.'

'Why's that?'

'Well, at that time I wrote the article in a bit of a light-hearted fashion. But since then, there's been a strong conspiracy theory going round.'

'Conspiracy theory?' Norton's ears pricked up.

'Yeah. Evidently he was a geneticist. And he was supposed to have discovered a cure for baldness. And this big German pharmaceutical company had him murdered so they could steal the formula.'

'Christ! That is a conspiracy theory, Gloves.'

'Well. Imagine what something like that'd be worth, Les. Millions. Fuckin' billions'd be more like it.'

'Yeah,' conceded Les. 'You're right.'

'I'll tell you what. While you're up there, I'll give you the phone number of a bloke I know with a yacht in Port Douglas. He might be able to help you with a few things. It's in my book here somewhere. You got a pen?'

'Yep. Right here.'

Gloves gave Norton the yacht owner's name and mobile phone number in Port Douglas. 'Anyway, Les. I have to get going. Good luck with whatever it is you're doing up there.'

'Yeah, thanks Gloves. I owe you a beer next time I see you.'

What about that, mused Les, after he hung up. Now we've got murder conspiracies. German drug companies. Baldies. Nazis maybe? Shit! Who knows where this may end? The bottle of mineral water was empty, so Les thought he might have a beer while he waited for the fax to arrive. He drank about half, put his tracksuit pants on and walked out to the office. The same smiling woman as before was behind the desk.

'Can I help you?' she asked.

'Yes,' nodded Les. 'Has a fax just come in for Norton?'

'Just one moment.' The girl went to a wire basket on a desk behind her and came back. 'There you are Mr. Norton.'

'Thankyou.' Les took the fax, folded it and walked back to his room.

Sprawled against the pillows on his bed, Les sipped some more beer while he read the newspaper article Gloves had sent him. The reproduction wasn't too bad, although the photo of the woman who found the message was practically a silhouette. The article stated how she found it and how she was certain the woman was one of the two missing divers. There was a bit more beat-up about the incident and how the two divers left some of their equipment at Wine Glass Cay, waited for the *Sea Trek* to leave, then snuck back amongst a larger group of divers on a boat run by Nimrod Diver Service. More of their equipment was found days later, washed up thirty kilometres north of Cooktown. A copy of the actual note the woman found said pretty much what Gloves had said it did over the phone. Fuck all. 'Everything is nothing. And nothing is everything.' That was it. Les read it a couple more times, stroked his chin thoughtfully then a half-smile flickered round his eyes. Sometimes it's those little bits of nothing that mean something. Or everything.

He placed the fax on the bed then got the photo Beryl had given him from the envelope in his overnight bag, turned it over and placed it next to the fax. The smile around Norton's eyes flickered even more as he slowly nodded his head. He was right. Although the note the woman found was more in capitals while the words on the back of the photo were in neat handwriting, whoever wrote both didn't dot their i's. They drew tiny circles over them instead. Les finished his beer and tossed the empty bottle in the waste paper basket. It could just be sheer coincidence. But it was possible Jade Biscayne might still be alive and kicking and still writing those funny little messages. What they meant, Les didn't have a clue. And didn't particularly care. He might as well try and decipher one of those books of Nostradamus quatrains. Still, it was nice to think there was a chance Beryl's daughter wasn't quite sliced bread — as Gloves so eloquently put it. Les looked at his watch. It was time to make a move.

Norton tossed his camera and a few other things into his overnight bag then changed into a lemon-coloured polo shirt, a loose-fitting pair of white shorts with a brown leather belt and a pair of tan loafers. After giving himself one last detail in the bathroom mirror he daubed on just a hint of Eau Sauvage. Ahh yes, he smiled, smelling the tips of his fingers. Is someone in for a spoil tonight or what. He got his swipe card and closed the door behind him. Just as the door shut a slight cramp, caused either by the run, his hunger pangs or the airline food suddenly hit the pit of Norton's stomach. He stopped and let go a fart that sounded like a sail tearing in a windstorm. Les blinked and shook his head. Okay, Woody the Rainbow Princess, Les the Wind Warrior is on his way.

Norton didn't quite know what to expect when the Rainbow Princess opened the door. But he wasn't surprised. Woody was wearing a tight, black, hot pants outfit sewn with gold and silver cobwebs, over rainbow-circled stockings tucked into the same shiny boots with pink shoelaces. The Bindi was gone, but she'd plaited tips of coloured feathers into her hair and added more glitter. Two earrings made from the same coloured feathers as in her hair bobbed across her boobs and almost down to her waist.

'Hello, Les,' she smiled up happily. 'I won't be a second.'

'Righto.' Les stepped back and waited in the passageway.

Woody soon returned closing the door behind her and put her swipe card in a blue handbag shaped like a dolphin. 'How are you, Les?'

'Good,' replied Norton. 'Hungry. What about you?'

Woody nodded emphatically. 'Did I tell you I was vegetarian?'

Les made an expansive gesture with his hands. 'Oh, Woody,' he said. 'I'd expect no less. In fact I'm surprised you eat at all and you don't just live off the universe and be done with it.'

'Yes, Les. Absorb and expand on the infinite nothingness of universal demand and supply.' Woody tucked her arm into Norton's. 'You're a really together guy, Les. You know that?'

'Woody,' replied Les. 'Sometimes I'm that together, I almost disappear right up my own astral plane.'

'Wow! Now that is really cosmic.'

Woody skipped along happily next to Les, rabbiting on non-stop about Tarot symbolism, astrological correspondence, tasseography and other assorted new age space junk. About the only earthly thing Les could glean from her was she designed web sites and was helping to pay off a terrace house at Newtown with her sister who wrote children's books. Somehow Les managed to slip in he lived at Bondi with a friend and did part-time security work. He also had some money from an inheritance.

They walked past the pool and through the beer garden up to the restaurant reception desk. Despite the happy hour there weren't all that many people around; however, those who were there gave Woody plenty of double blinks while they waited for one of the waitresses to come over. The waitress was all smiles and soon they were seated at the outside table Les had booked, menus in front of them.

'Why don't we have a drink first?' suggested Les.

'Good idea,' said Woody. 'I'd like a beer. Hahn Premium?'

Les nodded to the waitress. 'Two of those please.'

'Certainly, sir.'

The beers soon arrived and Les clinked his bottle against Woody's. 'Well. Here's to the cosmos, Woody.'

'Yeah. Cheers Les. To pyramidal balancing and the first density.'

'Exactly.'

Les took another mouthful of beer and perused the menu. It didn't take him long to settle on the chilled prawns for an entree and barramundi fillets for a main. He sipped his beer and looked up at the Rainbow Princess.

'See anything you fancy, Woody?'

'Yeah. Just the Chinese stir fried vegetables and rice'll do me Les.' Woody tapped a nail against her empty bottle. 'And another beer?'

Norton gave his half-full bottle and Woody's empty one a slow, single blink. 'Yeah ... righto. Would you like a bottle of wine too?'

'Ohh yeah. That'd be lovely.'

'Okay. You pick one out.'

'Gee. Thanks, Les.'

'It's my pleasure.' Les leant across the table a little. 'And it's all karma as well you know.'

'It is?'

Les nodded. 'You've got a lucky glow about you, Woody. An aura. I can sense it.'

Woody gazed into Norton's eyes. 'Les. Would you believe it? I found an energy grid running right through my room, and I've been channelling and spiralling all afternoon. Not only that ...'

While Woody prattled on about zodiac ascendancies, sacred geometry and the Sun God Ra, Les was convinced of two things. As well as talk, the Rainbow Princess could drink. She knocked off two more beers while they waited for their orders, then a bottle of Brown Brothers Chardonnay with her stir fry and another bottle of Hahn after that. She was probably the most boring person Les had ever met and there were moments when he could have reached across the table and strangled her with his bare hands. But at the same time Woody was also one of the most likeable. She meant absolutely no harm. It was if she had this crazy zest for life coupled with a bubbling enthusiasm for something she'd discovered that she wanted to share with Les. To help him. To teach him. Heal him if need be.

Norton had one more bottle of beer, then switched to mineral water and sat there almost mesmerised. They finished eating and had coffee; Les charged everything to his room, then they went into the beer garden.

He found a table next to the space in front of the whiteboard where a circle, roughly two metres across, was marked on the floor for the cane toad racing. He went to the bar and came back with a Jack Daniels and diet for himself and a mango daiquiri for Woody. He clinked Woody's daiquiri and took a sip and then, like some other people at a table near them, spluttered and nearly choked on his drink.

'Are you all right, Les?' asked Woody.

'Yeah. Yeah I'm fine,' answered Les. 'A bit just went down the wrong way, that's all.'

Norton couldn't believe what he just saw. The compere for the evening was the same boring dropkick driving the bus earlier that afternoon; only tonight he was wearing jeans, a black striped shirt, an old black Akubra and sunglasses. He stepped in front of the whiteboard and placed a cardboard carton in the middle of the circle marked on the floor.

'Good evening, ladies and gentleman,' he whined. 'Welcome to tonight's star-studded event. The Colony Resort cane toad races. My name's Richard, and I'll be your host for the evening. Now, For those of you ...'

Norton stared into his drink, a feeling of whimsical despair etched on his face. He'd just been punished non-stop by Woody. Now he had to put up with the horrible beast from the bus. He shot a quick glance across the beer garden towards the night sky. I know I've done something wrong. But what? Woody, however, didn't seem to mind. She actually kept reasonably quiet while Richard droned on and on taking half the night to explain what he could have got through in ten minutes. He rambled away starting with the cane toad's latin name, Bufonidae Horrubillus Bastardos or something, then its mating habits and how it secretes poison through the glands on its rotten leathery back. Norton recollected a version of cane toad racing they had at home when he was a kid. You got several cane toads, tied fire crackers to their backs with rubber bands then let them hop off. The last one to get blown to bits was the winner.

Basically, the deal tonight was:

There would be three races. But because it could be construed as illegal gambling, each cane toad was auctioned off for points. Ten points: Ten dollars.

Twenty Points: Twenty dollars. The cane toad was given a small, stick-on coloured patch, the bidder gave it a name, then the box of cane toads was placed in the circle, the box removed and the first one to hop out of the circle was the winner.

Three daiquiris for the Rainbow Princess and another delicious for Les later, Richard had finally explained everything and prepared the betting sheet on the whiteboard.

'Okay, ladies and gentleman,' he began again, pulling an ugly, sour-looking cane toad out of the box and holding it up in the air. 'Now how many points am I bid for this fine specimen?'

Les turned to the Rainbow Princess. 'Well, what do you fancy in the first, Woody?'

'I don't know,' she replied. 'What about you?'

Les shook his head. 'No. I can't bet against you, Woody. It'd be bad karma. Check the cosmic vibrations and pick out the one you like. Then I'll just do the bidding. Okay?'

'Okay.' Woody closed her eyes for a moment. 'The third frog he picks up.'

'Righto. The third one it is.'

Because Richard had taken so long getting his act together, a few more punters had drifted in and the bidding among the guests was reasonably spirited. The first toad went for fifteen dollars, got a red sticker and was named Ito. The second went for eighteen dollars, got a blue tag and was named Fritz.

'Okay. Now what am I bid for this one?' said Richard.

Norton waved his hand. 'Twenty-five points.'

'Twenty-five points. Any advances on twenty-five points?' Richard looked round the beer garden. Silence. 'Okay. To the gentleman over there for twenty-five points.' The compere gave the toad a green sticker, put it back in the box and came over to get the money. 'What do you want to call it?'

Les gave him the twenty-five dollars and nodded to Woody. 'Ask her.'

'What do you want to call it, miss?'

Woody thought for a second and smiled. 'Scruffy.'

'Scruffy the green it is.'

Les looked quizically at Woody as Richard walked back to the whiteboard. 'Scruffy?'

'Yes. That's my cat's name.'

'Fair enough,' nodded Les, taking a sip of his delicious.

He settled back to watch the proceedings as Richard auctioned off the three remaining cane toads and Woody got a bit of a roll going about predicting future events through theosophism and druid stones.

The bus driver-cum-compere finally had all six cane toads sold, the names and prices on the board and the pot counted for the first race — ninety-five dollars. In a way it suited Norton having the bus driver running things. Because he was more interested in the sound of his own voice and was wearing sunglasses there would be less chance of him noticing what Norton had in mind. Earlier in his room, Les had knotted three of the thick rubber bands he got from the office together as well as bending several paper clips in half. He put them in a resort envelope then placed them in his overnight bag next to his camera. About half a minute before race time he reached down into his bag, slipped two left fingers into the rubber bands and hooked on a paper clip giving himself a small but very effective slingshot.

'Okay,' said Richard, staring round the beer garden in his dark glasses. 'Is everybody ready?'

'This is it, Les,' said an excited Woody. 'Go Scruffy!'

'I can feel the vibes already, Woody,' replied Les, placing his right thumb and index finger over the paper clip.

'All right. Go!'

Richard took the carton away and stepped back, leaving six very ugly, very pissed off cane toads bunched together in the middle of the circle. The punters all started cheering and urging their cane toad on. Everybody else was mostly yelling or laughing, with quite a few horrified looks on the faces of the elderly women staying at the resort. His hands resting on his knees under the table, Les was still able to get a good view of everything going on in the circle. He spotted number three, adjusted his angle slightly, waited till the cane toads started moving round then let go a paper clip hitting three the green fair in its ugly green backside. The cane toad gave an angry hiss, then leapt straight out of the ring towards the restaurant underneath the tables of the screaming, startled women.

The Rainbow Princess leapt to her feet. 'Yeah! Go Scruffy! That was number three, Les.'

'My oath it was, Woody,' grinned Les. He punched the air with his right hand. 'We've got a winner.'

'All right,' said Richard, above the noise. 'Number three the green it is. Scruffy.'

The compere shuffled the remaining five cane toads back beneath the carton, then started crawling under the tables looking for three the green. Les slipped the rubber bands off and grabbed his camera out of the bag then stood up and started taking flash photos; managing to get the toe of his shoe over the paper clip, slide it out of the ring, pick it up and toss it back in his bag as Richard got hold of number three and put it back under the carton with the other cane toads. Les stepped back and got a photo of Richard giving Woody the ninety-five dollars, then sat back down next to her as the other guests settled down and Richard started getting things together for the second event of the evening.

'What did I tell you, Woody,' said Les, clinking her glass with his. 'I said you had a definite aura about you.'

Woody was a picture of joy as she counted her money. 'Look at this, Les. This is, totally cosmic.'

'Tell me something I don't already know.'

'Let me buy you a drink.'

Les shook his head. 'No, it's okay. I'm taking it easy. I have to be up before six.'

'Well, I'm having another one.'

'Go for your life, Rainbow Princess. It's your night. Celebrate.'

Woody weaved her way to the bar through the surrounding chairs and tables and got herself another mango daiquiri while Les stayed on what he had. By the time she got back, Richard, not having to go through all his palaver this time, was just about ready to start auctioning cane toads again.

'Righto, Rainbow Princess,' smiled Les, raising his glass. 'What do you fancy in the next?'

Richard got the points system rolling again. Woody concentrated hard and decided on the second cane toad. Les got number two for twenty-five dollars again, with a red sticker this time and Woody called it Amazonite. Before long all the names and prices were on the whiteboard, the bets were set and the pot this time was ninety dollars.

'Is everybody ready? Okay ... Go!'

Richard whipped the carton away leaving the same six, sour-looking cane toads bunched in the middle of the circle looking even more pissed off than they were before. The red tab on number two was easy to spot this time. Les waited till the toads started moving around again then let go another paper clip, slamming number two right in the ribs. It jumped up and tumbled over the other cane toads then leapt straight out of the ring under the chairs and tables towards the bar. The women sitting in front drew back and began shrieking at the ugly, angry cane toad squatted beneath them looking like it was getting ready to spurt venom everywhere.

Les slipped off the rubber bands, grabbed his camera and leapt to his feet. 'Yes. Amazonite by five lengths. Woody, you're a genius.'

Woody was on her feet too; daiquiri in one hand, coloured feathers bobbing all over the place. 'Yes! Yes! Yes! Creative visualisation. I can do it.'

'And the winner is Amazonite. Number two the red.'

Richard put the carton over the remaining cane toads again, then started crawling round after number two. Les took more photos, scooped up the paper clip as before and took another photo of Richard giving Woody her money. He sat back down alongside her.

'Well, jewel of the cosmos. I don't know what to say. Woody, you are truly the chosen one.' Les started making bows of worship at the table. 'I'm not worthy enough. I'm not worthy enough.'

'You know what, Les,' Woody began sincerely. 'I think I'm drawing some of my energy from you.'

'Help yourself, Woody. There's plenty to go round.' Les wiggled his empty glass. 'I might have another drink. You want one?'

'Okay.' Woody pulled a twenty from the last roll. 'But let me shout this time.'

'All right moneybags. If you insist.'

Les went to the bar and came back with another mango daiquiri and a Jack Daniels. Near the whiteboard Richard was getting things together for race three. Les placed the drinks on the table, sat down and gave Woody her change.

'You going to have another bet?' he asked, taking a sip of Jackies.

'I'll have to. The vibrations are just too strong.'

'Okey doke. So what does your mystical, metaphysical form guide say in this one?'

Woody concentrated and stared at Les. From Norton's point of view he couldn't tell if she was drunk or having some sort of out of body experience.

'Number four. Frog number four.'

Les nodded sincerely. 'Okay. Number four it is. And why don't we call it Rainbow Princess.'

'Yeah,' Woody clinked Norton's glass. 'Good one!'

Richard had the whiteboard cleaned and started auctioning off the cane toads again. The bidding was a little less spirited this time and Les was able to get four the white for twenty dollars. The pot finished up at eighty dollars, all bets were settled and Norton's hands went into his bag once again as another boozy, expectant hush went over the crowd.

'Is everybody ready? Okay. Go!' The compere whipped the carton away for the final event.

Les looked at the jumble of cane toads in the circle and gave them a quick double blink. I don't believe it, he smiled to himself. The great spirit is surely with me. Either that or Woody has got a lucky aura. Number four the white actually moved slowly away from the other toads, turned round and sat down with its backside facing Norton. Les couldn't miss. A noise rose above the crowd as the punters cheered on their respective cane toads. Woody then yelled, spilling more drink, and Les let go with another paper clip, whacking four the white right up the arse. It jumped straight over the other cane toads and out of the circle towards the beer garden. Richard, however, was a little more on the ball this time. He fell backwards like a slip fieldsman and caught number four before it got too far. Les eased the rubber bands off, grabbed his camera and jumped to his feet again.

'Woody. What can I say?' he grinned. 'You're not just a legend, you're a bloody immortal. You are out there.'

Woody was jumping around fit to bust. 'I told you, Les! I told you! You just have to tune into the energy grids.'

'And the winner is ... number four the white. Rainbow Princess.'

Les took a quick photo of Richard holding number four; he then gave his camera to a table of Japanese next to theirs, sat back down next to Woody and got them to take a photo. They were only too willing to oblige, before rattling off a few shots for themselves. One politely handed Les back his camera, as Richard came over with Woody's winnings.

'Your girlfriend's very lucky tonight,' he said, a somewhat mystified look on his face and more than a hint of suspicion in his voice.

'Luck? Listen mate, luck's got nothing to do with it,' said Les. 'This woman is the reincarnation of an ancient priestess from the city of Atlantis.'

Woody gasped and slapped Les on the arm. 'How did you know?'

'I don't know how I knew, Woody. I just did. It must be your aura.'

'There you go, miss.' Richard handed Woody another roll of money.

'Thankyou.'

'You're welcome.' The compere gave Les a suspicious look then went back to his travelling cane toad show to get ready to pack up.

Les downed the last of his drink and placed his glass on the table. 'Well, Woody,' he said, shaking his head. 'I don't know. Getting the first two up, yeah. But picking Rainbow Princess in the last, I honestly don't know how you did it.'

Woody smiled and placed her tiny hand on Norton's. 'I told you, Les. Creative visualisation. With a little magnetic polarisation too.'

'You don't think the bottle of wine, four beers and about two hundred mango daiquiris had anything to do with it?'

Woody gave Les a boozy, crooked grin. 'It probably helped.'

'How much did you end up winning?'

Woody had a look in her dolphin handbag. 'Over two hundred dollars.'

'Good on you.'

'Hey, but ... isn't some of this money yours?'

Norton shook his head. 'No. That's karma money. If I was to take that back, it would destroy all the auras. And I'd probably turn into a toad myself.'

'Oh. All right then.'

Les looked at his empty glass and noticed Woody's was empty too. He also noticed Richard had his sunglasses off and was looking at something near the edge of the circle that had caught his eye.

'Anyway, my little mystical friend. I've had about enough for the night, and I have to be up fairly early. How about I walk you to your room? Unless you want to stay here and celebrate?'

Woody gave her petite blonde head a little shake. 'No, I think I might go too.'

'Good idea, Rainbow Princess. This is a pretty rough part of town. You could get mugged around here with all that money.'

'You got anything to drink back in your room?'

Les looked at the Rainbow Princess for a moment. 'Exactly five small bottles of beer.'

'That'll do,' said Woody. 'Why don't we have a nightcap back at your place?'

'Why not indeed?'

They got up from the table and started walking towards the pool area. As they passed Richard, the compere had the bent paper clip in his fingers and was staring at it like a gorilla that had just picked up a green banana.

'Goodnight, Richard,' said Woody, waving her dolphin handbag under his face. 'I had a great night. Thanks a lot.'

'Yes. Goodnight miss. I'm glad you enjoyed yourself,' was the very sober reply.

'It was great, Richard. And so were you. I can't wait for the next meeting.' Les placed his hand gently in the small of Woody's back and ushered her past the pool in the direction of their rooms.

Les didn't quite know what to think as they walked through the landscaped plants and gardens and along the passageway. What was on the Rainbow Princess's mind wanting to go back to his room? Surely not the business. The idea of throwing Woody up in the air hadn't entered Norton's mind since he had first met her. She was cute and she certainly had sex appeal. But she was more like a colourful little kitten, like a friendly pixie, or a toy almost. Besides that, she'd talk you out of it before you got started. Also, it was bad enough that Les was two-timing Katherine a little with Evelyn. Now he'd be three-timing the both of them. There were a certain number of principles to be upheld here; along with ethics, honour and the Norton esprit de corps. No, Woody was probably just a bit pissed and wanted to have a mag for a while. Well, that was cool. One beer, a bit of human transformation, maybe slaughter a goat or a couple of chickens and read their entrails, then beddy-byes.

As they reached the passageway leading to Norton's room, Woody stopped. 'I'll just go to my room for a minute,' she said. 'I won't be long.'

'Okay. Mine's just down there. Last on the right.'

Back in the air-conditioned comfort of his room,

Les went to the bathroom, changed into a clean, white T-shirt and kicked off his shoes. He cracked two beers, placed them on the bar fridge then fiddled around sorting out what he'd need for the next day. Before long there was a knock on the door and Woody was back, still carrying her dolphin handbag. She placed it on the table and Les handed her one of the beers.

'There you go, mate,' he said, clinking his bottle against hers.

'Thanks.' Woody took a guzzle then belched softly into her hand.

'What do you want on? TV or the radio?'

Woody shook her head. 'Nothing,' she smiled. 'Lie back on the bed facing this way and put the pillows behind your neck. I want to give you a spoil.'

'A spoil?' chuckled Les. 'What've you got in mind, Woody?'

'You'll see. It's cosmic.'

'Okay. Let's get into some heavy cosmic.'

A little mystified, Les had a mouthful of beer then did as he was told with his feet almost over the end of the bed. Woody pushed the pillows firmly beneath his neck then took a small bottle of sandalwood oil from her bag and a small, circular piece of plastic that looked familiar.

'What's that plastic thing?' asked Les.

'The bottom of a rocket soft drink container. I put my fingers in the little lumps and it makes them feel harder and more penetrating.'

'Yeah, right,' replied Les, still none the wiser.

Woody smeared a little oil over the five points of moulded plastic, then sat on the bed and smeared some more oil across Norton's forehead and around his temple. She took another guzzle of beer, put her fingers inside the piece of plastic container and started rubbing it in circles around Norton's forehead.

Woody wasn't just talking space junk this time when she said it would be a spoil. The way she moved the smooth, plastic knobs over his head it felt exactly like someone's firm, penetrating fingers digging deep yet gently into his skin, giving him the most beautiful, relaxing scalp massage.

'Ohh yeah,' said Les from behind closed eyes. 'How good's this?'

'I told you it would be a spoil,' answered Woody.

'Mmmhh, reckon.'

'But I've had a lovely night, and you're a nice man, Les. You deserve it.'

'Mmhh. I ain't gonna argue with you.'

Woody added a little more aromatic oil and kept massaging away; Les felt that relaxed, at some stages he thought his head was going to float away like a balloon on a piece of string. Sometimes she'd hit a nerve spot near his temples and there would be a quick throb of pain. But just as quickly Woody would get her fingers going and gently massage the pain away.

'This will soon clear those blocked up chakras.' Woody's voice sounded like it was coming from miles away.

'Yeah,' replied Les sleepily. 'Clear up something.'

She massaged Norton's eyes, the bones down the sides of his broken nose, went into his sinus cavities. Les couldn't remember ever feeling anything like it. Eventually she stopped.

Les heard her have a drink and slowly opened his eyes. 'Woody ... that was absolutely sensational.'

'I'm glad you liked it,' she smiled.

'Like it?' Les reached over and put his hand on hers. 'I just wish there was something I could do for you.'

'You already have, Les.' Woody gave Norton's hand a soft squeeze. 'But there is something else you could do for me.'

'Sure, mate. What is it?'

'Would you have sex with me?'

Les gave Woody a dreamy, double blink. 'What was that?'

'Would you have sex with me?' Woody repeated.

Les couldn't help an almost imperceptible laugh. 'All right. If you insist. But shit, Woody. I'll probably squash you.'

Woody shook her head and the coloured feathers bobbed around her shoulders. 'No. Not if you do it my way.'

'Your way?'

'Yes,' nodded Woody. 'Stay as you are. But take your shorts off and put a pillow under your bum.'

'Okay, evil seductress,' said Les, undoing his belt. 'You're the dominant one.'

Les got down to the altogether and slipped one of the pillows under his backside. Mr. Wobbly was half flopping around not quite sure what was going on, but he started coming out of his slumber when Woody undid the laces down the front of her hot pants and slid them off over her boots. Underneath, she was wearing a shiny pair of crutchless, silver knickers with a delicate, pink trim that had Mr. Wobbly now thinking it was well and truly time to rise and shine, there was work to be done. The Rainbow Princess wasn't saying much now. She opened her blue dolphin handbag, took out a condom and daintily tore the packet open. Les couldn't help a quiet laugh; it was rainbow-coloured.

'Is that an organic condom?' he asked.

'Yes,' nodded Woody. 'And colour co-ordinated to fit any occasion.'

Woody sat down on the bed and gave Les a gentle kiss, delicately slipping her sweet little tongue in; she then reached down and started softly stroking Mr. Wobbly. Les kissed Woody back before she stopped, smiled and ran her tongue down his chest and over his stomach then around Mr. Wobbly. She didn't quite put it all in her mouth, just gave it lingering tongue kisses and tiny nibbles that caused several beads of sweat to form on Norton's forehead and a tear of joy to trickle out the side of one eye.

From her handbag Woody then took a bottle of sweet-smelling sandalwood oil and rubbed a little around Norton's steaming red boner. She then slipped the condom on and started rubbing a little oil over that as well, leaving Mr. Wobbly sticking up in the air like a rainbow-coloured candy bar that hard a school of piranhas couldn't sink their teeth into it.

'Now,' smiled Woody, as she placed her tiny hands on Norton's chest and started to straddle him, 'I'll just sit up here and do some different sort of channelling.'

Les smiled up at her. 'Go for your life, Rainbow Princess,' he said. 'Be my guest.'

Woody eased herself down onto Les and the last thing he saw before he closed his eyes and scrunched his head back onto the pillows beneath his neck was Woody's blonde hair and coloured feathers swinging from side to side, and a cute backside still in a pair of shiny, silver knickers going up and down on his rainbow-coloured old boy.

Woody didn't make a great deal of noise; mainly lots of oohs and ahhs and eehs and ohs with the occasional unnngh now and again. She started off slow then went a bit faster then slowed up again, but then began pushing down further. Les just lay on the bed with his eyes closed holding Woody gently by the elbows. He thought this wasn't too bad at all — but doesn't everybody fill up on beautiful food, have a sensational scalp massage then get a delightful porking on Wednesday night?

The Rainbow Princess started really getting into it and by then Norton was starting to come to the boil as well. He could hear her breath coming out in short, hard gasps, just as something inside Les was beginning to spiral up out of control also. Woody bent her head forward in a great flurry of blonde hair and feathers, moaned, then got her rocks off, while Les howled with delight, arched up and almost blew the end out of the condom. Woody gave it a moment or two then climbed off and lay down next to Les. He put his arm around her, kissed her on the lips then gave her another one on the cheek.

'Well, Woody,' he said, 'anytime I can be of assistance to you, you be sure to let me know. That was no trouble at all.'

'Thanks, Les,' she said, giving Norton a kiss on the cheek also. 'You're a nice, nice man. And that was really cosmic.'

'Yes,' conceded Norton. 'And in a way you could say I was pretty much the perfect lover.'

'The perfect lover? How do you work that out?'

'Well, I didn't blow in your mouth. There's no chance of you getting pregnant. And ...' Les pulled the condom off, tied a quick knot in it and flicked it across the room into the room tidy. 'I took the wet spot with me.'

'That's certainly one way of looking at it.'

'Now I'll walk you to your room.'

'There's no need to.'

'No,' Les shook his head defiantly. 'I insist. It's getting late and this is a bad part of town.'

'All right then. Thanks.'

Les put his shorts back on while Woody climbed into her hot pants; she placed the pillows back at the end of the bed and dumped the two empty bottles into the room tidy.

'Do you want to take a couple of those beers with you?' he asked.

'Yeah, okay. Thanks.'

Les put two of the beers in Woody's handbag, put his swipe card in his pocket and walked Woody arm in arm along the passageway to her room.

On the way, he told her about the bar in town with the two bands he was thinking of going and having a look at the following night. Did she want to come? Woody was keen, so Les said he'd ring her when he got back from whitewater rafting. Probably around seven. They had a sweet kiss goodnight and the last Les saw was Woody's pixie little smile disappearing behind her door. Five minutes later Les was stripped off in his room wondering if all that had really happened? He picked the rainbow-coloured condom up out of the room tidy and flushed it down the toilet. Yep. It had happened all right. After the massage and the empty Norton was totally and completely relaxed. His chakras were cleared and his bilges pumped. A minute later he was scrunched back into the pillows snoring his head off.

Les woke up a couple of minutes before quarter to six and was still quietly laughing to himself about Woody when the wake up call from the resort office came through right on time. He swung out of bed, cleaned his teeth then climbed into his Levi shorts, thongs and a plain white T-shirt. Most of what Les thought he'd need on the day he'd put in his bag the night before; all he added was the unopened packet of cashews and his book for a nibble and a read on the bus. He had a last look around the room, got his swipe card and walked over to the big dining room he'd passed the day before.

Inside it was all crisp white tablecloths and fans whirling beneath high ceilings with room for a hundred. But there were only about a dozen getting into the buffet breakfast when Les strolled in and gave the girl at the desk his room number. Breakfast was the usual eggs, sausage, bacon, fruit, cereal and whatever, but it was all fresh and delicious. Les had three plates plus toast with apricot jam and an extra coffee then walked out the front just as a small, red and yellow bus pulled up in the driveway towing a trailer full of blue and yellow, eight seater dinghies. The resort provided the guests with towels; Les took two, showed the bus driver his ticket then climbed aboard, joining about a dozen other punters from various resorts and hotels around Cairns. From there it was a short drive over to the Rolling Thunder depot, where they all got out and climbed into two bigger buses for the trip out to Tully.

Already the day was punishingly hot and humid with more fat, grey banks of clouds hanging over the green tops of the mountains surrounding Cairns and again for some reason Les was reminded of Hawaii. The bus, however, was nicely air-conditioned with the local radio station playing and about three-quarters full. Les found a seat half-way along, sat down and checked out his fellow thrill seekers.

Apart from the driver and a young river guide next to him who both looked more like surfies in their board shorts and T-shirts, Les appeared to be the only other Australian on the bus. The rest were a mixture of casually dressed Japanese, Europeans and pommies, all shiny and happy and looking forward to a day's whitewater rafting in Queensland.

They were a mixed bag of all sizes and denominations. None of the blokes would have got a start as extras on *Melrose Place* or *The Bold And The Beautiful* and the best rap you could give any of the girls would be plain.

The bus moved off last in a column of three. The river guide introduced himself over the microphone as Gary then went around handing out release forms stating the participants agreed whitewater rafting was a hazardous adventure sport and you accepted all responsibilities. In other words, if you drowned or went over a rapid and broke your back in six places and finished up a quadriplegic in a wheelchair for the rest of your life — stiff shit. Gary also asked if there were any epileptics on the bus to let the guides know because if they didn't and they saw you flopping around in the water or on the ground they might think you were having a good time or getting into some new dance and as the guides liked a good time too they'd probably join in. Hello, thought Les. Here we go again. Everyone wants to be a comedian. But Gary and the bus driver were two of your true blue, laconic, leg-pulling Australians. They waffled on with some light-hearted banter explaining safety procedures. Where to put your stuff and how to form into groups. Les liked the line he ended with: there was no smoking on the river and as they'd be out there for a fair while the best idea if you smoked would be to stick all your cigarettes in your mouth at once and take one huge drag before you left.

The bus slowed down due to some traffic. Gary explained that they were now approaching an army checkpoint where they were tightening up security for the coming Olympic Games and the bus would be thoroughly searched by members of the SAS. This brought all the Europeans to attention, while the poms exchanged surprised looks and the Japanese went into a huddle. Then it was a case of: 'seriously folks', as Gary explained it was only a fruit fly inspection station and an officer from the Fruit Fly Board would come on the bus and inspect all bags. You needn't worry if you had a fully automatic weapon in your bag or a kilogram of marijuana. That was cool. But if they found so much as an apple core or a banana peel on you, you were in deep shit. Worse than the bloke in *Midnight Express*.

Five minutes later a beefy woman in a blue uniform bustled on board, removed a half eaten Jonathon and they proceeded on their way again. The guide ran a video on the bus TV about whitewater rafting. But Les couldn't get all that good a view from where he was seated, and by now he'd had enough of jokes and safety lectures. So he unzipped his bag, took out his book and started reading. He was just enjoying the part where Frankie

Hearts got his legs blown off outside the Veterans and Friends Club when the bus pulled up at the Rolling Thunder souvenir shop and bar for a break.

There was a mini stampede out of the three buses when they stopped so the punters could queue up at the Rolling Thunder Roadhouse to get sandwiches and chocolates or whatever. Norton didn't particularly need anything, having had more than a good breakfast back at the resort. He settled for a quick snakes then checked the place out. There was a row of chairs and tables in one section where you could view a video of the day's events when the bus called in on the way back. A counter where you could buy a copy of the video, plus photos, Rolling Thunder T-shirts and shorts, a bar out the back and another counter selling food and drinks. After another quick look around at the place and the punters, Les bought a bottle of mineral water and got back on the bus. Before long the other seats filled up and they were on their way again. It was a two hour trip via Innisfail and Tully, through the canefields and forests. Les was nibbling cashew nuts, sipping mineral water and getting ready for Frankie DeCicco and his shooters to whack Paul Castellano at Sparks Steak House on the lower east side when the buses all ground to a halt in their special parking area a few hundred metres down from Tully Dam.

About eighty people got off the three buses and stood around taking in the rugged green beauty of the surrounding mountains and the Tully River roaring across the rocks below. The guides were going around marshalling everyone into groups and urging everyone to hurry because the more time you spent up here, the less time you got on the river. Les was handed a bulky, red safety jacket, blue helmet and paddle and told if he didn't want to wear his trainers on the river the company hired them for two dollars. Les found a pair of old Dunlop Volleys that fitted perfectly; he changed into them and his wet training shorts from the day before. He stowed everything else in his bag and put it in the lock up under the bus. Next thing Les was padded up, helmeted and standing holding his paddle wondering what group he should join. There were five blokes standing next to him under a number eight. An English voice said:

'Christ! What about these outfits? We look like those sperm cells in that Woody Allen movie about sex.'

Delta Force Eight'll do me, thought Les. 'Do you fellas mind if I join you?'

The brown-haired river guide with them gave Les a quick once up and down. 'You'll do perfect, mate. Righto fellas. Let's go.'

With their guide leading they joined the other groups down a rocky path through the bush to the river below. As they were clambering along in their bulky jackets, paddles over their shoulders or wherever, Les got a bit of a chit chat going while he checked out the other members of Delta Force Eight. There were seven counting Les and the guide. Two poms, a Swiss, a Belgian and a Canadian. They all had dark hair and all had the same medium to lean builds. The guide wore a white safety helmet with a green safety vest and matching board shorts and his name was Mick. Mick had a rugged face and a square jaw, with a lean, fit build like a gymnast. He also had an adrenalin junkie's eyes, and by his attitude and the way he spoke Les tipped that Mick might have quite a bit of Aussie larrikin in him. In fact, glancing around at the other ten or so river guides and safety men Les guessed they were all adrenalin junkies with a monster streak of Aussie larrikin in them. Good, he thought.

There were ten, solid, rubber dinghies tied to the bank; they found number eight and Mick looked at his crew. 'Can everyone swim?' Les and the Canadian nodded; the rest exchanged glances. 'Well, it doesn't matter,' said Mick. 'Your vest'll float you. But remember one thing — if you fall out of the boat, keep your feet up as you're going along.'

'Why is that?' asked the Belgian.

'Because if your foot jams under a rock, you'll break your leg.'

'Oh.'

'Okay. Now everybody jump in the water first and get wet.'

Like the others, Les plunged into the safe little eddy where the boats were tied at the edge of the river. You couldn't go under far because of the bulky life jacket, but Les couldn't believe the water. It was fantastic. Like floating in beautiful, bubbling champagne; fresh and invigorating, but definitely not cold. Les floated around for a minute taking it all in. The cool, green water, the roar of the river rushing over the rocks and boulders, the weathered cliffs towering up through the emerald forest towards the clusters of grey clouds drifting across the blue sky above. Even if Les had just lain there doing nothing till the sun went down, it still would have been a great day.

'Okay, fellas. Everybody in the boat.'

Getting in the boat with the bulky life jacket on was a bit tricky. Mick showed them how to pull up on the ropes then kind of slither in on your side. Then he showed them how to paddle and how to hold it under your other arm when you weren't paddling so it didn't fly loose and knock someone's front teeth out. How to go left, go right, down the middle, and other tips. Then they all sat up on the edge of the boat, Les and the Canadian in the front, the others round the middle and Mick up back. He had a look around at the other boats then undid the rope.

'Okay. Here we go ...'

They were the third boat out and there was more to it than just drifting along in the current. You had to paddle backwards and forwards as well as all together, otherwise you would have just spun round in circles before bouncing off the rocks sticking out the middle of the river and the cliffs and boulders on the sides. Plus you had to paddle into the rapids to clear the bubbling, churning whitewater at the bottom, which was as much air as it was water. If you didn't, you got stuck there because of the hydraulics. They paddled fairly leisurely along, then Mick spoke.

'Righto, fellas. We call this first one the alarm clock.'

'Why's that?' asked one of the poms.

Mick smiled. 'Because it wakes you up. Okay. Rock'n'roll.'

They paddled furiously between two rows of boulders and Les stared at what looked like a surging waterfall looming up ahead. He just had time to furl his paddle and grab the rope when down they went hitting the bottom with a thump and a great spray of water that drenched the lot of them. Solid as it was, the dinghy jack-knifed in the middle and the Swiss went flying over the front like he'd been fired out of a slingshot. By the time the rest of Delta Force Eight got their shit together and started paddling, the Swiss was on his back tumbling over the rapids.

'Righto. Let's pick him up,' said Mick.

Everybody started paddling and they soon pulled up alongside the Swiss. The Canadian took one side of his jacket, Les the other, as the Swiss grabbed the rope and they swung him inside on his back.

'You okay?' asked Mick.

'Yes. Yes. I am fine,' answered the Swiss. His eyes looked like a giant squid's, he was spluttering water and not able to swim and he'd obviously been terrified. But once he realised it was just about impossible to drown with his jacket on, the safety helmet protected his head and his trusty team mates were with him in an instant, he was okay. He picked up his paddle and rejoined the others on the side of the boat.

Mick thrust his fist into the middle of the boat. 'Righto. Hands together for that one, boys.'

Delta Force Eight gave a cheer, thumped their fists together then took to their paddles again.

Next up was a long set of shallow rapids with another drop at the end called The Double D Cup. Mick said this got its name from a blonde German backpacker who decided to undo her life jacket for a moment or two. Her boat hit the rapids and she want arse over head losing her jacket plus the top of her bikini and the only thing that kept her afloat were her two massive tits. Every river guide on the Tully plunged in to save her and she finished up written into whitewater rafting folklore.

'Okay. Paddle left boys... Now right...'

Delta Force Eight did as they were told. They spun round in a circle, bounced off several boulders, then hit the drop at a slight angle in another great splash of white water, jack-knifing the dinghy. This time it was Norton's turn to get flung out of the boat.

Whether he wasn't sitting right or he didn't grab the rope on time, Les wasn't sure. All he knew was that his feet went up in front of him and he bounced backwards, to finish up in the hydraulics under the boat. His first instinct was to dive down and swim away. But the surging wash and the bulky jacket prevented that. Using his hands, Les starting inching his way beneath the bottom of the dinghy. With his lungs bursting, his heart pounding and his life flashing before his eyes, Les crawled under the bottom of the dinghy for a full two and a half seconds before bobbing up near the front with a nose full of water. The two poms helped him in and the Swiss smiled and handed him his paddle.

'Shit!' said Mick, a half-smile on his face. 'I dead set thought we'd lost you then. I was starting to panic.'

'Don't worry,' said Les, snorting water out of his nose. 'I've got a knife in my jacket. I would have cut the bottom straight out of the boat and crawled in.'

'Hands together for that one, boys.' Delta Force Eight thumped their fists together then paddled to a small bay at the side of the river to wait for the other boats.

Les took his helmet off and sat back on the edge of the boat to watch the other rafters. Everybody was having the time of their lives. Laughing, yelling and cheering. A boatload of Japanese were the best to watch. They'd hit the rapids and the drops with looks of absolute terror and horror on their faces. Then, as soon as it was over, they'd all start laughing fit to burst. River guides would stand on the rocks with ropes to make sure everybody was safe while another one would appear out of nowhere with a camcorder and capture everything on film. To top it off a boatload of girls came down the last drop at the wrong angle and the lot of them went in the river.

'Quick men. To the rescue,' said Mick.

Les jammed his helmet on and they paddled out to the middle of the river to start dragging spluttering, startled backpackers into their boat. The last one in had just about lost the bottom half of her bikini revealing the biggest, hairiest map of Tasmania Les could ever remember seeing. Moses couldn't have parted it. Delta Force Eight looked at it, looked at each other then as one thrust their fists into the middle of the boat.

'Oh yeah,' said Mick. 'Definitely hands together for that one, boys.'

After taking the backpackers they'd rescued back to their boats, Delta Force Eight waited till everyone had caught up then paddled off again. They bounced off some of the boulders in mid-stream, hit the cliffs now and again along the banks of the river. The two poms went over the side going down The Maze and they lost the Belgian when they hit the bottom of The Corkscrew. The only two who hadn't hit the drink so far were Mick and the Canadian. A big thrill among the various boat crews was to try and splash the living daylights out of each other with your paddles as you came alongside. The first time Les tried it he nearly got blinded by a faceful of water from the Japanese boat. They were the sneakiest. After several losing encounters, Les finally realised the idea was to get in front of your opponents and splash backwards; that way you could jam your paddle harder into the water. Another thing that brought howls of delight was when the river guides fell out of the boats. It made everybody's day. However, after watching some of the guides' more spectacular tumbles into the water, Les had a droll feeling that a few of them were staged.

One thing the guides couldn't stage, however, was their enthusiasm and sense of humour. They had to be the greatest bunch of good time Charlies Les had ever come across. Barrelling down the Tully River in rubber dinghies was a mountain of fun by itself; but the guides with their joke-cracking and antics were definitely the icing on the cake. They came to a wide, gentle, tree-shrouded bend in the river, tied the boats up and stopped for lunch.

Everybody got out of their life jackets and filed up to a sheltered area Rolling Thunder had built beneath the trees. Lunch was monster hamburgers or sausage sandwiches, help yourself to the salad, and all washed down with coffee, tea or cordial. Les settled for a sausage sanger with BBQ sauce and a mug of tea and, like everybody else, wore what he didn't eat. While everyone was stuffing themselves, two of the guides roamed around with a camcorder and a microphone doing quick interviews with the punters. Eventually they got to Les.

'Hello. What's your name?'
'Les.'
'Having a good time, Les?'
'Reckon.'
'First time rafting?'

'Yep,' nodded Les, then pointed his finger into the lens. 'But like the man said in the movie. Hasta la vista baby. I'll be back.'

Les meant it too. If he couldn't get back up here with Katherine, he'd shout either Billy or Warren. Whitewater rafting down the Tully was too good to experience only once and on your own. A thought crossed Norton's mind as he leant on the wooden railing and gazed down on the cool, green water flowing past. I'd like to bring Evelyn up here and undo her life jacket going down The Double D Cup. I think the guides might rename it something else after that. Les had time for another half a mug of tea and they were on their way again.

Delta Force Eight was the first boat away and after about ten minutes of easy paddling Mick pointed to a sheer cliff face coming up a hundred metres or so on their left.

'I think we'd better give the poms a shower,' he said.

They drew up against the cliff beneath two crystal clear streams of water cascading down from the rocks fifty metres above. It gently tumbled and splashed into the boat and the water around them and felt absolutely glorious. Les let it fall on his face, cupped some in his hands and drank it, caught some in his helmet and dumped it over his head. Mick said this was called Champagne Falls. After he put his helmet back on and they paddled off to let some other boats under, Les wished he could have bottled about two hundred litres of Champagne Falls and taken it back home with him.

Delta Force Eight paddled on zipping down different rapids with different names while Mick shouted orders to paddle left, paddle right, move left, move right and so on. Les fell out again at the bottom of one rapid, so did the two poms and the Belgian; and still the only one who hadn't fallen out so far was the Canadian. They came to another spectacularly beautiful section where the river seemed to narrow on the left between two huge boulders. Mick told them to stop just before one of the boulders.

'Okay, fellas,' he said. 'This next one's called The Ninja Drop.'

'This is also called the guide's revenge, yes?' said the Belgian.

'No, it ain't. Now fellas,' assured Mick. 'The only way to go down this one, is to do exactly what I say.'

Mick told them to leave their paddles down the back of the boat with him, then all sit up the front in a circle with their heads down and their arms around each others shoulders. Everybody did as they were told, but somehow Norton's instinct, sense of balance and water to weight ration told him this was a gee up.

'You right now, fellas? Okay. Here we go.' Mick kicked off from the boulder they were up against and gave a few quick stabs at the water with his paddle.

Les felt the boat start to move then pick up a little speed. He had a quick peek to his right to see a sheer, five metre drop of rushing water coming up. I knew this was a gee up, was his last thought as the boat slipped over the top, careened down the rapid then ploughed nose first into a deep hole of bubbling water and, as if in slow motion, jack-knifed in the middle. Everyone, except Mick, went arse over head into the river. The spluttering members of Delta Force Eight bobbed to the surface and almost in one voice heaped a torrent of abuse on their river guide. Mick just sat there grinning, then shook his head.

'Don't bother putting your hands together for that one, boys.'

Everyone got back in the boat then sat back against the cliff face watching the guides do the same thing to all the others. Ironically, the only ones who managed not to get tossed out was the boatload of women. After a while they all paddled off again. There were one or two more rapids, after which they all pulled up at the side of another sheltered bend in the river and that was it. Seventeen kilometres and five hours of sheer fun and exhilaration over. Well, thought Les happily, as he floated around with the others soaking up the last few moments of the river before they got out, that has to be the best hundred dollars I've ever spent. Thankyou sweet Katherine Hannan.

It didn't take long to help bundle the dinghies up to where the buses were waiting for them. Everybody handed in their life jackets and helmets, retrieved their dry clothes from under the buses and got changed. After putting on the same clothes he wore earlier, Les took one or two photos of the fellow rafters then climbed aboard. A safety check to make sure no one had drowned and they were on their way.

Most of the others on the bus looked like they'd just finished a fifteen rounder and were glad to get their backsides on a dry seat. Les, on the other hand, felt great. His skin was still tingling from the beautiful, clean water, he had no muscle soreness; it was as if he'd just finished an easy workout then gone swimming in the fountain of youth. The guide with the driver ran another rafting video for those who were interested; half of whom nodded off before it finished. Les watched it for a while reliving some memories still fresh in his mind, then went back to his book. Sammy's pal, Joe (Stymie) D'Angelo had just got whacked by a Colombian in Tali's bar when the buses pulled up again at the Rolling Thunder Roadhouse and everybody got out for drinks, nibblys and souvenirs if they wanted them.

Norton's team, plus Mick, congregated at table eight amidst all the other punters. Les got a bottle of Fourex for himself and one for their river guide. They all toasted each other's health and discussed the day's events over cheese and bickies, then Rolling Thunder ran fifteen minutes of the day's video set to Creedence Clearwater Revival and compered by two of the guides who sounded like Martin and Molloy. It was hilarious and every boat was in it; including Les going arse over head at The Double D Cup.

As soon as it finished, Norton was first in the queue with his plastic to get a copy, plus photos and T-shirts to be sent to his home at Bondi. He had time to shout Mick one more beer and shake hands with the rest of Delta Force Eight, then everyone got back on the buses.

It was dark when they arrived again in Cairns to change into the smaller buses for the lifts back to where they were all staying, and everyone around him was pretty much on the nod. But Les was still full of beans when he was dropped off at Colony Resort. He was still whistling happily when he walked into his room and was heading for a shave and a shower when the phone rang. It was the Rainbow Princess.

'Hello, Woody. How are you?'

'Unreal, Les. Totally, totally cosmic.'

'I thought you might have been.'

'What about yourself?'

'Good. I just walked in the door, to tell you the truth.'

'Did you?'

'Yep. Just this very second.'

'Unreal.'

'So what's doing tonight, Woody? Do you still want to come and see those two bands with me?'

'Yeah. For sure. But I'm still out at my friend's place at Kamerunga and I'm going to have something to eat here. How about I meet you at nine o'clock?'

'Okey doke. You want me to call round to your room?'

'If that's all right by you.'

'Couldn't be creamier, Woody.'

'Okay, Les. I'll see you at nine o'clock.'

'See you then, Woody. May the force be with you.'

That suits me, thought Les. I got plenty of time and all I got to do is feed myself. Good one. He hung up the phone, stripped off and climbed under the shower.

After daubing himself with just a smidgen of Eau Sauvage, Les figured the place they were going would be both casual and smoky. So he gave the same blue T-shirt he wore on the plane a quick press then threw that on with his Levis and a pair of black, Nautica gym boots. The only question was whether to take the car and stay sober, or get a taxi and tie one on a bit. You could bet the Rainbow Princess would be hitting the bar like the Australian submarine fleet on shore leave. It might be best to stay sober and keep an eye on her. Les got the car keys and his swipe card and walked across to where he'd had breakfast that morning.

This time the dining room was about half full and the evening fare was satay, curry, cold cuts, rice pasta, and plenty of vegetables and sweets. Les got a table near the servery and had five small plates, bread rolls, all washed down with coffee and OJ. He finished off another orange juice and looked at his watch; it was time to get the Rainbow Princess. What'll she be wearing tonight, he wondered, as he went round to knock on her door. Actually I thought she looked pretty good last night with those feathers in her hair.

'Hi, Les. I won't be a moment.'

'You're right, Woody. There's no mad hurry.'

Woody returned in a few seconds carrying the familiar dolphin handbag and locked the door. She was wearing the same Egyptian motif T-shirt tied in the middle with a maroon, snakeskin belt, skin tight red pants covered in little black and white bats, and pink plastic shoes done up with rainbow shoelaces. Two turquoise crocodiles hung from her ears and perched on her head was a pointy, rainbow beanie. She looked like a cross between Queen Nefertiti and a gumnut baby.

'How are you tonight, Les?' she said, beaming up at Norton as she slipped her arm in his.

'Firing on all cylinders, old mate,' Les smiled back at her. 'So you had a good day, did you, Woody?'

'Oh, wait till I tell you about it, Les. It was full on cosmic.'

'That's good. No doubt you'll be having the odd drink or fifty tonight Rainbow Princess?'

Woody shook her head. 'No. No way. I'll just drink mineral water.'

'Mineral water?'

'Yes. I'm feeling too spiritual to get out of it tonight, Les. Mineral water'll do me.'

'Really?' Les looked at the Rainbow Princess happily bouncing along beside him. 'Hey, Woody. Have you got your driver's licence with you?'

'Sure. It's in my handbag. In my wallet. Why?'

'How would you like to take a spin in a brand new four-wheel drive? With power steering and five on the floor?'

'Oh, cool. I'd be stoked.'

'Good.'

Cool all right, thought Les as he handed Woody the keys. Saves me having to catch bloody taxis and this way I can have a few bourbons instead of having to drink gallons of unleaded all night. Plus the insurance is kosher as long as I'm in the car if she rolls it. And while she's driving it might shut her up for five minutes. Les walked Woody across to the parking area and opened the car door for her.

Woody was all excited as she got behind the wheel and adjusted the seat up as high as she could. Les clicked her seatbelt for her and explained the gear shift, then worked the windscreen wipers as a little light rain started to fall. Woody kicked the engine over and slipped the Overlander into reverse. Oh well, thought Les, making a mental sign of the cross as Woody backed out of the parking area and the headlights cut through the drizzle in front of them, this couldn't be more dangerous than whitewater rafting. And I'll be half pissed coming back so I won't give a stuff anyway.

However, Norton need not have worried. Woody handled the four by four like an old pro, slipping through the gears with ease while her pink shoes bounced lightly over the pedals. He gave directions and picked up an old Marc Hunter and Dragon track on the radio and before he knew it Woody had reversed easily into a parking spot on The Esplanade just past where they were going.

'It's a bit early to go straight in,' said Les, as they got out and locked the car. 'Why don't we have a drink somewhere first and check out the night markets? I might buy a couple of souvenirs for some friends back in Sydney.'

'Okay,' she agreed. 'That sounds like a good idea.'

There was a different crowd now to what Les had seen in town the day before. The hippies appeared thin on the ground and there were well-dressed couples among the people walking past plus a few drunks and Japanese with their hair dyed blonde. The restaurants all seemed to be doing an even trade and a police car sat on the taxi rank while another cruised past in the steady flow of traffic. The restaurant where Les stopped for coffee had a liquor licence; they found an empty table out the front and Les got a bottle of Fourex for himself and a mineral water for Woody.

'Well ... Here's to the cosmos again, Woody,' he said, clinking her glass.

'Yes. To the cosmos Les,' replied Woody.

As Norton took a mouthful of beer he could see Woody was almost breaking her neck to tell him something. He took another and smiled at her.

'So what happened today, Woody?' he asked.

'No. You go first,' answered Woody.

'Okay.' Les told her as briefly as he could about

his day on the river. Falling out of the boat, the guides with their antics and joke cracking, stopping for a meal. How he'd ordered a video and that if they caught up in Sydney he'd show it to her. 'Yeah. It was a good day all right Woody. But next time I go, I'll take one of those disposable cameras with me.'

Woody laughed at Norton's description of the day's events then started up. Her girlfriend Mercia called round and after buying some extra crystals with the money she'd won, they drove out to a canefield somewhere between Ravenshoe and Tully.

'And there it was, Les. About two hundred metres in from the road. A beautiful, perfect agraglyph.'

'Go on,' said Les. 'And what was it in the shape of Woody? An FJ Holden? The Sydney Opera House?'

'No. Just a perfect circle eight metres across. With two smaller ones next to it. But the sugar cane was all interwoven not flattened and you could still feel the plasometric energy in the soil.'

Les had another mouthful of beer and looked up at the passers-by for a moment. 'So they'd definitely landed, Woody?'

'Oh yeah,' she replied. 'A magno-propulsar craft had been there all right, Les.'

'Bad luck you arrived late, Woody. You could have got a mag on with the driver and found out where it came from.'

'I already know that, Les.'

'You do?'

'Of course. Pine Gap.'

'Pine Gap? I would have thought the Bermuda Triangle.'

Woody shook her head. 'No. They used to fly out of Area 51 in Nevada. But too many people got onto them so they shifted operations to Australia.'

'Fair enough,' agreed Les. 'The way the Aussie dollar is they'd get a lot more ballistic, beta-particles for their buck.'

Woody went into a quick rave about magno-propulsar vehicles, anti-gravitational energy grids and interlinking power crystals. She lubricated this with mineral water then looked directly at Norton.

'Have you ever seen a UFO, Les?' she asked. 'You said your friend Warren had.'

Les wasn't quite sure how to answer this because he had seen something strange one night back home in Dirranbandi. He was looking after his brother's house for a few days while Murray had taken the family to Brisbane. It was late one night, he'd just switched off the TV and thought he heard a noise in the backyard. There was nothing there when he went out to investigate and seeing it was such a clear night Les thought he might as well have a leak and do a bit of star gazing while he was at it, because you often caught glimpses of meteorites and the family considered them lucky. Les was happily splashing away when he noticed a shooting star coming up on his right in a northerly direction and travelling parallel with the horizon. This one seemed a little unusual, however, because it had no tail and was just a glowing, white ball of light moving across the sky at some phenomenal speed. How high up it was Les couldn't tell. All he could think was that this was a good one because he'd been watching it for about four seconds and generally if you saw a meteorite you caught a quick glimpse and that was about it.

The object went past his right shoulder and Les watched it for at least another four seconds while it went on to pass his left shoulder. Then, without any loss of speed the object did an abrupt ninety degree turn to the right and disappeared into the stars. No sound. Nothing. One minute it was going in one direction. Then in less than a split second it was going in another. The only thing Les could compare it to was during a game of pool or snooker when you took a shot off the end cushion to cut a ball sitting in the middle of the table into a side pocket. What blew Les out completely, however, was he roughly calculated the object went five kilometres across the sky in five seconds — which meant in a minute it would go sixty kilometres, and whatever that was, multiplied by sixty, was how fast it was going an hour. At the time, Les just stared up at the night sky for a few minutes in disbelief wondering what he'd just seen. Whatever the glowing, white object was, it definitely wasn't any shooting star or meteorite. Les never told anybody what he'd seen and he thought now that he wouldn't bother telling Woody either or she'd probably have him there all night talking about it.

'No, Woody,' he said, shaking his head. 'I've never seen any UFO's. All I've seen is a few shooting stars out in the bush at night.' He drained the last of his Fourex. 'I might have another beer. You feel like another mineral water?'

'Okay. Can I have sparkling this time?'

'Sure.'

Les returned with the drinks and decided to change the subject. He took a sip of beer and nodded at the front of Woody's T-shirt.

'What about the pyramids, Woody,' he said. 'Have you figured out who built them?'

Woody took a sip of mineral water and nodded. 'Martians.'

'Martians? As in ...' Les pointed to the stars.

'That's right, Les. Martians.' Woody's eyes almost seemed to glow as she stared directly at him. 'You know what the pyramids are, don't you Les?'

'Yeah. Great big blocks of stone all piled up on top of each other somewhere in Egypt.'

'They're anti-gravitational battery chargers.'

'Battery chargers.' Les gave Woody a slow double blink. 'Sort of like ... Egyptian Alka-Nile Energisers?'

'You got it, Les. Only the Egyptians never built them.'

'They didn't?'

Woody shook her head. 'You see, Les, we originally came from Mars when its atmosphere burnt out. One tribe went to South America and built pyramids there. The other tribe went to Egypt.

Originally the pyramids were capped with polished limestone with a huge, copper conductor on top. The spacecraft used to lock onto this and recharge their gyro-propulsion units.'

'I see. So ... where did all this energy come from, Woody?'

'From the weight and the alignment of the pyramids. You see, Les, the pyramids weigh millions of tons. That all pushes down with incredible force, which is gravity. When the Martians built the pyramids, they aligned them due north and directly along the Earth's magnetic energy grids. Then they worked out the isopin quantum number, and with the use of interlinking crystals, were able to harness the forces of both anti-gravity and anti-matter. Simple.'

Yeah simple, thought Les, taking a good swig of beer and glad Woody was only drinking mineral water tonight. 'How come there were never any records kept of all this?'

'Well, there were. But the Spanish priests destroyed all the ones in South America when the conquistadors conquered the Aztecs. They said they were teachings of the devil. Likewise the ancient Egyptian priests destroyed any records of the pyramids being built. When they found them, they conned all the Pharaohs into thinking they were the key to eternal life. And they managed to keep themselves in power and a cushy job for years doing body embalming. Same with the Aztecs. They found their pyramids and got a good thing going with human sacrifices. People were pretty dumb then, Les, and believed anything priests or holy men told them. The old fear of the unknown.'

'They still do,' mused Norton, taking another swig of beer.

Woody's eyes were still glowing as she went into a rave about the giant face at Cydonia on Mars, the Nazca patterns in Peru and Synchotron Particle Accelerators. Les let her go for a while then finished his beer and looked at his watch.

'That's all very interesting, Woody,' he said. 'But the night market'll be closed soon. Why don't we go and check it out before it's too late.'

'Good idea,' replied Woody, clapping her tiny hands together. 'Let's go.'

Although the night markets were just about getting ready to pack up, there weren't too many punters around and business looked a little slow. They strolled round the four rows of shops and stalls selling T-shirts, clothes, wooden motorbikes and mini-guitars, second-hand books, Chinese massage and such like. A stall selling metal puzzles had a knot of punters watching a demonstration and there were a few in front of two glass blowers. The rest of the stall holders were mainly reading books or magazines, and those who weren't looked like if you pulled a twenty dollar bill out they'd chew your arm off to get it. Les wasn't all that keen on a cap or a T-shirt with either a crocodile or a tropical fish on the front when he saw the ideal souvenirs he wanted a few seconds before Woody.

'Hey, look at this, Rainbow Princess,' he said. 'It's last night's losers. They must have just got back from the glue factory.'

They came to a stall selling crocodile skin belts, leather hats, wallets, vests and things of that nature. Stacked out the front was a pile of dead cane toads that had been made into key ring holders. They'd been tanned and had little glass eyes. Some even had their arms still attached in the front. With the tiny glass eyes catching the light they almost looked as if they were still alive.

Woody picked one up. 'Oh dear ... I hope this isn't Amazonite.'

'No way, Woody,' assured Les. 'Your three toads were all champions. They'd be retired to stud by now.'

Les bought four cane toad key rings and Woody got two. Les also weakened and bought a T-shirt with Cairns and a coloured, Aboriginal crocodile motif on the front. They bundled all their souvenirs into one plastic bag then walked back to the car and left them on the front floor.

'Well Woody,' said Les, locking the doors and handing her the car keys, 'why don't we go and see if these bands are any good?'

'Good idea, Les,' said Woody. 'In fact, you're full of good ideas. I like you.'

'And I like you too. The fin might be a bit loose on your surfboard. But you'll do me for an old mate.'

A big lump of a bloke with dark hair and a white shirt with a security patch on the sleeve gave Les a smile and Woody a double blink as they walked into Jimbo's Blues Bar. They climbed two or three flights of stairs and came out on a landing where a man in a white shirt and tie sat behind a reception desk. It was five dollars entry. Les gave the man a ten and they walked inside past a wall that was the back of the stage. The interior was dark, dingy and mainly black decor. Shark jaws and drum kits hung off the ceiling and every wall was covered in either old rock posters or ones advertising booze. The stage faced a glass brick wall with an open landing behind it, to the right was a smattering of chairs and tables with several pool tables behind them. Left of stage a railing ran round a couple of steps that led up to a semi-circular bar area. Two blonde bar staff in black T-shirts hovered in front of the punters and off to their left was another smattering of stools and tables and a pool table near a wall covered with more rock band memorabilia. The crowd of about fifty, including the four couples on the dance floor, looked very casual and partial to a drink and a cigarette; they had faces that said not to get too far out of line with any of them unless you liked chewing your corn on the cob with no front teeth.

Up on stage some bloke dressed like an American Indian, complete with a war bonnet, and playing a rainbow-coloured guitar, fronted a band belting out a good solid lick of down home blues. In front of the stage two wary looking bouncers moved around through the cigarette smoke picking up glasses. Les pointed up from the dance floor to some empty stools on the right between the bar and the one pool table.

'Why don't we prop up there, Woody,' he said. 'We can get a good view of the band.'

'All right.'

They weaved their way amongst the other punters and found two stools with a drink stand. Les went to the bar and came back with a mineral water for Woody and double delicious for himself. As he sat down the band was tearing into 'Okie Dokie Stomp'. Les took a hit of Jack Daniels and started tapping his feet.

Woody watched him for a moment. 'Hey Les...' she said. 'Can you dance?'

'Can I dance?' replied Norton. 'Does Little Richard play the piano with both hands? Let's go!'

There was plenty of room on the dance floor, where Woody's style turned out to be some kind of jazz fusion and funk; Norton's was more rock'n'roll boogie with a bit of boot scootin' thrown in. Somehow they got a weird routine going and had some fun.

'Hey Les,' said Woody, as the song finished, 'you're the ultimate groove machine, baby.'

'You should have seen me before I lost both my feet from frostbite climbing Mount Everest.'

The band started into 'Rock This House' and Woody and Les funked and boogied all over the dance floor again. Les had her hand as she just came out of a triple spin when the band finished and the bloke in the American Indian outfit held his guitar up.

'Thankyou. That's it from us,' he mumbled. 'Now stick around for Rock Solid Steve and The Scorchers.'

'Ahh, bad luck, Woody,' said Les, as they walked off the dance floor. 'I was just starting to get warmed up.'

'Yeah. Me too.'

'We'll wait and see what the next mob's like.'

'Whatever you say, big daddy.'

They sat down again, sipped their drinks and got to talking about this and that, music and cars mainly. Woody told Les she drove a yellow beetle with a clapped-out gearbox. Les said his last car was stolen and he was in the market for another. He didn't bother mentioning the mighty Datty still parked out the front of Chez Norton. Woody finished her mineral water and insisted it was her shout. Les didn't argue.

While Woody was at the bar Les was thinking he wasn't wrong when he guessed earlier the place would be smoky. It was absolutely diabolical and his eyes were starting to sting already. Les was also thinking he was getting some very strange looks from several people around him. Unfriendly looks. Les made eye contact and smiled at two Aboriginal women who were staring at him and for his trouble seemed to get a look bordering on open hostility. Then Les thought maybe he was imagining it, because apart from having a yahoo on the dance floor he certainly hadn't done anything objectionable since he'd been there. But for some reason he definitely seemed to be picking up some bad vibes.

Woody returned with the drinks just as band number two started up. They were a full-on, fifties style, rock'n'roll outfit. The lead singer wore Buddy Holly glasses and skin tight pants with a riggers belt full of harmonicas round his waist. The guitarist had hair like Elvis and threw his big Fender around like Chuck Berry. The drummer at the back was a bit of a ring in with hair longer than Rick Wakeman. But the bass player was the best — he was a big, happy-faced bloke with a goatee beard, wearing black pants and a yellow Hawaiian shirt. And he didn't just play his big double bass, he slapped the shit out of it, making the thick, fat strings click like castanets. They'd just started ripping 'Twenty Flight Rock' apart when Woody looked at Les and nodded to the dance floor.

'Come on,' was all she said.

'Doesn't look like I got much choice, does it?' replied Les.

Woody and Les hit the dance floor with the other punters and did whatever came naturally. The band slipped into 'Thirteen Women' followed by 'The Race Is On'. Did a scorching version of 'C.C. Rider' then slowed down for a ballad. Woody suggested they sit this one out and she also wanted to go to the loo. Les sat back down with his delicious as Woody picked up her bag and headed for the ladies.

While she was away, Les couldn't believe some of the looks he was now getting. Especially from two blokes in jeans and check shirts who had just arrived on the scene — a white bloke and an Aborigine. They were really giving him the evil eye. Something weird's going on here, thought Les. I don't know what it is, but I got a bad feeling, he took a quick look around. Yeah, these cunts have got it in for me for some reason. I might grab the Rainbow Princess when she gets back and split. Fuck the heroics. Not when you're on your own and a long way from home. He took another sip of Jackies and looked up to see an overweight, Aboriginal woman of about thirty wearing a cheap yellow dress glaring down at him. She wasn't looking very happy, and she wasn't looking very sober either.

'So,' she said, at the top of her voice, 'you havin' a fuckin' good time, are you? You cunt, Allan.'

'What?' Les stared at her and screwed up his face. 'Are you talking to me?'

'Yeah. I'm talkin' to fuckin' you all right. You fuckin' low cunt. I've been home waitin' for three fuckin' hours. And here you fuckin' are, fuckin' down here. You fuckin' low dirty fuckin' cunt. Cunt!'

Les could see he wasn't dealing with an indigenous person, a Koori or an Aboriginal woman. Yellow dress was just a foul-mouthed, drunken thing in need of a good smack in the mouth; woman or not.

'Look,' said Les. 'You got the wrong bloke, all right? Now piss off and leave me alone, will you.'

'What? Got the wrong fuckin' bloke? Don't give me the fuckin' shits.'

Woody returned from the ladies, had a quick look around, then sat down sensing something was wrong. The woman in the yellow dress glared at her as the two men wearing the check shirts edged a little closer.

'Hey. Here's your fuckin' white bitch now,' said yellow dress, still yelling at the top of her voice. 'Ain't I white enough for you? You fuckin' cunt. Joycey too fuckin' black for you, you cunt. All right when you want something to fuck though. Aren't I? Joycey's all right then Allan. You fuckin' cunt.'

Les put his arm around Woody, then turned to Joycey or whatever her name was. 'Listen, you heap of shit. Piss off before I get the bouncers to throw you out on your arse. And take your friends or whatever they are with you.'

Les turned to tell Woody not to worry when out of the corner of his eye he saw yellow dress pick up a Corona bottle from the glasses stand and swing it down towards his head. Les just had time to ride it, but the bottle still broke over his skull sending shards of glass everywhere and giving him a slight scalp wound.

'Shit! You fuckin' moll,' he howled.

'Now have fuckin' this,' she spat at him.

Yellow dress pulled her arm back to jab the bottle neck into Norton's face. Fuck this, thought Les. He banged his left hand down on her wrist knocking the jagged piece of bottle to the floor, then gave her a stiff backhander with his right. Not hard enough to knock her out, but solid enough to send her on her backside in a cursing flurry of cheap yellow dress and tatty orange knickers.

This was the cue for her two friends in the check shirts to start giving it to Les. They came at him throwing all sorts of punches and they weren't little blokes either. Les managed to tuck his chin in, but he copped a few round the head and shoulders and they stung. He set himself and jabbed two quick, short lefts into the mug on his right then turned around and fired a looping right into the other mug's face. He was just about to follow this up with a good left hook, when yellow dress got up from the floor and jumped on his back. Shit! This is nice, thought Les. He barely had time to pull her arms off his throat when the mug he'd just hit came charging in to tackle him round the waist. Les brought his right knee up at pretty much the same time and mug number two caught it flush in the face, sitting him on his backside in amongst the broken glass. Les reached up, grabbed yellow dress by the hair then quickly bent at the waist sending her flying over his shoulder onto a table of punters in front of him. They all cursed and swore as their drinks went everywhere in another swirl of cheap yellow dress and orange knickers as she bounced off their table onto somebody else's, sending more drinks flying. The place was already in a bit of an uproar. But after the flying gin, that was it. The domino effect.

Now everybody started fighting; including the two bouncers who'd been over the other side of the room keeping the lid on another fight that looked like developing over a game of pool. Les turned round in the sea of brawling men and women to look for Woody and caught a punch that was intended for his face on the back of his head. There was no sign of the peace-loving, vegetarian Rainbow Princess. She'd packed up her crystals and vanished. Les didn't know where she was, but wherever she was, Les thought he might join her. Hopefully back at the car. He turned around and kicked a bearded bloke wearing a battered leather hat who had just thrown the punch at him in the balls, then started pushing and fighting his way to the door. As he got past the bar he turned around for a moment and across the melee he saw yellow dress and her two friends in the check shirts pointing in his direction before starting to push through the crowd towards him. Christ! They're keen, thought Les. But I'm stuffed if I'm going to stick around here. If they catch me down the front I'll fight them there where there's more room. Les strode past the empty reception desk and started taking the stairs two at a time. He had almost reached the bottom when he stopped dead in his tracks.

Coming up the stairs was a typical red-headed Queenslander who could almost have been his twin brother. He had Norton's height and build, and the same ambling walk. He had the same craggy jaw and half-crooked smile along with a broken nose. He even had a scar on his chin in the same place as one of Norton's old football wounds. To top it off he was wearing a blue T-shirt and jeans like Les had on. The only difference was his eyes were more hazel in colour and his hands weren't as big. Whoever the bloke was, he looked half drunk and in a fairly good mood.

'Allan?' asked Les.

'Yeah,' replied the bloke. He looked a little surprised, but didn't seem to notice the same similarity Les did.

'Where've you been? Joycey's upstairs looking for you.'

The lop-sided smile spread a little over the bloke's face. 'Ohh. I been playin' cards with some blokes from work. And I ended up gettin' on the piss.'

Les gave the bloke an understanding nod. 'There's a couple of other blokes upstairs looking for you too.'

'Is there? Okay. Thanks, mate.' The bloke gave Les a smile and went on past him up the stairs.

Well I'll be fucked, thought Les, shaking his head. I don't believe that. Les had made it to the foyer and was still shaking his head when he heard a sudden burst of yelling and swearing and Allan, or whoever he was, came tumbling back down the stairs with the two blokes in the check shirts trying their best to punch and kick the tripe out of him; and from where Norton stood, it didn't look like they were doing too bad a job.

They fought out into the street where a small crowd had started to gather. With a cut mouth and blood running out of his nose Allan managed to pull back from his two assailants.

'Hey, what the fuck's...'

That was all the red-haired bloke had to say before he fell back under another hail of punches and kicks. Les stared at the action from the sidelines, still not quite believing what he was seeing. It was almost like watching himself get beat up. Having to fight two men and getting taken by surprise, the red-haired bloke wasn't doing too bad, but in all reality his luck was fast starting to run out. Les winced slightly as some more solid punches landed and was thinking of making a move either one way or the other when a noise behind him caught his eye. It was Woody in the four by four. She screeched to a halt out from the parked cars and swung the passenger door open.

'Hey, come on Les,' she called out. 'Get in. Quick.'

'Yeah... righto,' replied Les, a little absently. He walked over to get in the car then stopped. 'Hey, Woody,' he said. 'Just wait there a minute.'

Fuck this, Norton brooded to himself as he turned back around. Those two morons just tried to give it to me upstairs. Bugger it. The two men just about had Allan on his knees by now. The Aborigine had him by the collar of his shirt thumping him in the side of the head with his right fist while the white bloke was kicking him in the ribs. Les walked up, cocked his right and smashed the Aborigine in the side of the face. He didn't know what hit him. One second he was standing there. The next he was flying across the footpath with his teeth falling out and his jaw swinging round the other side of his head. The white bloke looked up right on time to see Norton's massive left fist land fair on his nose, spreading it across his face like a burst plum. His eyelids just started to flicker when Les hit him with a right uppercut that cracked his chin bone open up to his bottom teeth. He pitched sideways on his knees then face first onto the footpath, oozing blood and out like a light.

Allan stood up groggily shaking his head. His T-shirt was almost torn off his back and blood was trickling down his face and off his chin. He ran a hand over his mouth, looked at the two men out cold on the footpath then looked at Les. 'Hey shit! Thanks, mate,' he slurred, spitting out a gob of blood. 'Thanks heaps.'

'That's okay,' replied Les. 'I couldn't stand there and see you getting two outed.'

'Yeah, right,' heaved the bloke. He looked at the two men on the footpath again. 'Fucked if I know what that was about. That bloke there's me girlfriend's brother.'

Les shook his head sympathetically. 'Yeah. You just can't trust anyone these days. They'll turn on you for no reason at all.'

The red-headed bloke was facing Les who was facing the deserted nightclub foyer. He didn't notice an apparition of absolute, drunken madness in a yellow dress come charging down the stairs. She didn't notice the red-headed bloke who had his back to her. All she saw was Norton as she burst out the doorway.

'So there you are Allan, you cunt!' she screamed. 'Thought you could fuckin' get away did you? Fuckin' come here, you cunt.'

'Certainly my treasure,' replied Les. He walked up to yellow dress as he was told and left hooked her right on the jaw. There was another flurry of cheap yellow dress and a goodly display this time of tatty orange knickers and dear Joycey landed out cold in between her two friends.

The red-haired bloke looked at yellow dress, then looked at Les. 'Hey, what did you do that for? That was me girlfriend.'

Norton shook his head. 'That wasn't your girlfriend. That was my uncle Eugene. He's a transvestite.'

'What?'

'Like I said mate, you just can't trust anyone these days. See you.' Les doubled back across the footpath, got in the Overlander and slammed the door. 'Righto, Rainbow Princess. Colony Resort. Let's get out of here before the cops come.'

'I think that might be a good idea too, Les.' Woody shoved the gear lever into first and floored it.

They sped along The Esplanade, then Woody took a left onto Mackenzie in the direction of the resort. Les turned to her not sure whether to laugh at the night's events or not.

'Did you see what happened back there?' he asked.

'I certainly did,' replied Woody. 'That stupid woman hit you with a bottle for no reason at all.'

'Bloody drunken moll.' Less pulled a hanky out and daubed at his scalp. There was very little blood. 'Christ! I'm lucky she didn't split my head open. Then she tried to glass me with the broken bloody bottle.'

'She was totally uncool.'

Les gave a grunt of satisfaction. 'She was cool the last time I saw her. The moll. She was out cold.'

'Yes. And I don't blame you one bit, Les. She was a monster.'

Les wiped his face and put his hanky away. 'So what happened to you?'

'Well, bar room brawls aren't my forte in life. I would have only got in your way. So I split for the car and brought it round.'

'You did the right thing,' said Les, giving Woody a pat on the leg. 'Good on you, mate.'

'But the freaky part is, Les, when I ran down the front. There was a guy there getting out of a taxi and I thought it was you. He was the spitting image. I thought for a moment I must have slipped into a dream sequence and you'd materialised out of nowhere and were getting into a taxi. I said to him, "Hey, Les, wait for me", then he just looked at me and went inside. Like he'd vanished. It was ... it was cosmic.'

'Yeah, I know,' Les nodded his head emphatically. 'I bumped into him coming down the stairs. He even had the same clothes on I had. I spoke to him.'

'Did you?'

'Yeah,' laughed Les. 'Evidently that hump in the yellow dress was his girlfriend and she thought I was him out two-timing her.' Les shuddered. 'Christ! I'm glad he's got her and not me. What a beast.'

Woody slipped the Overlander back into second as they came to a roundabout. 'Les,' she said. 'That was a cosmic vibration, you having a twin brother there tonight. An omen.'

'You think so?' asked Les.

'I know so. A celestial augury. He was a parallax entity.' Woody looked evenly at Les. 'I'm going to read your stones when we get back to the hotel.'

'What? My kidney stones?'

'No. The alchemist's stones. I've got a funny vibe, Les.'

'Well all I got, apart from a few bruises, is one beer in the fridge.'

'You drink that while I cast the stones.'

'Okay, Rainbow Princess. Whatever you say.'

Back at the resort, Woody reversed the Overlander into almost the same parking space, switched off the engine and handed Les the keys. As they walked past the main office, Les told her to give him fifteen minutes while he had a quick shower and got changed. Woody replied that suited her, as she stank of cigarette smoke and intended doing the same thing.

Back in his room Les got out of his clothes and hung them on the balcony to air, then gave himself a good going over in the shower. Apart from a tiny cut in his scalp, a few bruises on his head and possibly the makings of a black eye, he hadn't pulled up too bad. Better than poor bloody Allan, Les laughed as he got out and wrapped a towel round himself, or his silly bloody girlfriend. A few minutes later Les had tucked a clean white T-shirt into his Levi shorts and was sitting on the bed drinking his one bottle of Cairns Draught. He'd finished about half and was wishing he had a couple more when there was a light tap on the door.

Woody was wearing a pair of white shorts and a light blue T-shirt with an Indian elephant god on the front and carrying her dolphin handbag. 'God. You think I didn't stink of cigarette smoke! It was all in my hair and everything.'

'Yeah I know. It's punishing isn't it?' agreed Les. 'We were only in the place an hour.'

'The band was good though.'

'Yeah. What about that bass player.' Les took another swallow of beer. 'Sorry I can't offer you anything to drink Woody. There's nothing in the fridge. Not even a mineral water.'

'That's okay. I brought something with me.' Woody opened her bag and took out a bottle of mineral water and a small, black leather pouch with a drawstring, something like a marble bag. 'All right. Sit up the other end of the bed.'

'Okay.'

Les finished his beer and tossed the bottle in the bin, then squatted cross-legged in front of the pillows. Woody did the same thing opposite him, then placed the leather bag on the bed between them.

'I'm only going to do a three stone read. What I want you to do is shake the bag, then take out three stones and place them on the bed. One in the middle first and then put the others on either side.'

'Okey doke.' Trying his best to take things seriously, Les shook the bag then put his hand inside and rattled the stones around. They were shaped like flat, blunt teardrops, were very light and felt like roughly hewn pieces of quartz. When he placed them on the bed in the order he was told, they were an opaque, very pale green.

'Okay. Let's see what we've got here.' Woody turned the one in the middle over first. It had a symbol of a gold circle on it with a smaller circle inside. 'Adept,' Woody nodded. 'That's very good. You trust your skills and abilities and acknowledge your achievements. You trust yourself, Les. And you have the skills you need. Now. Let's see number two.' Woody turned over the stone on her left. On it were two gold X's. 'Alembic,' said Woody. 'Observe what you have set in motion. Be patient. The path you're setting out on is both reflective and transparent, Les. So be careful. There could be danger.' Woody seemed to think for a moment as if she was hesitant to turn the last stone over. The symbol this time was an inverted triangle with a skinny T sticking out of it. 'Nigredo,' said Woody. 'Night descends. Darkness. Death.' She paused for another moment. 'But maybe not physical death. Sometimes the darkest moments hold the power of healing. It could even be a rebirth. In a strange kind of way.' Woody smiled up at Les. 'Okay. Now cup the three stones in your hands and hold them out in front of you. I'll do a channelling.'

'Okay.'

Les scooped up the three stones and held them in front of him as he was told. Woody placed her hands around his and closed her eyes. A few moments passed then she spoke.

'I sense danger, Les. I can see a wolf. And water. Tumbling water. I can see jewels. A third jewel. You're looking for two jewels. But the third jewel is the key. The danger. And to find what you seek Les. You'll find the writing is on the wall. The writing is on the wall.' Woody opened her eyes and took her hands away. 'I'll write that down.'

Woody got up off the bed and wrote what she said down on two pieces of paper. She folded one up. Then placed the other in her hand and lit it with a match. Then she passed the burning piece of paper from one hand to another till there was nothing left but ashes. She rubbed the ashes against the palms of her hands then blew the black dust across the room. Satisfied, Woody got the piece of paper she'd folded up and poked it in the fob pocket of Norton's Levi shorts.

'By burning one message that should burn off some of the danger. And if you keep that other piece of paper near you it should ward off any other danger.'

'Woody,' said Les. 'I'm only going up to Cooktown for a couple of days. I'm not parachuting into Cambodia.'

'I know. But we were only going in to see a band tonight. And look what happened.'

'Yeah. Fair enough I suppose.'

Woody got back on the bed and snuggled up against Norton's chest. 'Besides, I wouldn't like to see anything happen to you, big Les. You're nice.'

Les put his arms around Woody. 'I wouldn't like to see anything happen to me either.' He kissed her on top of her head. 'And you're nice too, Rainbow Princess.'

Woody smiled up at Les like a mischievous little kitten, then kissed him. 'Would you like to do it again?' she purred.

Les kissed Woody back then smiled at her. 'Yeah. I'd like to do it again Woody. What have you got in mind this time?'

'How about I rest my sweet little face in those pillows? And put my sweet little backside up in the air?'

'A doggy, Woody.'

'Mmmhh. Think of it more as a pussy catty, Les.'

'Okay.'

Woody took off her shorts and this time her crutchless knickers were black with a white lace trim. She got another rainbow-coloured condom from her bag and in no time Les was sheathed up and ready to go, while Woody was face down on the bed, her firm behind and juicy, little ted poking up in the air and looking sensational. As soon as Mr. Wobbly spotted it he started drooling at the mouth, breaking his evil little neck for a piece of the action. Les placed his hands on either side of Woody's bum and slipped into her, slowly at first, then started pumping away. It was delicious; firm, warm and absolutely delightful to the senses. Woody moaned and sighed and gripped the pillows while Les kept pumping away at a steady, even stroke enjoying every second of every minute of it. Les would have liked to have lasted all night, but it was too good and he started to hit the vinegar strokes. He arched his back, gripped Woody's backside a bit tighter, then gave a great shudder and a moan himself as it felt like he emptied out everything inside him except maybe the quicks in his fingernails.

Les got rid of the condom and they lay on the bed together for a while as Les got his breath back and Woody's eyes stopped spinning around like toy shop gyros. Les settled down with Woody cuddled up next to him and he was almost thinking of dozing off when both he and Mr. Wobbly started coming to life again.

'Hey, Woody,' said Les.

'Yes,' replied the Rainbow Princess.

'Have you got another one of those technicolour prangers in your bag?'

'I think so. Why?'

'Well, I don't know whether it was all that talk about flying saucers and pyramids ... but I'm still horny.'

'Are you?'

'Yeah. I'd like to ... do it again.'

'Would you?'

'Yeah. What about yourself?'

Woody smiled at Les. 'All right.'

'Beauty. But seeing as I'm a bit of an old-fashioned, Queensland country boy, how about we do it this time in the old-fashioned missionary position?'

'On my back with my knees up?'

'Yeah,' nodded Les. 'That's the one.'

Woody gave a dainty little chuckle. 'All right. Seeing as you've put it so nicely. How can I refuse?'

Woody found another rainbow-coloured condom, Les slipped it on and after a little bit of foreplay they got into it again. The earlier time was good, but being able to kiss Woody and run his hands softly through her hair and over her firm petite body, this time felt just that much better. Woody slipped her tongue into Les's mouth and ears and Les did the same to her. He pumped away as before but a bit longer this time, until once again it got too good. Les arched his back as Woody brought her knees up and for the second time Les moaned and shuddered and emptied everything out of him except what felt like maybe the retinas in his eyes.

Les got rid of condom number two and once more they lay on the bed together for a while. After a few minutes, Les felt that relaxed he knew if he didn't make a move soon he'd never get up. 'Come on Rainbow Princess,' he said, scrabbling Woody's hair. 'I'd better walk you home.'

'You don't have to,' said Woody.

'All right.' Les picked up the phone. 'I'll ring you a taxi.'

'What?'

'Come on, you hulking great brute.' Les got Woody to her feet and put his Levis on. 'Hey, how about having breakfast with me in the morning before I leave for Cooktown?'

'All right. Cool.'

They got dressed, Woody put her stones back in her handbag and Les walked her the short distance to her room. He kissed her goodnight, said he'd ring her about seven-thirty and the last he saw of Woody was a tiny hand waving goodbye before the door closed.

Back in his room, Les suddenly felt very tired. It had been a fairly long day and an eventful one. And this time tomorrow night I'll be in Cooktown, he thought. He got under the sheets with the bed light on and had a look at the piece of paper Woody had written on in nice, neat print. She is a nice girl and she definitely doesn't mean any harm. There's no two ways about that. But what a load of shit ... Les studied the piece of paper. Wolf. Well, that was me telling her about 99FM in Bondi. And tumbling water. What the fuck was I doing all day today, making sandwiches? Jewels? that could mean anything. And the writing's on the wall. Well, it always is. Isn't it? It's like saying you can't see the forest for the trees. Or 'look before you leap', how about 'he who hesitates is lost'?

Les shook his head, smiled then folded the piece

of paper back up and placed it next to the bed. But she means well. And if she gets a kick out of all that mumbo jumbo, good on her. In fact I wouldn't mind catching up with Woody in Sydney. I don't know why, but I quite fancy the little nut. Les closed his eyes and scrunched his head into the pillows. In no time the big Queenslander was snoring like a baby.

Les woke up about six-thirty feeling pretty good considering what had happened the night before. He cleaned his teeth then got his clothes from the back patio and checked out the weather while he was there. The sky was completely clouded over and it looked like there'd been more light rain overnight. Like the previous two days it was still ferociously humid; too humid to even contemplate a run. Les changed into his Speedos, grabbed a towel and walked out to the nearest pool.

There, apart from a cleaner on the other side, he found he had it all to himself. After a few stretches Les swam around for a while, giving himself a chance to mull things over in his head. He was still half-mulling things over as he towelled off and walked back to his room. After a quick shower he changed into his Levi shorts, Nikes and another plain white T-shirt, then rang the Rainbow Princess.

'Hello, Woody, me old China plate. How are you this morning?'

'Hi, Les. I'm good. How are you?'

'Terrific. You hungry?'

'Mmmhh. A little bit.'

'Okay. Then let's do breakfast.'

'Can you give me fifteen minutes?'

'No worries. I'll see you then Woody.'

Les hung up then looked at the phone. While I'm at it, I may as well ring that mate of Gloves in Port Douglas and see what he's got to say. It's on the way to Cooktown if he knows anything. Les found the phone number and pushed the corresponding buttons.

'Hello,' came a toneless, gruff voice at the other end.

'Yes. Is that Bill Gibbons?'

'Yeah.'

'My name's Les Norton, Bill. I'm a mate of J. D. Gloves. I'm in Cairns at the moment and he said to ring you.'

'Yeah?' There was a pause for a moment. 'What about?'

Strike me hooray. This sounds like a live one, thought Les. Les went on to say he was a friend of the Biscayne family back in Sydney and he'd promised them he'd make a few enquiries while he was in Cairns in the faint hope Jade might still be alive. 'Anyway, Gloves gave me your phone number and said you might be able to help me.'

'Yeah? I don't know how,' came the dull voice at the other end. ''Cause I don't know nothin'.'

'I didn't think you would,' said Les, ready to hang up. 'Don't worry about it.'

'Then again, I might know something,' Bill said quickly. 'Did you say you were in Cairns?'

'That's right.'

'Why don't you come for a run out to Port Douglas? You can talk to me on my yacht.'

Les thought it over for a moment. 'All right. How do I find you?'

'It's easy. You got a biro?'

Bill gave Les directions as to how to find his yacht on the marina at Port Douglas. He couldn't miss it. It was called the *Eden* and it was a white timber job with heaps of character. 'Okay Bill, I'll see you in a couple of hours or so.'

'Two hours? It won't take you two hours to drive here from Cairns.'

'I got to have my breakfast.'

'Breakfast?'

'That's right, Bill. A lot of people are doing it this time of the day.' What sounded like a contemptuous snort came from the other end of the line. 'See you when I get there.'

Les shook his head as he put the phone back. Christ! What a fuckin' lemon. I'll bet the only reason he wants me to come out to Port Douglas is so he can show me his yacht and waste my time. Les glanced at his watch and gave his rumbling stomach a pat. Anyway, time for breakfast — and with someone who sounds much nicer over the phone. Les then picked up his swipe card then walked round to Woody's room and knocked on the door.

Woody was carrying her dolphin handbag and wearing the same T-shirt and shorts as the night before, the only addition being a pair of sparkling, gold slippers turned up in the front. She closed the door behind her and slipped her arm into Norton's.

'Hello, Rainbow Princess,' said Les, as they strolled along the passageway. 'You're looking very bright-eyed and bushy-tailed this morning.'

'Thankyou, Les,' smiled Woody. 'You're looking very cosmic yourself.'

'I've never felt cosmicer.'

'How long before you leave for Cooktown?'

'Straight after breakfast, Woody. What about you? What are your moves today?'

'Mercia's coming round in about half an hour and we're going back out to Tully.'

'Uh huh. When do you go back to Sydney?'

'Just after lunch tomorrow.'

'I'll get your phone number before you go. And maybe we can catch up in Sydney for a lentil burger and a schooner of aloe vera juice.'

'Okay. I'd like that. I'll get your number too.'

The dining room was about half full; Les signed for both of them then found a table at the front not far from the servery. Woody got into the muesli and fruit and juices, Les did the same only taking about four times as much.

'I'm glad to see you're into health foods too, Les,' said Woody, daintily picking away, while Norton shovelled it down like he was expecting food rationing to start that afternoon.

'Oh yeah,' replied Les. He spooned down the last of his muesli followed by two pieces of rockmelon and a fat strawberry. 'For starters.'

Les went back to the servery and returned with two plates full of bacon, scrambled eggs, sausage and everything else he could fit on them, plus toast, jam and coffee. Woody got a coffee and watched almost fascinated as Les steadily chomped his way through it all.

'You know who you remind of when you eat Les?' she said.

'No Woody,' answered Les, skewering another small sausage. 'Who? Godzilla?'

Woody shook her head. 'Kramer.'

'Kramer? You're kidding?'

'No. You shovel it down. But you do it with a definite style.'

'Thanks.'

Woody got another small glass of pineapple juice while Les finished the last of his toast and coffee. She sipped half of it and looked at her watch.

'Well, Les. I have to get going. Mercia'll be here soon.'

'Yeah. I'd better start making tracks myself.'

'Just remember what I told you last night. You be careful up there.'

Les nodded. 'I will, Woody. And also the writing is on the wall.'

'That's right. Keep your eyes open. And avoid any bad vibes.'

'Don't worry, Woody. If I see any bad vibes up

there I'll take absolutely no notice. I won't even ignore them.'

'Exactly, Les. Exactly. Everything is nothing. And nothing is everything.'

Norton's face dropped slightly. 'What did you just say, Woody?'

'I said, everything is nothing. And nothing is everything.'

'Where did you hear that?'

Woody shrugged a reply. 'It's an old Zen saying.'

'What's it mean?'

'What does it mean?' Woody gave Les an enigmatic smile. 'It means ... exactly what it says.'

Les tried to match Woody's smile. But for some reason he couldn't. 'Thanks,' he said quietly.

'I'll split the bill with you,' said Woody, opening her handbag.

Les shook his head. 'That's okay, Woody. It's on the house.'

Les walked Woody to her room, kissed her goodbye and said he'd see her in Sydney. Woody told him she was looking forward to it.

Back in his room Les was just about ready to go. He nicked a small towel from the bathroom to wipe any sweat off his face while he was driving, then without bothering to call for a porter again, grabbed his bags and walked round to the front desk.

The meals, drinks and phone calls had certainly put a dint in the five hundred dollars advance Beryl had given him. Bloody hell, thought Les, as he used his plastic and signed the bill. The way I'm spending money, I'll have to find that granddaughter of Beryl's and pick up the twenty-five grand on offer just to break fuckin' even. Now I'll probably have to buy that miserable prick in Port Douglas a coffee too. Les picked up his bags and walked out to the car, stopping on the way at the store for a large bottle of mineral water. Fair dinkum. Does it ever end? Les fired up the Overlander and drove out of the car park; he pulled up out the front for one last look at Colony Resort and another check of his map. Even taking his time he'd be at Port Douglas in no more than an hour. He had a mouthful of mineral water and headed north.

Les had no trouble finding the Captain Cook Highway out of Cairns. After that it was just a matter of keeping an eye on the traffic while he negotiated roundabouts that made the ones he and Jimmy Rosewater found on the Central Coast look like pinheads. Once the roundabouts ended, it was mountains and forest on the left and canefields and more trees on the right. Les was cruising along listening to the car radio, not thinking about a great deal when he rounded a bend and, almost like someone had pulled a huge screen back, the coastline opened up on his right. Kilometres of beautiful sandy beaches and bays dotted with small, bumpy headlands and quiet inlets. Although the sky was clouded over and the onshore wind with a low tide had muddied the green water and spread the surface with foaming whitecaps, it still made for a pleasant drive all the way to Port Douglas.

The council had the road up about a kilometre before the turnoff. Norton slowed down for the traffic then turned right at another canefield, getting a quick view of a small rainforest-style resort on the opposite corner. From there it was a few more kilometres of resorts, greenery and home units till the road finished at Macrossan Street. Les got a glimpse of ocean on his right then turned left. Motoring slowly past boutique clothes shops and restaurants and cars parked in the middle of the road and others angle-parked against the footpath with the usual tourists wandering around wondering where to go and what to spend their money on. It all looked very nice and laid-back. But Les wasn't interested in any of the touristy things. In fact, after talking to Bill Gibbons on the phone he wouldn't have been there at all except that it was on the way. He drove to the end, where on the corner of Wharf Street an old white-painted hotel with an Australian flag wafting languidly in the breeze faced a war memorial in the park opposite. He turned left and checked the instructions the bloke had given him over the phone again. He was supposed to go past the jetties to the big marina at the end. Les drove on a couple more kilometres past some fairly large buildings spread along the water's edge before finally coming to a parking area full of cars and tourist buses. This area faced a long, glitzy shopping mall built around the marina he was looking for. Les parked the car under some palm trees and walked towards the nearest entrance.

A sliding glass door swished open and Les stepped inside into the air-conditioning and towards an old-fashioned weighing machine sitting on the cream tiled floor. Everything was cream and green with shops running to the left and right. In front of him was an office for Golden Ocean Dive Services and beyond that another sliding glass door that led out to the marina. Les walked across, the door swished open and he stepped back out into the heat.

The outside area was bigger than Les expected. A spacious boardwalk, edged in by a green and brown fence dotted with brown lamp rails, offered more shops with a large coffee bar and bistro to his right. In front of him two long rows of boats and yachts bobbing gently at their moorings made quite a pretty sight as they ran off towards the cloud-covered, green mountains of Dickson Inlet in the background. Les strolled right towards a row of ads overlooking the marina saying CATCH AND RELEASE MARLIN FISHING. GET HIGH PARAFLY. DAY SAILS LOW ISLES. Near these was a wooden walkway painted with anti-slip, which made it look like galvanised iron. Les stood in front of it and looked down at the yachts as a girl in a pair of shorts and a straw hat came up the walkway on a pushbike.

Les glanced around the boats sitting at their moorings, half-catching the attention of several yachties who were sitting around reading, playing guitars or painting whatever needed painting. There was no shortage of expensive-looking yachts and boats. But it didn't take him long to find the *Eden*. It was wooden all right and white — about six different shades all trying to fade into each other. Two masts pushed up from the deck above a row of corroded, green portholes running round the galley with two rolls of tatty-looking sails furled loosely beneath. The deck looked about seven metres long and needed painting, all the stainless steel fittings had a white, corroded look about them, and even the lifebuoy tied to the rail looked like it wouldn't work; on the bow the 'd' was missing out of Eden. So that's what character means, mused Les.

As he was looking down at the yacht, a bloke came up from the galley carrying a small plastic bucket with a length of rope tied to the handle. He was lean, about average height with unkempt, dark hair and a fleshy, jowly face folding in towards a sour, down-turned mouth that had a couple of teeth missing, and from what Les could see of the others they might as well have been. The bloke was wearing a pair of thongs you could shoot peas through, a crumpled, dirty, white T-shirt, crumpled, dirty white shorts and a cheap, yellow cotton baseball cap even more crumpled than the rest of his clothes. Les had worn better gear when he used to bone kangaroos back in Dirranbandi. The wretched figure in the cotton cap took a glum half-look around him then flung the bucket into the harbour, rinsed it then pulled it back in again and folded the rope up.

'Are you Bill Gibbons?' Les called out.

The bloke looked up in the direction of Norton's voice. 'Yeah.'

'I'm Les Norton. I rang you earlier.'

The bloke nodded as he folded the remaining rope. 'All right. Come aboard.'

Aye, aye captain, thought Les as he walked down the ramp, crossed the concrete marina and stepped onto Bill's yacht. Up close it looked as if the yacht's main building material — besides old wood — was gaffer tape.

'Nice boat, Bill,' said Les, watching for splinters as he placed a hand on one of the railings.

'Yeah, you noticed.' Bill tried for a smile but his face couldn't quite do it. 'Leaves the rest of those stink pots and plastic piles of crap for dead.'

Les absently picked at some gaffer tape covering a hole in the canvas awning above the helm. 'Yes. Like you said earlier, it's sure got character.'

Bill stopped in front of Les to check him out. He didn't offer Les his hand and in return Les didn't bother either. After a second or two Les got the feeling Bill had been out on the ocean on his own for too long; he also smelled like he hadn't taken a bath since the battle of the Somme.

'So you're a mate of J. D. Gloves are you?' said Bill.

'That's right,' nodded Les. 'Where do you know him from?'

'I don't. My brother does.'

'Oh. Oh well. He's not a bad bloke anyway.'

'Yeah.' Bill's mouth dropped some more. 'They're all good blokes, aren't they?'

Shit a brick, thought Les. This is going to be a lot

of fun sitting out here with this wet blanket. 'Anyway, why don't we go over to that bistro up there Bill? And I'll shout you a cup of coffee.'

Bill scowled towards where Les was pointing. 'Fuck going over there with all those poxy fuckin' posers. I'll make you a cup of coffee here.'

'Yeah?' smiled Les. 'That's very generous of you, Bill. I'll have a latte.'

'A what?'

'I said I don't want a large one.'

Bill stared at Les for a moment. 'Come below.'

'Thanks.' *You miserable fuckin' prick.*

Les followed Bill as he took the bucket and climbed down a short flight of steps into the galley. A quick gust of air coming up told Les what had been in the bucket, before it was tossed over the side. The galley was cramped and just as much in need of repair as the deck. In the middle sat a decrepit freezer with a board on top that served as both a kitchen and a navigating table. Above this were several dusty food and book racks and some navigating equipment that looked like it came from a turn of the century Hong Kong ferry. A stove next to one wall had two rusty units and a buggered grill, and Bill's grimy sink wouldn't have held more than two plates at a time.

'So this is life on the ocean wave, eh Bill,' said Les. 'It sure is a nice boat. You had it long?'

Bill tapped the table. 'Twelve years. And it's still as good as the day I bought it.'

'I can see that,' acknowledged Les.

'How do you like your coffee?'

'White with two sugars, thanks Bill.'

Bill switched on an electric kettle and placed two plastic mugs on the table. While Les checked his for dirt and dead insects, Bill started getting out the ingredients. Les could hardly believe his eyes. Every label was of the black and white, Pay Less kind. Pay Less coffee, Pay Less sugar, Pay Less dried milk. Les looked up at the food racks and everything in them was Pay Less also — from the jam to the salt and pepper.

'You should call your yacht the S.S. Generic, Bill,' said Les.

'What?'

'I said, it must be terrific living on a yacht, Bill.'

'Yeah. It is.'

The kettle boiled and Bill placed it on the table. As he did, Les let a small roll of fifties fall from his pocket to maybe keep Bill interested. Bill noticed them while trying his best not to. Les bent down to pick up his money and as he did the boat rocked slightly and this loud, crashing, BANG!... BOOM! came from beneath them.

'Shit! What the fuck was that?' said Les.

'I got a loose baffle in the water tank,' said Bill. 'I been meaning to fix it.'

'Can you sleep with that?'

Bill looked surprised. 'Yeah.'

Les picked up his money and put it back in his pocket. 'I could have a loose pocket in my jeans,' he said.

Les made himself a mug of coffee, but no matter what he did to it, it still tasted like ferret piss. While he added more powdered milk, Bill produced half a packet of stale Pay Less biscuits and placed them on the table.

'Why don't we go upstairs and sit in the open?' suggested Les.

'What's wrong with down here?'

'Nothing. I just think upstairs would be nicer.' Another loud BANG!... BOOM! shook the deck beneath them. 'You bring the biscuits.'

Les climbed the steps and found a seat near the helm; Bill sat down opposite him and leaned forward, cradling his mug between his knees. He had a strange, cocky sort of attitude, as if he'd put one over on Les by making him come out to his yacht. And he also knew Les was after information and obviously had money to pay for it. All Les was interested in by now was finding out what he could and getting as far away from the old bucket and its skipper as he could.

'So if you don't mind me asking, Bill,' Les began directly, 'what do you reckon happened to those two divers?'

'They're dead,' replied Bill bluntly.

'Dead?'

'Yeah. The sharks've got 'em by now.'

'What makes you say that, Bill? Were you on the *Sea Trek*.'

Bill shook his head. 'No. I was on the other one. The boat they were supposed to have snuck back on.

I do a bit of dive work for Golden Ocean now and again, I go down after all the tourists get on board. Look for stragglers and pick up any straws or drink containers that might get dropped over the side. We did three body counts that day and there was no way they were on the other boat.'

'So what did happen?'

'That prick at Sea Trek left them behind I reckon.' Bill almost spat out the words. 'They drowned.'

'You're positive about this Bill?'

'Of course I'm fuckin' positive.'

Les thought for a moment. 'Did you ever do any work for Sea Trek, Bill?'

Bill's mouth curled even further. 'Work for them? I got that prick started. Lined up the boat for him. Told him all the best reefs. Then as soon as he got going he dumped me. The poxy cunt.'

Gee, I wonder why, thought Les. 'Yes. There sure are some arseholes out there, Bill.'

'But fuck him anyway,' sniggered Bill. 'His arse is in a sling. Not mine.'

'Yeah, fair enough.' Les tried to take a sip of coffee, but couldn't. 'But tell me this, Bill. Say you wanted to pull a stroke like that? How would you go about it?'

Bill shrugged. 'Get someone to pick you up in a rubber ducky I suppose and head straight for the coast. Piss off from there. Or just find a place nearby to hide and disappear forever.'

'Disappear forever?' Les glanced towards the surrounding mountain range. 'I know it's a bit remote up here. But it's not the end of the fuckin' world.'

'Are you kidding?' retorted Bill. 'There's places out there still haven't got names. Haven't even been walked on yet.'

'Yeah?' Norton was genuinely surprised.

'Plus the joint's swarming with bloody crocodiles. People vanish up here all the time. Never to be seen again. Cars, boats. The fuckin' lot.' Bill looked at Les and gave him a contemptuous laugh. 'You're not with your cappuccino crowd down in Sydney now fella.'

Les glanced at the mug of swill in his hand. 'No. Obviously not.'

Norton let his eyes drift across to the mountains behind them once more while he quickly went over a few things as they stood. Bill was obviously convinced Jade and her partner Hordern Genting were dead. He was also filthy on the owners of the *Sea Trek*, the boat Jade and Hordern had disappeared from, because the owner had given him the punt. And his only claim to fame was his living on a grubby yacht, getting round looking like a shithouse, dirty on the world. Les should have known over the phone. But Bill had been useful to a certain extent. Les hadn't realised just how wild it was up here. And that if you did want to pull a scam, like disappearing from a dive boat, you actually might get away with it with a bit of planning. He tipped the rest of his coffee over the side and watched the milky stain seep into the green water near the boat.

'All right, Bill,' said Les. 'I'd better get going.' He placed the plastic mug on the seat beside him and stood up. 'Thanks for your help anyway.'

Bill gave him a supercilious smile. 'Sorry you had to drive all the way out from Cairns for nothing.'

Les smiled back. 'No, not really, Bill. I'm on my way to Cooktown.'

'Cooktown?' Bill's sour face suddenly looked as crumpled as his old clothes.

'Yeah? Christ, you don't think I'd especially go out of my way to talk to a miserable prick like you then sit around on a floating pigsty and drink coffee that tastes like Count Yorga pissed in it, do you?'

'Well, I'm sorry if me and my yacht ain't up to your highfalutin Sydney standards.'

Les shook his head. 'Don't be, Bill. You've been more than a gracious host. And to show my appreciation ...' Les took the roll of fifties from his pocket then dug out a couple of two dollar coins. 'There you go, mate,' he said, tossing the two coins onto the deck in front of Bill. 'Get yourself a jar of fuckin' Nescafé. And if there's enough over, buy yourself a cake of soap. They've got packets out there with the instructions written on the back, especially for old sea dogs like you.'

'Why you ...'

With a look of indignant rage all over his face, Bill jumped up from his seat to order Les off his boat. As he did, the wash from a large, passing yacht hit the *Eden* followed by another loud BOOM! ... BANG! from below. Bill whacked his head on the folded up main sail, then his feet went from under him and he landed heavily on his rump.

'Ow — shit!' he yelped.

Les looked at him flopping around on the deck and laughed out loud. 'What's happened skipper? Your sea legs going on you? You fuckin' walrus gumboot.'

Bill was still laying on his side rubbing his behind when Les climbed back behind the wheel of the Overlander. The first thing he did was have a mouthful of mineral water to take away the taste of Bill's Pay Less coffee. Bloody hell! What about that hump. Suddenly a smile creased the corners of Norton's eyes. You can bet that rotten Gloves has sent me out there for a gee up. The bastard. Les had some more mineral water then screwed the cap back on and glanced at his watch. Anyway. Next stop, beautiful downtown Cooktown. Les started the engine and headed off back up Macrossan Street towards the Captain Cook Highway.

It began to rain as Les took the Rex Range Road at South Mossman and started climbing the steep curves and hairpin bends towards Mount Molloy. Sitting high off the road, the big four by four might have been ideal in the mud. However, on a winding road full of sudden bends, Les may as well have been driving a double decker bus. But the power steering was spot on and the gear shift smooth and it was fun in a way. The rain stopped and started, still thickening the air with humidity as Les crossed the Kelly St. George River and headed onto the Peninsula Developmental Road with its spectacular views across the Great Dividing Range. Les smiled as he hit a patch of muddied, red dirt road just before the truck stop at Lakeland and the cabin filled with the familiar smell of rain spattered, outback dust. It had been a while. Just past Lakeland, Les arrived at the Cooktown Developmental Road and now it was all red mud, loose rocks and precipitous cliffs as the narrow road descended towards the Barrons Range.

Shit! This is nice, thought Les, as the Overlander banged and bounced around more curves and hairpin bends, slowing him down to no more than ten kilometres an hour. I hope it's not still raining when I'm driving back. Eventually the road evened out and now Les had to slow down for small herds of cattle clustered on either side of the road and no amount of horn blasting or abuse out the window would hurry them as they ambled across or along it like they owned it. The road turned bitumen again as Les approached the Helenvale turnoff and Black Mountain National Park then passed through the mysterious Black Mountains, also known as the Mountains of Death. Stacked up on either side of the road, the millions of black granite boulders looked quite eerie as they loomed up out of the thick, green bush towards the low, grey clouds hanging over them like rising steam. Les had remembered reading stories about the Black Mountains and the stockmen and people who had disappeared into them, along with the rescue parties and black trackers sent to find them. To this day no one knows what lies under the Black Mountains. That secret is still guarded by the rock wallabies and giant rock pythons that inhabit the towering slabs of black granite.

There was another patch of dirt road then bitumen again and before long Les was bumping over the rickety, one lane wooden bridge across the Annan River, waving to a few Aboriginal people sitting on either side in the light rain fishing for barramundi. Les wiped some more sweat and dirt from his face with the towel he had stolen from the resort and the next thing he was on the outskirts of Cooktown and it was late afternoon.

Inadvertently, Les went left at the Hopevale turnoff which steered him towards Charlotte Street, Cooktown's main road. The rain seemed to ease as he went past a sign saying Two Mile Creek and the local cemetery on his left. There weren't many cars or people about, then houses and a caravan park appeared amongst the trees and palms on either side of the wide bitumen road. Mount Cook and another range of green hills loomed up on the right and a flat, bushy plain ran towards the Endeavour River on his left with another range of low mountains in the distance. A bakery appeared on his left opposite a community centre and shops. An old, wooden, colonial-style hotel with a leafy, open beer garden sat on the next corner to his right. On the opposite corner was a white and green fibro building divided in two by a window, with Waldo's Cafe on the right and a sign above the footpath on the left saying

Amethyst Reading Room. There was a newsagents and a tiny mall up from the first hotel, then another old wooden hotel with a verandah and gables above. On the left was the local butcher and a few more shops, opposite was the old bank and another restaurant and a TAB. Across the road was the local post office and back on the corner opposite, near the TAB, was a palm-fronted bar belonging to the resort where Les was staying. Les was about to hang a right and book in, but decided to have a quick squiz from the car at the rest of Cooktown; there didn't appear to be all that much, but what there was looked extremely pretty.

After the post office was an arts centre, the local RSL, a bowling club then a park with a shelter and a children's play centre, then another park facing a beautiful, wide harbour where the Endeavour River runs into the Coral Sea. A cannon and a sandstone memorial sat in the park near a statue of Captain James Cook facing down towards the boats moored alongside Cooktown wharves. Les motored past the wharves and a floating restaurant a little further on. He did a U-turn and came back past another private hotel, houses, the local courthouse and police station, all built backing onto a mountain; some vacant land and then he was back at the resort corner. Les noticed a sign on the corner pointing up the street alongside the main entrance to the resort towards the steep hill above Cooktown Harbour. It said Grassy Hill. He thought he might as well check that out while he was at it. He slipped the

Overlander into second, took another left past some shops and an art gallery, then started the steep climb up to Grassy Hill Lighthouse.

The big Overlander lurched and bumped up the narrow, winding road to the top, where Les pulled up next to the railing opposite a small, red lighthouse. He got out and climbed a short flight of steps past another memorial to Captain Cook and stopped beside a plaque with some information on it about Grassy Hill. It was well worth the effort because the view was somewhere between breathtaking and spectacular.

To the south, Mount Cook jammed straight up against the coast and back from it two small sandy bays faced the ocean and the distant shadows of the Barrier Reef. From the west, the Endeavour River wound its way into Cooktown Harbour, forming a long strip of white sand running along the water's edge on the opposite side of the bay. The sand ended where the bush plains stopped against another range of mountains to the north that pushed into the sea, before running on and on into the seemingly endless and silent distance. Staring at the northern view gave Les goosebumps. He found himself almost lost for words. This was the end of the line. The only way to describe it would be to say it was like looking back in time. A light drizzle started as Les stared at the view almost mesmerised and tried to imagine what Captain Cook must have felt all those years ago when he beached the *Endeavour* and climbed Grassy Hill with his telescope to try to find a way out through the Barrier Reef. Not too confident. Les soaked up the view a while longer then got in the car and drove back down to the resort to check in.

The front of Endeavour Resort was white with varnished louvres and, although nowhere near as big as the one he stayed in at Cairns, much brighter and modern-looking. Les swung the Overlander into the drive, jumped out and stepped up to the reception and rang a bell on the desk. A few moments later a blonde woman in a neat white dress appeared from an office at the rear and gave him a welcoming smile.

'Hello,' she said. 'How can I help you?'

'Hello,' Les smiled back. 'My name's Norton. Have you got a booking for me?'

'Just a moment.' The woman consulted the register. 'That's right. Two nights with a possible third. Through BB and L Holdings in Sydney.'

'Yep. I'd say that's it,' nodded Les. He gave the woman a smile and stretched his arms while he had a quick look around.

'Now, if you could just fill this standard form out, Mr. Norton, I can show you to your room and explain our facilities.'

'Okay,' replied Les, picking up a pen from the desk. 'Is this an old hotel you've done up?' he enquired as he printed his name and address.

'Yes. It used to be the old Gold Diggers Arms.'

'Well, it looks pretty good now.'

'Thankyou,' smiled the woman. 'And I can promise you, our restaurant is the best in town.'

'That's good, because I'm not real bad on the tooth.'

'Then you won't be disappointed,' assured the woman.

Norton filled out the form, the woman pointed to where his room was opposite the parking area at the rear then gave him his key and a hotel brochure. He thanked her then drove the short distance round to his room. It was about the same size as the one at Colony Resort with a TV, a fridge and a comfortable double bed, only this one had a tiled floor, and pastel blue walls hung with paintings of old sailing ships. A louvred wooden door at the rear slid across a double glass one that opened out onto a patio overlooking a lovely, freeform pool surrounded by palm trees and landscaped gardens.

This looks all right, thought Les. Thankyou Bouncing Beryl baby. The rain had eased but it was still oppressively hot and humid and Les was tempted to dive straight into the pool. Instead he thought he might have another quick look around Cooktown before it got dark, maybe take a few photos and have a beer at one of the other pubs then come back, have a beer at the resort and wallow in the pool. He left the same sticky clothes on, got his overnight bag and locked his room.

The resort had a bottle shop near the main entrance and the public bar was on the corner next to that. Les strolled round the corner and headed left past the TAB, a few other shops, the bank and a restaurant. The middle pub didn't look all that inviting; gloomy, hardly anyone in there and a jukebox in a room at the side belting out some pop song. Les drifted up to the end pub, then crossed the road to check out the Amethyst Reading Room and Waldo's Cafe in case it might have something to offer. The reading room was closed but all it had to offer was a few shelves full of second-hand paper backs and a couple of tables in the middle. The cafe had a dusty, homely look about it and was open with no customers and no sign of the owner. Several plastic chairs and tables were dotted round in front of a red, laminex counter, with an ancient, metal, coffee urn sitting on it. A few dog-eared, Queensland travel posters were pinned to the walls, and outside, some fixed bench tables sat under the trees in a small garden. Waldo's didn't look all that 'haute cuisine' although something chalked up on a small blackboard menu behind the counter looked interesting. Fish pies with coconut. Les had another look then turned for the hotel on the opposite corner.

As you walked in a bank of stainless steel fridges behind the bar on your left faced the customers and several chairs and tables spread around some well worn, red carpet and the pool tables against the opposite wall. There was a dining area at the rear and a beer garden; there were also the usual beer and spirit posters on the walls alongside the football pennants and photos of the pub fishing club. Fans hovered slowly above the noise, while across a panel hanging down from the ceiling between the pool tables and the bar was a painted mural of Captain

Cook raising the Union jack as a troop of redcoats fired a salute from their muskets. The patrons were both whites and Aborigines; mainly men with a sprinkling of women. Shorts or jeans with T-shirts either tucked in or hanging out was the main dress, along with battered Akubras, R. M. Williams and plenty of good old Aussie thongs. Most of the men were propped along the bar looking laconically into their beers. A group of Aboriginal women hovered drunk over the pool table, giggling one minute then screaming at each other the next. Everybody seemed to be smoking, including the two barmaids. Les got a mug of Fourex and found a stool in a corner between the bar and the pool table.

Now what am I supposed to be doing up here again? Les mused, as he sipped on his beer. Looking for Jade Biscayne and her daughter Amy. And the boyfriend, Hordern. He ran his eyes round the hotel. I can't see them in here. Maybe I should go over and ask those three blokes at the bar in the Akubras. Excuse me fellas, have you seen Jade Biscayne around lately? Brunette. Pretty face. Good body. She and her boyfriend disappeared while they were scuba diving off Cairns about a year ago. She's got her daughter with her. You haven't? Oh well, thanks anyway ... Les chuckled to himself. Yeah, that'd be right. Going by the looks of some of these blokes in here, all I'd get for my troubles'd be a good kick in the nuts.

Les took another sip of beer, then got this weird feeling of deja vu. He closed his eyes for a moment then shook his head in disbelief. No, I'm wrong. I'm seeing things. I've gone bloody troppo already. It has to be. But Les wasn't seeing things. He raised his head as if he was looking at the ceiling and out of the corner of his eyes saw that two blokes seated on stools on the opposite side of the room away from the pool tables were staring at him. They weren't only staring at him, they were talking about him as well. One had on a white T-shirt and the other wore a grey T-shirt that could have been white at one time. Both wore dirty jeans and old trainers with baseball caps jammed above grainy, unshaven faces. The looks they were giving Norton were the same kind of looks he'd got on Thursday night in the bar in Cairns. Les took another mouthful of beer and stared into his glass. I don't fuckin' believe this. I've never seen those two wallys before in my life. But I'll bet they've got me mixed up with somebody else. I haven't got a twin brother up here. We're triplets. Probably bloody quads. Or quins. He knew one thing — he was not in the mood for any more of this shit.

Les was about to go over and front the two blokes cold and get it sorted out there and then, but changed his mind. No, bugger it. I'll head back down to the resort and have a few beers there, then go for a swim. He finished the last of his drink, picked up his overnight bag and started for the door. It's a pity though, he sighed. The beer's pretty good in here.

Les left the hotel and didn't notice anybody following him down the street. From the direction of the second hotel however, he did notice a lot of bad language. As he approached, he saw a beefy woman in a blue dress with her arm in a plaster cast standing out the front arguing with a skinny Aborigine. He was wearing a filthy pair of pants, a dirty shirt, an old baseball cap and no shoes and he was doing all the swearing.

'Get fucked, you fuckin' moll,' he cursed at the woman. 'I'll drink where I fuckin' want to.'

'You will not,' said the woman, defiantly. 'And you won't come in here and try to assault the publican either.' The woman waved her plaster cast towards the other side of the street. 'Now get!'

'You get fucked. You fuckin' cunt,' slurred the Aborigine. 'I ain't fuckin' goin' nowhere.'

The Aboriginal man puffed up what there was of his chest and went to shove the woman in the blue dress aside. She scowled, shoved him back then swung her left arm and hit the man flush on his jaw with the plaster cast. His arms went up in the air as his feet went from under him and he fell back on the footpath, arms by his side, out cold as a lamp post. While the woman glowered down at the man, now snoring peacefully on the footpath, Les whipped out his camera and took a quick photo then stepped carefully between them.

'That's not a bad left hook you've got there, madam,' said Les.

The woman looked up at Norton. 'Yeah, not bad eh,' she beamed. 'I've been saving it up.'

'I'm sure you have,' replied Les, slipping his

camera back into his overnight bag as he continued on to the resort.

There was a surprisingly well-stocked health food shop almost next door to the resort; Les stepped inside just as the owner was about to close and bought two packets of Vege-Chips to munch on while he had a beer in the bar. The bar itself was quiet. Besides the couple and their dog who were almost hidden among the palm trees out the front, there were only about half a dozen or so drinkers plus the owner and the barmaid inside. The barmaid had dark hair and was wearing a blue Endeavour Resort T-shirt, the owner had on a white sports shirt and grey trousers and the all-male patrons were dressed pretty much like the ones in the hotel up the street. The owner also had a neatly trimmed beard, dark hair and lidded eyes and reminded Les of Commander Riker out of *Star Trek*.

The room itself was bright and spacious, half-tiled and half-carpeted, with an angled bar on the left as you entered from the main street. There was no shortage of chairs and tables among the white columns. A silent jukebox with a TV set above it sat next to a couple of pool tables in a tiled area at the rear where another entrance led outside. Pinned to the walls above a neat arrangement of indoor plants were a number of framed glass, beer and rum posters, fishing photos and maps of Cooktown, while another TV set was playing above a corner near the front door. Les got a mug of Fourex from the barmaid and found a chair and table facing the main street.

If Les thought the beer at the other pub was pretty good, the one he just bought was even better again — cold, creamy and smooth as honey. Les downed it in about three swallows then went back to the bar and got another two. He almost finished another one in record time, then slowed down and opened a packet of Vege-Chips. This is all right, Les smiled to himself, as he drank his beer and nibbled on some chips. There's no one in here to annoy me, the beer's the absolute grouse and I sure haven't got far to go home. He chuckled quietly at what he'd just taken a photo of up the road. And so far the entertainment's not bad either.

Feeling a little mellower and relaxed after the cool ones, Les stared out across the sleepy main street, just as what little sun there was began setting among the grey clouds in the distance. Yes, humid and all as it is, I think Cooktown's my kind of town. Don't know about finding this Jade sheila though. That's just a waste of time if you ask me. She could be bloody anywhere up here, even if she is still alive. And where does Beryl want me to go while I'm up here? Cedar Bay. Okay. Then what do I do when I get there ...? Les finished his second beer then went to get his map out of his overnight bag so he could check exactly where Cedar Bay was from Cooktown, when three shadows fell across his table. He looked up to see the two men in the T-shirts who'd been staring at him in the hotel up the road. This time they had a third man with them; a taller one with the same grainy, unshaven face and old jeans, only he was wearing a black T-shirt. None of them looked very happy finding Norton and Norton wasn't all that rapt in having an enjoyable beer spoiled either. He closed his eyes for a moment and shook his head. I don't fuckin' believe it. These morons must have followed me down from the hotel or something. Oh well, I suppose I may as well go along for the ride then put them straight before anything happens.

Les looked up at the three men and gave them a crooked, half-smile. 'All right fellas. You've found me. Now who am I this time?'

The three men exchanged glances then Black Shirt spoke. 'You've got a fuckin' hide puttin' your head in Cooktown again, Hollier,' he said.

'Hollier. Well that's a start,' answered Les. 'And have I got a first name?'

'Yeah. How about cunt,' said White Shirt. 'But we'll call you Greg if you like. Cunt.'

'Greg Hollier. Fair enough,' nodded Les. 'And exactly what have I done. Would you mind telling me?'

The three men exchanged glances of angry disbelief. They were all huffing and puffing and trying to look tough. But from Norton's point of view they just looked like three boofheads. Tall and lanky and full of themselves seeing there were three of them, but boofheads all the same. In fact, the one in the grey T-shirt looked like he was stoned.

White Shirt puffed out his chest indignantly. 'What have you done? You fucked my sheila and got her pregnant,' he spluttered. 'Then stole her car and left us to pay for the fuckin' abortion.'

'Shit! Did I?' Les had to stop himself from laughing.

'I know it was you shot my dog and sunk my boat,' said Grey Shirt.

'Bloody hell!' said Les.

'And best of all,' hissed Black Shirt. 'You ripped me off for ten pound of dope.'

'Good Lord!' Norton was aghast. 'No wonder I never heard from you over Christmas.' He ran his eyes over their angry faces. 'I don't suppose ... "sorry" would help, would it?'

The tall man's face started to turn as black as his T-shirt. 'Can you believe this cunt?' he said, turning to the others.

'Yeah,' nodded White Shirt. 'I can.'

'Anyway, we're not here to play games with you,' said Black Shirt. 'We're going to give you what we should have given you six months ago before you skipped town. You arse.'

Norton held up his hands. Things were starting to go a bit too far, but he still couldn't help but see the funny side of it. And this Greg Hollier bloke, whoever he was, was certainly a twenty-five carat, one hundred and ten percent dropkick. Although going by the heads on the three mules standing at his table, Les could see how he had got away with what he did.

'Okay, fellas,' said Les. 'It looks like you got me. But before give me this terrible pasting that I so richly deserve, could you do me a favour?'

'A favour?' said Grey Shirt. 'Like what?'

'Would you mind giving it to me in the park across the road? I want to come back here and have a feed later.'

'Come back here and have a fuckin' feed?' said White Shirt. 'When we're finished with you, you cunt, you won't even be able to eat soup.'

'I could still use a straw,' suggested Les.

'No. Over in the park's okay,' said Black Shirt. 'And I'll even do you another favour,' he smiled.

'You will?' Les returned Black Shirt's smile.

'Yeah. I'll buy you a beer.'

'Gee thanks,' said Les. 'That's decent of you considering.'

Black T-shirt picked up Norton's remaining mug of Fourex and slowly tipped it over Norton's head. 'There you go.'

Les closed his eyes as he felt the cold beer run down his face and soak into his T-shirt. Suddenly Les stopped seeing the funny side of things. He wiped the beer out of his eyes and then rose from the table picking up his overnight bag at the same time and stared daggers at Black Shirt.

'And now I might do you a favour,' hissed Norton.

'Yeah? What's that?' replied Black Shirt.

'I'll fight you first.'

'I can't fuckin' wait.'

Les slung his bag over his shoulder and nodded to the front door. 'This way, fellas.'

Until Black Shirt had tipped the beer over his head, Les was ready to come clean and tell the three men there'd been a case of mistaken identity. He had been acting a bit smart, geeing the blokes up; but dumb and all as they were, they did have a legitimate beef with the Hollier bloke. So Les had been about to produce his driver's licence then take the three of them round the front desk to prove who he was before it went any further. But getting the beer shampoo was making the cup of tea just a little too strong. That made it personal.

The three mugs were still keen to give their adversary the flogging he had coming. But they were just a little mystified at the pace he was setting as they crossed the street onto the opposite footpath. They expected him to run off or at least start begging for a bit of mercy, instead it was as if he was keen to get the job done. He'd also put on a little weight in the right places since they saw him last. Les was confident that he could take the three of them out. He'd rip into the biggest one first and get him out of the road. Then he thought he might even try a couple of techniques he and Billy Dunne had been practising after watching a couple of Steven Seagal videos round at Chez Norton's one rainy afternoon. Despite his earlier anger and his hair and clothes being still wet with beer, Les was in a fairly buoyant mood as he led the three men past the RSL, the bowling club and Endeavour Lions Park with its electric barbecues, big fat trees and children's play station.

With a lively step, Les walked the boys past an old well, another sign saying Warning Estuarine

Crocodiles Infest This Area, some ancient sandstone monument, a cannon then into another park edged with low, white railings where the bronze statue of Captain James Cook standing with his telescope and maps stared towards the harbour mouth. Across the road was the brown police station with its red trim and green, galvanised iron roof. But Les couldn't see any police about or anyone else much for that matter, except one or two cars going past now and again. It was a lovely park and although the skies were grey and foreboding there was still a beautiful view across the harbour of the distant ranges and the small boats rocking gently at their moorings. Norton however, wasn't there for the view. He slipped his watch off, put it in his bag and dropped the bag under a nearby tree.

'Okay. Who's first?' he said, clapping his hands together. The statue of Captain Cook was behind him, Black Shirt was in front of him, White Shirt was to his left and Grey Shirt to his right. Les pointed at Black Shirt. 'You. The man with the beer shampoo. Let's go.'

Black Shirt wasn't quite ready. He looked at his two mates, and brought his fists up. But before he had time to look again Les stepped up and pulverised his nose with a perfect straight left. Black Shirt screwed his face up with pain as his eyes filled with water and his nose burst with blood. Then just as quick, Les slammed a left hook into Black Shirt's mouth, mangling his lips into his smashed teeth. His knees started to buckle and, already defenceless, he threw his hands up in front of his face and half turned away from Les. Les stepped in front of Black Shirt, locked his elbows together, and pushed up then kicked his right leg behind Black Shirt's kicking them from under him. Black Shirt spun across Norton's hip like a Catherine Wheel, before slamming down headfirst onto the grass out cold.

Les left him and turned to White Shirt. 'Now, your turn.'

White Shirt gave Les a double blink. This definitely wasn't the Greg Hollier they used to know and love. Before he got his hands half-way up Les slammed his right foot up under White Shirt's floating rib. White Shirt gasped with pain as all the air was belted out of him. He doubled over clutching at his stomach, trying to breath. Les stepped in front of him, bent slightly at the knees then took him in a double front headlock; he then bent backwards, lifting with both his arms and legs. White Shirt's feet left the ground and he went sailing straight up over Norton's left shoulder. Norton let go just as White Shirt was perpendicular, so that he slammed down on the grass almost breaking his back. Les bent down and gave him a quick, right hammer fist across the bridge of the nose. Apart from the bleeding, that was the end of him. With his back to the statue of Captain Cook again, Les turned to Grey Shirt, whose face was now starting to look like a bowl of sour goat's milk.

'I guess that just leaves you and me,' smiled Norton.

'Yeah ... well. I mean ... like ... you know, Greg,' spluttered Grey Shirt.

'Hang on. I shot your dog,' said Les.

Grey Shirt gestured with his hands. 'Hey, it was an old dog. It had no teeth.'

'What about your boat?' said Les. 'Don't forget I sank it too.'

'It would have sunk anyway. It was fucked.'

Les shook his head. 'No, come on. You can't just stand there. You got to do something.'

With worry all over his face Grey Shirt stared at Les, then in desperation did exactly what Les thought he'd do. He charged at Les hoping maybe to knock him over and get a headlock on him or just run for his life. Les stood in front of Grey Shirt as he ran at him, then bent down as he reached him and took hold of Grey Shirt's right wrist then stood up again. Grey Shirt went sailing over Norton's back and crashed into the statue of Captain Cook.

Les walked over and looked down at Grey Shirt who seemed to be in a lot of pain. 'How are you feeling?' asked Les.

Grey Shirt had his face screwed up and his eyes clamped shut. 'Not real good,' he groaned. 'I think I've twisted my knee and busted my ankle.'

Les shook his head in sympathy. 'Gee, that's no good. And there's worse to come.'

'Ohhhhh.'

Les bent down and gave Grey Shirt a short, jolting right to the chin. Not enough to hurt him too much, but enough to knock him out. 'Sweet dreams, handsome.'

Les stepped back and surveyed his handiwork. Apart from some claret coming from a couple of noses and a few scratches, there wasn't all that much blood; what there mainly was was concussions and bruised bones. Then an idea struck Les. He stacked Black Shirt and White Shirt alongside their mate beneath the statue of Captain Cook, got his camera from his overnight bag and took some photos. A tourist couple in shorts and straw hats walked past and Les asked them if they'd be so kind as to take a photo of him next to his mates. They were a bit drunk and had passed out. The couple were only too willing to oblige, thinking it a bit of a hoot. So Les folded his arms and put his foot on Black Shirt's chest like a big game hunter and had two photos taken; after that, the tourists took a couple of photos for themselves. Les thanked them then put his camera back in his bag and went for a quiet stroll towards the wharves just to see if there was anything worth seeing.

There was another memorial a little further on where Captain Cook had beached the *Endeavour* for repairs on 18 June 1770, and not far from that a memorial to the Aboriginal people of the area called the The Milbi Wall. An irregular shaped wall of painted tiles depicting all the events that had happened to the local indigenous people over the years. It was very colourful and skilfully constructed, but the light was getting a little faint to read the inscriptions so Les moved on. After spotting another warning sign about estuarine crocodiles, Les was at the wharves.

The first thing Les noticed as he walked up the ramp was a sign saying 'Give The Groper A Go', which also said that giant Queensland gropers and Potato Cod are protected. No spearfishing and if you do happen to hook one, you had to cut your line. That would be for the fishing boats, Les imagined, because there was no more than a few feet of water under the wharf and big fish like that only hung out on the reefs. There were a few kids fishing round the piers, the tide was up so you could see into the water a little and there were a surprising number of small and not so small fish swimming lazily around. Les stared at them absently when a huge groper appeared out of nowhere, rolled over taking a mouthful of fish then with a flick of its tail disappeared in a swirl of muddy, green water. Les couldn't believe it. The groper had to be at least two and a half metres long and over three hundred kilos in weight. Well, don't that beat all, he thought. Les got his camera from his bag hoping it might come back and he could get a photo. But it didn't. Les waited till it was almost dark, but when the rain started again he put his camera away and walked back to the hotel on the opposite side of the road to the park. Whether his three mates were still there keeping Captain Cook company Les didn't know and wasn't the slightest bit interested.

I don't believe this, Les muttered to himself, as he shook his head and stared at the bathroom mirror. That's the bloody second time now. How many blokes are there up here who look like me? Did my parents have me cloned or something when I was born? Maybe they all need glasses up here? He was stuffed if he knew. One thing Les did know — it was still hot and punishingly humid and the resort pool looked awfully inviting when he walked past. So he climbed into his Speedos, got a towel and walked back outside.

The water in the pool was heavenly and Les didn't just dive in, he waded out and dissolved in it. The rain spattered down around him while Les wallowed and splashed around as if the world owed him a living; something like that big, old groper under the wharf. After flopping and swimming around for what seemed like ages, washing away any bad vibes, as well as the odd sprain or bruise, Les got out, shook some water off himself then went back to his room for a shave and a shower. By now his stomach was starting to rumble like a Harley-Davidson revving up. He changed into his Levis and the black 99FM T-shirt he had won and hurried out of the rain along the wooden walkway to the resort dining room.

The well-stocked bar was on your right as you walked in facing an indoor and outdoor dining area with a set of stairs to the left leading to another entrance below. It was all polished wood and comfortable wicker cane or wooden chairs set against the shiny wooden tables. The timbered walls and ceiling housed a nautical atmosphere, from the paintings on the walls to the intricately carved models sitting in glass cabinets amongst a generous placement of flourishing indoor plants. Soft white railing around the outside dining area offered a view directly across the street to the council chambers alongside the post office and the night time reflections of Cooktown Harbour in the background. The dining room was over half full and was being looked after by about six staff in white T-shirts including the manager and the woman from the front desk. Les found a stool at the bar near three other men, ordered a Fourex Gold and an outside table to be charged to his room.

Norton's first beer didn't even touch the sides going down. He vaporised that, got a second and had almost finished that one when a waitress led him to a table on the balcony. Les went for a Caesar salad for starters then coral trout fillets in lime and dill butter; he ordered another beer to sip while he watched the rain spattering down onto the main street and waited for his meal.

The woman at the desk wasn't lying about the food. It was just a bit more than good. Les demolished both plates and the vegetables, then topped it off with a tangy, mango gelato and a coffee. Content now from the three beers and with the rumbling in his stomach finally silenced, Les thought he might prop up at the bar and have the odd delicious before he went back to his room and hit the sack.

Things had settled down a bit in the restaurant and Les had the bar almost to himself. He ordered a Jack Daniels and unleaded from the blonde woman who'd checked him in and told her he enjoyed the meal very much. The woman was genuinely pleased. The manager with the beard introduced himself. He said his name was Arnold, but everybody called him Arnie. Les and Arnie had a bit of running conversation about Cooktown and the resort. Les said he ran a security firm in Sydney, he'd been holidaying in Cairns and had driven up to Cooktown to get the seaplane out to Lizard Island and do some snorkelling. But the rain wasn't getting any better, so he would probably brush it and drive back to Cairns on Sunday. After three delicious, Arnie shouted Les one and a Corona for himself then joined Norton on the other side of the bar where the conversation somehow switched round to bird-eating spiders.

'Mate. You ought to see the size of the bloody things,' said Arnie. 'Bigger than a man's hand. Sometimes they get in the rooms and the guests nearly go through the roof.' Arnie chuckled into his beer. 'I just about have to go in with a whip, a chair and a gun and get the bastards out. They're good for brandy sales but.'

'You'll need more than brandy if one crawls into my bed,' said Les, taking a slurp of his delicious. 'Christ! Between that and the crocodiles, this is the last frontier.'

'Did you see the signs alongside the water?' asked Arnie.

'Yeah. There's one about every five metres. Is that fair dinkum?'

'Too right. There's millions of the things out there. And big ones too. People are always going missing.' Arnie had another mouthful of beer. 'Yet we've also got the sweetest, prettiest little frogs you've ever seen.'

'Not bloody cane toads, Arnie.'

Arnie shook his head. 'No. You have a look in the skinny fronds of the palm trees near the pool. They sit on them. No bigger than your fingernail.'

'Go on.' Les had another sip of Jackies. 'Hey, talking about people going missing,' he half joked. 'That was a funny one about those two scuba divers.'

Arnie tossed his head back. 'Oh Christ! Didn't that cause some dramas. It still is.'

'Yeah. It was all over the papers in Sydney for weeks,' said Les. 'Didn't they find a dive bag up here somewhere?'

Arnie nodded. 'They're always finding something. Last one was a flipper near Cape Flattery.'

'Where's that?'

'About fifty kilometres north of here. On the way to Lizard Island.'

'Right,' replied Les, not much the wiser.

'Then there's all the conspiracy theories,' said Arnie.

'Yeah,' nodded Les. 'I was just about to mention that. They've been seen more times than Elvis and

Lord Lucan. Everywhere from Townsville to Hell's Gate Roadhouse.'

'Some of the town drunks even reckon they saw them up here. The woman anyway.'

'Fair dinkum. Whereabouts?'

'Up near the top pub one night. And outside the post office.'

'Outside the post office?' said Les. 'What was she doing there, Arnie? Sending a postcard?'

'Probably picking up a dole cheque.'

Les laughed as he had another drink. 'So where do you reckon they are?'

Arnie glanced towards the ocean. 'Out there. Shark shit.'

'Really?'

Arnie nodded. 'Or if they did make it to land, crocodile shit.'

Les shuddered. 'That's a pleasant thought.'

The blonde woman from the front desk came over and said something to Arnie about one of the beer lines icing up. Arnie downed the rest of his Corona and stood up. 'I'd better go and fix this. Nice talking to you, Les.'

'Yeah, you too, Arnie. I might have another one with you tomorrow night.'

'Tomorrow night I'll be flat out,' said the manager.

'Yeah? Why's that?'

'We've got fifty pilots flying in from New Guinea.'

'Fair dinkum?'

Arnie nodded. 'The New Guinea Light Plane Association people are staying here for a conference. And they like to party.'

'Fifty of them. Shit!' said Les.

'So if you're thinking of having dinner tomorrow night, I'd advise you to get here early. Or you might have a bit of a wait.'

'Okay, Arnie. Thanks. I'll remember that.'

Les watched the manager disappear towards the kitchen, then finished the last of his drink. He thought about another one and found himself yawning instead; the big meal, the beers and the delicious had slowed Les down more than he thought. He signed the tab, took a bit of ice from his glass to chew on and headed for his room.

It was still raining outside. But on the way Les stopped near one of the skinny palms by the walkway and looked at one of the fronds in the faint, drizzling light. Sure enough. Sitting along one of the fronds were four tiny frogs, each one no bigger than a jelly bean. They didn't move a centimetre and didn't seem disturbed one bit by Les staring at them. Well, don't that beat all, thought Les.

'Hello, fellas,' he said, even giving one of them a bit of a pat. It still didn't move.

Les would have liked to look at the frogs a while longer, they were that cute, but a sudden downpour splattered onto the walkway. He left his tiny green friends, went round to his room and put the key in the door.

After giving his teeth a quick going over, Les checked the room for mosquitoes and bird-eating spiders, then adjusted the air-conditioning, turned off the light and lay on the bed in his jocks and T-shirt. Outside the rain was still falling steadily and it looked like being a hot, sweaty, and no doubt muddy drive to Cedar Bay in the morning. For what? More than likely nothing, yawned Les. He yawned a couple more times and the next thing Les was snoring peacefully.

Les could have been tireder than he thought, or maybe it was the quiet coolness of the air-conditioned room, but it was close to eight o'clock when he blinked his eyes open and wondered for a moment where he was. He got out of bed, slid open the louvred, wooden door and had a look around. The rain had eased momentarily, but going by the thick, grey banks of cloud filling the sky more was soon on its way. The resort pool still looked inviting, however. Les cleaned himself up then climbed into his still damp Speedos hanging in the shower and with a towel over his shoulder walked out to the pool and flopped straight in.

He swam a few crooked laps at first to get his muscles going then, as he'd done the day before, just wallowed around until his stomach said it was time to get out and have breakfast. Back in his room he had a quick shower and changed into his Levi shorts and a grey, Easts T-shirt; then, with his road map under his arm he walked out to the dining room.

There were about a dozen or so people having breakfast, seated mainly around the balcony and taking advantage of the brief respite from the rain. The food was spread out much the same as at the resort in Cairns, only on a smaller scale. Les showed the waitress his room key, found a table on the balcony with a view towards the wharves, and helped himself. He started off with the fruit and cereals then mowed his way steadily through the sausages, bacon, scrambled eggs, tomatoes and other hot goodies, washing it all down with coffee and fresh orange juice. Who did Woody say I reminded her of when I ate? Les smiled to himself, as he scooped some more scrambled eggs onto his fork. Kramer in *Seinfeld*. Well that's fair enough. Kramer's a man who seems to enjoy life. And so do I. Especially when someone else is picking up the tab.

There wasn't much to go by on his map. Les studied it over another cup of coffee. Cedar Bay looked to be about forty kilometres back down the coast and part of a national park. It also said on the map, 'Cedar Bay accessed only by walking tracks through national park or by boat. Bush campers take fuel stove.' The closest point from the road to the coast looked like at least a five kilometre walk, too. Great, thought Les. That'll be real good if it starts to rain. I'll probably never get back. If a snake doesn't bite me, the bloody crocodiles'll get me. And for what? How are you going to find a woman and her daughter in there? From what I saw up on Grassy Hill yesterday, you could hide a Qantas 747 up here and no one would find it. Les shook his head and took another sip of coffee. This is just going to be a waste of a day if you ask me. Beryl's off her bloody head.

Les was about to fold the map when he stared at the name Cedar Bay again and picked his chin for a moment. He remembered reading something about this place once. Something happened there? What was it? A murder? Shark attack? Did a plane go down in there or something? He shook his head again and folded the map. Buggered if I know, he thought. And I'm buggered if I care, to be honest. He finished his coffee and stared down the road. How do I let people talk me into this shit? I might tell Beryl the car blew up or something. I said I'd ring her too. Buggered if I know ...

Les was still staring down the street when he noticed movement amongst the trees in the park with the shelters, next to the bowling club. There were stalls and people hovering around stuff laid out on plastic sheets. Hello, Les smiled to himself. Looks like they've got some kind of Saturday market going on in beautiful, downtown Cooktown. Les watched the movement in the park for a while then rose from the table, folded his map and put it in his back pocket. After signing the tab, he walked down to check out the market. Anything to kill some time before taking a reluctant drive out to the middle of nowhere in the rain to try to find nothing.

Probably due to the rainy weather, stallholders were a little thin on the ground. There wouldn't have been much more than a dozen people selling various odds and ends and half of them were clustered around a blackened, iron kettle boiling away on an open fire in one of the barbecue pits. There didn't appear to be any hippies. Mostly solid, country women in their forties with two young, Scandinavian girls who'd set up by the roadside selling pink grapefruit for forty cents each and fat, yellow passion fruits at six for a dollar. Les got a dollar's worth to bite into while he had a look at what was on offer. Cakes, scones, homemade chutneys and jams. Pots, pans, mirrors, books, a couple of old radio cassettes, and some wooden statues. A woman was selling fresh, hand-squeezed orange juice from the back of a small brown, four by four. Although Les had orange juice coming out his ears from breakfast at the resort he bought a paper cupful and discovered that, like the passion fruit, it had plenty of tang. He browsed through some cartons of paperbacks and found one to his liking: *The Bruiser*. 'A novel of the prize ring — with all the excitement, chicanery, brutality and glamour of professional boxing. Jim Tully.' It had two and sixpence printed on the cover next to a drawing of a boxer with a bloodied face and cauliflowered ears and at twenty cents seemed like a reasonable enough price. Anyway, if I don't like it, I'll sell it to Billy Dunne for fifteen cents. He'll love it. That way I'll only be out of pocket five cents, then paid the woman and strolled off back towards the resort.

Les was definitely still in no hurry. He meandered up the market side of the street till he came to the post office. In an alcove on the right were the post boxes and a noticeboard pinned with ads and other pieces of paper. Outside the post office was a large tree with more ads and pieces of paper, only those were smaller and pinned to the bark. A woman in a straw hat was emptying one of the post boxes; Les gave her a smile and thought he'd check out the ones inside first.

They were mainly ads or notices for Cooktown Shire Council, a rodeo, a police charity golf day, the Baptist church kindergarten. A dance, a community literary programme and things of that nature. Les gave them a fairly uninterested perusal and walked out to check the ones pinned to the tree. These were more of a personal nature. Someone had lost a dog. There was a guitar for sale, as well as a home brewing kit, two tennis rackets and a bike. There were ads for walks in the bush, trips along the Endeavour River. Work wanted. Several missing persons. One was sort of interesting. 'Be Bill Kyte. Like to earn $500 for thirty minutes work? Meet Frank and his daughter at the Daintree Ferry. Prove you are Bill Kyte and walk away with $500. This is a genuine private offer.' There was a phone number and instructions to arrange a time and a place. Shit! thought Les. That hump in Port Douglas was right. They do go missing up here.

Then Les pushed his face closer to the tree. And what he saw made him gape slightly. There it was, a small piece of thick, white paper just above an ad to share a house on Grassy Hill. A little faded, but pinned securely at the corners with four brass thumbtacks. 'Everything is nothing. And nothing is everything.' The same neat script and the same tiny circles above the letter 'i'. Les folded his arms and stared at the piece of paper. Unless that's just a very strange coincidence, she's here! The local drunks could have been right. Now all I got to do is find her and I'm twenty-five grand in front. Les pulled the piece of paper off the tree, folded it and put it in his pocket. It might be worth taking a run out to this Cedar Bay after all. He crossed the street to the health food store, bought a bottle of mineral water and two Summer Rolls then went to his room.

Feeling a little keener now, Les changed into his cotton tracksuit and black gym boots. If he was going to go hiking down bush trails in the wet, it was no use twisting an ankle or getting bitten all over by mosquitoes. His chances of finding Jade and her husband were still on the slim side. But at least Les was convinced it wasn't going to be a complete waste of time. He tossed a few things in his overnight bag, clamped his Bugs Bunny cap down on his head, and then, after locking the door, walked out to the Overlander and kicked over the motor.

Apart from a few cars and a small cluster of people outside the newsagents, there wasn't a great deal of movement in Cooktown. A cleaner was at work outside the top hotel. There was no one in the Amethyst Reading Room and Waldo's wasn't open for breakfast. Les had gone about two hundred metres past the bakery when it started to rain. It didn't just rain. It came down in buckets. Bathtubs would be a better description. Apart from that time in Florida, Les couldn't ever remember seeing rain like it. There was no wind and it wasn't cold — just solid grey sheets of water belting down from a blackened sky and with no sign of easing. Inside the Overlander it sounded like a meteor storm and even with the windscreen wipers on full, visibility in front of the car was barely a few metres.

When Les rattled across the old wooden bridge, the Annan River looked like the Amazon compared to the day before, and on the dirt road on the other side there was more than just huge puddles of water — it was a winding porridge of red mud. Shit! Les cursed, this is going to be nice. And this is the graded road into town. What's the one into Cedar Bay going to be like? With the rain bucketing down, Les slipped and slid his way to Black Mountain National Park, where the famous mountains, big and black as they were, were just visible on either side of the road. A bit further on was the turnoff to Cedar Bay. Les was almost at a crawl as he hung a left in the mud and managed to make out a sign saying VISIT HISTORICAL TIGERS LAIR HOTEL. Yeah, I might just do that thought Les, as he straightened the Overlander up again. I'll need a drink of some description after this.

The rain eased slightly and as he slewed up, down and around the bends in the road he was able to make out some farmhouses and a range of jungle-covered mountains on either side. Concentrating more on the road than the scenery, he crossed a little wooden bridge over some raging stream whose name he didn't manage to see. Then the bush seemed to plateau out for a bit against the mountain range on his left, and further on an old, single-storey wooden hotel with a galvanised iron roof appeared amongst the trees on his right. Parked next to a phone box out the front were three four-wheel drives coated with red mud that thick even the torrential rain seemed incapable of shifting. The only clean spot Les could see was an arc across the back windows from the rear windscreen wipers. See you on the way back, thought Les, and slowly ground on into the rain and mud.

He went down dips and up over rises, fording what once might have been rivulets but were now streams of water flowing over the road. A few kilometres on, Les drove up a rise then slid round the bend at the top, and where it levelled off slightly, he came to his first bogged car sitting next to a field on the right-hand side of the road; the driver and passengers were still sitting inside. Les mentally wished them luck and drove on. The road twisted, rose and dipped then narrowed again to almost nothing and Les thought if another four by four comes the opposite way, we're both stuffed. Further on Les came to a Suzuki Sierra, angled into a ditch on the side of the road and up to the doors in mud. There was no one inside; where its occupants were was anybody's guess. The jungle covering the hills on either side of the road got thicker, and the road itself managed to get worse. Les decided it was time to engage the four-wheel drive. He waited till the road levelled off momentarily then widened before pulling up; he then stepped out into ankle deep mud and a sudden, murderous downpour to lock the front wheel hubs. He was out of the car about two minutes, but that was enough to get soaked to the skin. He got back inside, kicking mud all over the floor, and drove on. The traction was a little better. But if he was going slow before, in four-wheel drive he may as well have been walking.

The road was now just a rough track through the mountains and jungle, with a swollen river tearing through a ravine a hundred or so metres down on his left. The track was either thick mud or deep puddles of water with rocks sticking out. What wasn't rocks sticking out, was more holes going down. It would have been bad enough driving over it on a good day. But now it was nothing less than dangerous.

With the demister blasting and the windscreen wipers going flat out, Les crawled on at a snail's pace for ages just getting nowhere. Despite him concentrating on the job ahead and gripping both the gear lever and the steering wheel for grim death, the big car kept sliding all over the place and it was no fun at all. Where the coast was Les didn't have a clue and where he was he didn't have a clue either. He wasn't game to stop and wasn't game to take his eyes off the road for a moment to check the map. Then, as he almost lost control chruning round another bend, a chilling thought struck Les and he started to get a little worried. If he did get bogged out there, he'd be there a long, long time. And if he did lose control and slid down the side of the road into the ravine on his left, he'd possibly be there forever. A couple of beads of sweat began to form on Norton's forehead and it wasn't from the humidity. He topped another rise then broadsided around a bend of nothing but loose mud, almost coming to a halt.

'Fuck this,' cursed Les, gripping the steering wheel as he just managed to straighten up the Overlander.

A bit further on, the track hipped a little on either side. Les double shuffled the Overlander back into first, slowed down as much as he could without stopping and managed to pull off a slithering U-turn.

'That's it. Mission aborted.' Les gripped the wheel and straightened the car back up. 'It's all yours, Jade baby, wherever you are.' He smiled grimly and slipped the gear lever into second. 'And as for you Beryl, you can go shit in your handbag for all I care.' With the rain bucketing down worse than ever, Les headed back the way he came.

The return journey was no better or worse; he just felt slightly more relieved. Les slowed down almost to a crawl, making sure he got out of there even if it took him till midnight to get back to Cooktown. It was absolutely no fun. It was simply driving for survival. Bloody hell, Les sweated, as he broadsided into another patch of mud then churned through another great puddle of water, what if I had a blowout?

But Les didn't have a blowout and he eventually made it back to a section of road he recognised, where he got back out and disengaged the front wheel hubs. The Ford and the Suzuki were still sitting at the side of the road. But as Les went past the old hotel the four by fours were gone from the front. He didn't bother to stop for a drink. Next stop would be Cooktown and a cool beer in dry clothes at the resort.

As soon as Les hit the bitumen road the rain eased and by the time he drove past the bakery it had stopped altogether. Les shook his head as he turned off the windscreen wipers. What a nice waste of bloody time that was, he cursed, I should have bloody known. Anyway, that's it for Cooktown — I'm out of here in the morning. If that rain keeps up I'll never get back to the main road, he thought. Apart from a few cars parked outside the top hotel there were hardly any people around. But the cafe across the road was open and, as Les hung a right past the bottle shop, he saw there were a few drinkers in the bar at the resort. He swung the Overlander into the parking area, grabbed his overnight bag and went straight to his room. The first thing he did was hang his wet tracksuit out on the balcony then climb into his Speedos to throw himself into the pool.

After flopping around and swimming a few strokes Les started to feel a little better. The drive might have been a bastard, but in all reality he was lucky to get back. Les couldn't even imagine what would have happened if he'd got bogged. He looked up at the sky where a few cracks of blue were already starting to appear behind the grey clouds and winked a quick thanks. He lazed around a little longer just enjoying being able to relax now, then got out and went back to his room.

After a shave and a shower, Norton felt pretty good. He changed into a pair of white, denim shorts, deciding to give his 99FM Bondi T-shirt another run. As he combed his hair in the mirror, he knew there was something else that would make him feel even better again. A nice cool one. He got his room key and some money and walked down to the bar.

There were about eight blokes clustered round the corner, talking and half-watching another two blokes playing pool at the back. Adam Brand was playing on the jukebox and the dark-haired barmaid in her blue T-shirt was cleaning some glasses. No one gave Les a second look and, apart from the barmaid, Les didn't make eye contact with anyone either. Les bought two mugs of Fourex and sat in almost the same place as the day before and gazed out the window. Beer number one disappeared down Norton's throat almost as if by magic and half-way through beer number two he began to mellow out and started looking at things a little more objectively. Yes, he thought, with a slow nod of his head, Cooktown's a nice place, just bad luck I cracked it for some dud weather. And all Beryl's favour has got me so far is a fight with three idiots and almost stranded in the middle of nowhere. I'll have a quiet one tonight so I can't get into any more strife, then bail out in the morning. That ticket's open so I might spend a couple of days in Cairns lying round in the sun before I head back to the old steak and kidney. I won't bother ringing Beryl. I'll give her all the good news when I get home. If she wants her daughter and grandkid, she can come up and find them herself.

Les finished his second beer and looked at the empty glass for a moment. I've still got a strong feeling they're up here somewhere though, he thought. Les got a third beer and when he'd almost finished that, he started to get another strong feeling. Hunger. While he was concentrating on driving he never went near his Summer Rolls or the packet of Vege-Chips he had left over from the day before. And breakfast was just a memory. So where can I get a quick feed in Cooktown? he wondered. Les smiled and snapped his fingers. I know. What about those fish and coconut pies in that place across from the pub? Beautiful ... He downed the rest of his beer and left.

After being in the car all day Les felt like stretching his legs and it was just a few minutes pleasant stroll up to Waldo's. He walked in through a curtain of coloured plastic strips and stood between the counter and the few plastic chairs and tables. Under the counter was a display cabinet stocked with chocolates and chips and behind that was a glass-doored fridge half full of cold drinks, with a blender sitting on a table next to it for making smoothies. An open door on the right led out to more tables in the garden and on the left, rows of empty shelves, more rooms and a toilet. The reading area was closed off by a thick gauze curtain but behind it Les could see the shelves of books and empty tables he'd noticed the day before. A blackboard menu with not much on it looked down from behind the counter. Les couldn't see the owner or any other customers and Waldo's didn't give the appearance of being the gastronomical hub of Cooktown. Les studied the menu. Apart from sandwiches and fish pies there wasn't much else to choose from, and you could have any flavoured smoothie you liked as long as you liked banana. A thin, dark-haired girl wearing a blue T-shirt and black jeans appeared from the door leading to the garden. She had a very young, shy-looking face and probably worked there after school.

'Yes please,' she said. 'What would you like?'

'Two fish pies and a banana smoothie thanks,' replied Les.

The girl shook her head. 'Sorry. No smoothies. The machine's broken.'

'Okay. Two fish pies and a carton of orange juice.'

The young girl took two pies from a small oven and placed them in a paper bag on the counter along with a carton of orange juice. Les paid her and thought he might as well eat sitting at one of the tables. The pies were different and quite good — plenty of fish pieces in a creamy sauce, with a hint of satay amongst the coconut and a light, flaky pastry. Les was seriously thinking of a third when a woman walked in with a large caterer's can of coffee and placed it next to the broken blender. She was tall, with straight brown hair brushed either side of an angular, attractive face; two small wrinkles in her cheeks formed tiny half-circles at the sides of her mouth. She was in good shape, wearing tight blue jeans and a loose knit, orange top, with a thin cluster of red coral round her neck. Les didn't notice any makeup and judged her to be somewhere in her thirties. She noticed Les and gave him an odd kind of once up and down from behind a pair of studious, hazel eyes. Les caught her eye and smiled.

'Hey, these fish pies are good,' he said.

'Thanks,' she replied. 'I'm glad you like them.'

Les took another bite along with a swallow of orange juice as the young girl returned from out the back and approached the woman in the orange top.

'I might take my break now, Miss Waldren, if you like,' she said. While it's still quiet.'

'Okay, Bettina,' replied the woman. 'That'd be good.'

Les looked at the young girl as she walked away, looked at the woman in the orange top then, still chewing on his fish pie, went out the front and stared up at the green and white sign. Waldo's. There's a young bloke down the surf club called Waldren and all his mates call him Waldo for short, he recalled. Waldren. Waldo. Cafe. Chef ... I'll bet that sheila behind the jump's Sherry Waldren. Jade's friend. Les went back inside and sat down. He took a mouthful of orange juice and noticed the woman watching him. Les stared back at her.

'Is your name Sherry Waldren?' he finally asked.

The woman nodded slowly. 'That's right,' she answered.

'I suppose your friends nicknamed you Waldo.'

The woman smiled. 'As a matter of fact, they did. Yes.'

Les took another sip of orange juice and placed the carton in front of him. 'Are you a friend of Jade Biscayne's?'

The smile disappeared quicker than the first beer Les had earlier at the resort bar. 'What makes you say that?' the woman said.

'I'm a friend of her mother's,' answered Les.

'Her mother?'

'Yeah, Beryl. I know her from Bondi.'

The woman's hazel eyes seemed to study Les for a moment. 'I knew Jade when she lived in Cairns. But I don't ever remember meeting her mother. What does she look like?'

'Dumpy, violet eyes,' shrugged Les. He gave the woman a quick description of Beryl.

The woman continued to study Les, her eyes moving briefly to his T-shirt. 'Are you from Bondi?'

'Yeah.' Les got up and offered his hand. 'My name's Les.'

'Sherry.' The woman shook Norton's hand then continued to watch him as he resumed his seat. 'I used to live in Bondi,' she said.

'Did you? Whereabouts?'

'In Warners Avenue. About fifteen years ago.'

'You'd probably find it a lot different now.'

'Yes, I imagine I would.' Sherry seemed to busy herself behind the counter. 'So, what brings you to Cooktown, Les?'

'I've been whitewater rafting in Cairns. And I thought I'd take a run up here and go diving out Lizard Island. But the weather's been no good.'

'When did you get here?' asked Sherry.

'Yesterday afternoon. I'm staying at the Endeavour Resort.'

'It's nice there.'

'Yeah. It's good.'

'When are you going back?'

'Tomorrow morning.'

'That soon.' Sherry seemed a little surprised. 'You wouldn't have got to see much of Cooktown?'

'Enough,' replied Les, evenly.

Sherry moved something from one side of the counter to the other. 'So this is your last night in Cooktown.'

'Yep,' replied Les. 'It sure is.'

'What are you going to do?'

'Not much,' shrugged Les. 'Have a quiet one. I might have a few drinks at the resort. That's about all.'

'I get out of here about nine-thirty tonight. Why don't you come up, and we might go and have a cup of coffee, or something? It's not often I get to talk to someone from Bondi,' she added with a smile.

Now it was Norton's turn to study Sherry. 'All right,' he said. 'Sounds good.'

'If the front door's locked, come round the back. And leave your car. We can take mine.'

'Okay.'

'Oh, and Les,' Sherry placed her index finger over her lips, 'this is a very small town you know.'

'I understand perfectly, Sherry,' smiled Norton.

The strips of coloured plastic parted and two men in old Akubras and scruffy jeans came in. Les thought this might be his cue to leave. He gathered his rubbish up from the table and moved towards where the two men just entered.

'Thankyou,' he said, and pushed a hand through the coloured strips.

'Anytime,' replied Sherry. She looked up at the two men who had just entered. 'Yes? What would you like?'

Outside the cafe, Les tossed his rubbish into the nearest bin and had a thoughtful stroll back to the resort. So that's Sherry Waldren, eh? Jade's friend from Cairns. Waldo. And now she wants to take me for a cup of coffee — or something. But don't tell anybody. I suppose that's fair enough, she's probably got a boyfriend and he's out of town. But if we're going to have a coffee somewhere, somebody's going to see us. Unless 'or something' means back at her place. Maybe she hasn't got a boyfriend. Maybe she's just a bit fruity and wants to sneak me home, fill me full of dope and drink and have her filthy way with me. I'll be in that, smiled Les. She's not half a bad sort. Les reached the souvenir shop and had a quick look at the crocodile skin belts and T-shirts in the window. I still reckon she's foxing a bit though. The look on her face as soon as I mentioned Jade and the glib way she danced around it and started asking about Jade's mother — I wouldn't be surprised if Waldo was up to something. Not that it should worry me. I'm out of here tomorrow. Anyway, we'll see what happens over coffee tonight. Who knows? Maybe my last night in Cooktown could go off with a bang. Les crossed the road to the resort. He had half a mind to stop at the bar and have a couple of beers, but went to his room instead.

After having a glass of water, Les started sorting out and packing his clothes. He left his tracksuit hanging over a chair on the patio to dry and cleaned the mud from his gym boots in the shower. He switched on the TV and managed to find a rugby league replay on some ABC regional channel. Since he'd stopped playing league, Les wasn't as interested in football as he used to be. But he still followed the Roosters with Warren and if any other good games came up he'd generally watch them. This one wasn't too bad. Brisbane versus Newcastle and the forwards were showing each other no mercy. Les was half-watching and half-sorting out his gear. Brisbane had just gone in near the posts when Les heard this noisy, whirling, clatter going over the resort. It sounded like a helicopter. He was about to open the back door and have a look, but the video replays of the try were on and he wanted to watch the conversion so he didn't bother. He decided it was probably one of those pilots from New Guinea Arnie was talking about last night. Les finished sorting out his clothes, then sat back and watched the rest of the game. By the time the Broncos ended up winning by six points, the two fish pies and worn off and Les was getting hungry again. He switched off the TV, got his room key and walked out to the dining room.

The manager wasn't kidding when he said they'd be busy. The dining room and the bar were packed. Most of the regular tables were full but the pilots had two long banquet tables out on the balcony where they were all wining and dining and having the time of their lives. Four of the pilots, including one woman, were standing in front of the banquet tables wearing woven headpieces and native clothing over their own. They were banging native drums, singing silly songs about each other, dancing around and jumping up and down like mad things. The ones at the tables howled with laughter, got roaring drunk and egged the other four on while they took photos and shot videos. To Les it looked like a good time was being had by all. But the staff were being run off their feet keeping up the supply of food and drink, so getting a meal would probably be a slow process. Les decided to brush the resort dining room and eat somewhere else. But where? What about the rissole across the road? No matter where you are, you always get a good, cheap feed at the local rissole. Les left the New Guinea pilots to it and walked across the road to the Cooktown RSL.

The front door was open and the welcome mat out. Les signed the visitors book and stepped inside. On the left as you walked in was the bar with a sign above it saying 'Offensive Language Will Not Be Tolerated'. There was a bank of poker machines to the right, plaques, flags, old rifles and a host of other war memorabilia pinned to the white-painted walls. An old Spitfire engine sat in an alcove near a glass cabinet full of medals and over the cabinet was a red ensign.

There was an array of chairs and stools and in the far left-hand corner was the bistro with the usual, dour photo of Her Majesty above the counter. Across from the bistro were more chairs and tables and a beer garden out the back. The place was quite full of men and women in fairly casual attire. Sitting at the end tables across from the bistro a small crowd of people seemed to stick out from the rest. They had longish or punk hair, ratty clothing and bumbags and two of the men had black T-shirts with clapper boards on the front. Les tipped them to be film crew of some description; they and their actions had it written all over them. Les felt like a beer, but he thought he'd walk across to the bistro and order first. He stood behind a man in a check shirt and old shorts and waited his turn.

The menu was fairly extensive and Les had just about figured out what he'd have, when he happened to turn to his left and who should be standing next to him but Roy Steelman; the presenter of *Roy Steelman's Big Country Adventures*. You couldn't mistake him. Dark hair, big dark eyes, not very tall, solid build. He was wearing a black cowboy shirt, black jeans, a black belt with a silver buckle and black R. M. Williams Cuban heel boots. Les had watched his show on TV a few times and liked it. But both he and Warren couldn't figure out how Roy and the people who appeared on his show could use the word 'mate' so much. 'G'day, mate. 'Ow are ya mate. Or'right mate. I got some mates over 'ere wanna see ya, mate. Yeah righto, mate. I'll bring me mates over too, mate.' Les used the word 'mate' himself a bit. It was a unique part of Australian terminology. But he also liked an expression he picked up from some surfies at Bondi, who often used to greet or refer to each other as plain 'Me old', short for 'Me old mate'. And not flogging the word 'mate' all the time.

Nevertheless, it was definitely Roy Steelman from television fame standing next to him. Only this time, he had that hunted look TV celebrities often get when they're out in public. Trying to avoid eye contact with the punters so that they don't have to put the happy hat on and be everybody's best friend, answer inane questions and sign autographs. Les looked at Steelman for a moment. Steelman looked back at Les. Les looked back at Steelman again, while Steelman looked back at Les as if he was waiting for the inevitable. Les left him staring and turned to the woman behind the counter.

'I'll have the grilled perch, thanks.'

'You want chips and salad with that?'

'Yes please. And some lemon.'

'I'll call your number when it's ready.'

'Thankyou.'

Les took his ticket and absently turned around to find Steelman had vanished into thin air. I hope I didn't frighten him, mused Les. I can be a bit intimidating at times, they tell me. There was a spare seat at a table across from the bistro where a bloke in a pair of grey trousers and his grey Saturday night shirt had just about finished a piece of Scotch fillet. He looked about twenty-something, with thick brown hair and a happy, plump face.

'All right if I sit here, boss?' said Les.

'Yeah. You're right mate,' answered the bloke.

'Thanks.'

Les put his cutlery on the table and sat down. The bloke in the grey shirt had strong, working man's hands and seemed to be enjoying his meal.

'The tucker looks all right,' said Les.

'Yeah. This steak's the grouse,' nodded the bloke.

'I'm going for the grilled perch myself.'

'Whatever you get, you can't go wrong in here, mate,' said the bloke, sounding a little proud of the fact.

'That's what I like to hear, me old,' smiled Les.

The bloke seemed a friendly enough type so Les thought he'd offer him a drink. 'I'm going over to the bar. Can I get you one while I'm there?'

'Yeah, righto,' said the bloke. 'Just a Fourex'll do, thanks.'

'No worries.'

Les returned with two sparkling cold glasses of beer and put them on the table. The bloke thanked Les. Les told him his name and found out the bloke's name was Jim.

'Jesus, we had some rain today, Jim.'

'Yeah, we had a drop or two,' replied Jim, laconically.

'A drop or two?' said Les. 'I never seen nothing like it! I was driving around out near Cedar Bay earlier. Bloody creeks were overflowing. There was mud from arsehole to breakfast time. I was bloody lucky to get back.'

Jim shook his head. 'You just got caught in a shower, mate. You go back there tomorrow and that'll be all cleared up. Roads'll be okay. Creeks'll probably be back to normal.'

'Fair dinkum?'

'Yeah. It runs away quick up here.' Jim took a solid pull on his beer and gave Les a knowing look. 'You want to see rain, you come up here in the rainy season. We get cut off for days, sometimes weeks at a time.'

'I imagine you would.' Les gave Jim a grudging look of approval and had a healthy swig of beer himself.

'You up here on holidays, Les?' asked Jim.

'Just for a couple of days. I'm going back tomorrow.'

'Where are you from?'

'Sydney.'

'I got a cousin lives there. Parramatta.'

'I live at Bondi.' Les nodded to the team with the clapper board T-shirts and bumbags a couple of tables away. 'Hey, Jim. Is that a film crew sitting over there?'

'Sure is,' nodded Jim. 'Haven't you heard the big news?'

Les shook his head. 'I thought I saw Roy Steelman in here a few minutes back though.'

'You probably did,' said Jim. 'That's his film mob. They all drove into town a while ago. He flew in, in his helicopter.'

Les nodded. 'I heard it go over my hotel room when I was watching the footy.'

'He landed it opposite the police station. The fuckin' thing's got a ruptured fuel line.'

'That'd be handy,' said Les.

'Reckon. I'm a mechanic and they wanted me to work on it tonight. I told them to shove it up their arse. I'm not working on my Saturday night off.'

'Fair enough, Jim,' smiled Les. 'What are they doing up here anyway?'

'They're filming something to do with a big mob of light planes, just flew in from New Guinea.'

'Yeah. The pilots are all staying over the road where I am,' said Les.

Jim shook his head adamantly. 'They can stick those light planes up their arse for mine. I like my feet on solid ground.'

'Me too,' agreed Les.

'Planes and crocodiles,' said Jim. 'They're the only two things that put the wind up me.'

'I noticed plenty of signs down by the harbour saying watch out for crocodiles, Jim. Are they that bad up here?'

'My oath,' answered Jim. 'That bit of rain we just had might flush a few out too.'

Les was about to say something when he heard the woman in the bistro call out his number. 'That sounds like me I think, Jim.'

Les walked across to the bistro and came back with a plate stacked with fish fillets and surrounded by coleslaw and salad. He put it on the table and sat down as Jim finished his steak and pushed the plate aside.

'Can I get you a beer, Les?' he asked, pointing to his empty glass.

'If you're going that way, Jim. Thanks, me old.'

As Jim went to the bar, Les attacked his grilled perch and salad. It was delicious. The fish was cooked to perfection, the coleslaw wasn't too soggy, and the salad was crisp and fresh.

Jim the mechanic returned and placed a beer on the table next to Les. 'I gotta catch up with some mates out the back. I'll see you later, Les.'

'Yeah, you too, Jim,' replied Les. 'Nice talking to you.'

Les watched Jim disappear out the back door into the beer garden and continued with his meal. It didn't take him all that long to eat it, although when he had finished he was quite full. Nothing wrong with that, he thought, washing it down with the last of his beer. What I wouldn't mind now is a cup of coffee. But, he remembered, I'm supposed to be going somewhere for coffee with Sherry Waldren.

Les drummed his fingers on the table and had a look around him. The film crew were still nattering away and smoking their heads off; and so was just about everybody else in the club. Besides that, it seemed to have filled up more and was getting very noisy. Les glanced at his watch and pushed his legs out under the table. They were still a bit stiff from being bounced round in the Overlander half the day, and so was his back. In fact, Les felt a little stiff and uncomfortable all over from too much food and lack of exercise. I know what I might do, he thought. Take a stroll down to the wharves and back. Walk the meal off and give my legs a bit of a stretch. By then it'll be time to head for Waldo's. He wiped his mouth with a paper napkin and left the way he came in.

On the opposite side of the road, a little further down from the RSL, Les had noticed a couple of shops with curious names that he still hadn't checked out. The Texas Clothing Shop and the Billy Billy Store. Now that he was going in that direction, Les thought he might as well cross the street and have a look. The Texas Clothing Shop was exactly that. A big shop full of clothes; second-hand working gear and all sorts of other stuff. The Billy Billy Store had lights on out the back and arranged across a partition behind the front window were photos of old Cooktown. It was a bit dark, but Les could make out the old butchery, steamers docked at the wharves, some old hotels. He couldn't quite make out the dates, but it appeared Cooktown must have been quite a thriving place before the gold ran out. He gave the photos another quick once over and walked off.

The lights were on at the police station, but there was no sign of the local constabulary. However, sitting in the park across the road near some trees, like Jim the mechanic had said, was Roy Steelman's helicopter. A small, black two-seater with blue and white markings, a bubble front and struts underneath. Nothing to get too excited about. Les thought he'd stroll on down to the wharves and maybe have another look on the way back.

Les crossed the road diagonally and was surprised at the lack of cars and people around for a Saturday night; especially down that end of town. I'll bet even that old groper's either in bed or watching TV, thought Les, as he looked around the deserted wharves. A few stars shone from among the breaks in the clouds drifting across the night sky, and the sound of the water lapping against the shore was very soothing; and that was about it. Les turned and walked back through the parkland and trees along the harbour.

Les had almost got as far as Steelman's helicopter when he suddenly found himself caught short. The last two beers on top of all that fish and salad must have gone straight through him. He found a convenient tree and unzipped in the shadows. Les was happily splashing away, instinctively keeping an eye out for passers-by when he heard someone coming from the other side of the helicopter. Whoever it was they were trying to sing, but all that was emerging was a garbled, drunken slur. Les peered into the darkness and, if he wasn't mistaken, it was the same skinny old Aboriginal bloke the woman wearing the plaster cast on her arm had flattened outside the middle pub. Except for an unironed white shirt hanging out, he had the same dirty clothes on, and was holding an open bottle of Bundaberg rum in one hand and a lighted cigarette in the other. He got to the helicopter, took a swig of rum then weaved around on his feet looking at it.

'Hey! Get that fuckin' cigarette away from the helicopter! You bloody idiot!' an angry voice came from near one of the trees. It was followed by a movement amongst the shadows and out stepped an overweight man with a thick neck and a blonde ponytail, wearing a black T-shirt and a bumbag. Whether he was part of the film crew or just some bloke hired to keep an eye on the helicopter, Les couldn't tell.

The Aborigine spun drunkenly around at the sound. 'Wha ...?'

'I said fuck off with that cigarette.'

The old Aborigine puffed out his non-existent chest again. 'Who are you tellin' to fuck off? You fuck off, you cunt. If I wanna look at the plane, I'll look at the fuckin' plane. Get fucked.'

'Ohh, what's the use of talking to you cunts when you're pissed.' Bumbag walked across and slapped the cigarette out of the old Aborigine's hand.

'Hey, fuck you. Who d'you think you are? You white cunt.'

With a wild-eyed look of belligerent, drunken defiance, the old blackfella raised the bottle of rum above his head. Bumbag chopped him across his skinny arm, sending the bottle of rum flying from his hand and causing it to smash against the side of Steelman's helicopter. Rum splashed all over the plastic bubble and inside the cockpit, the rest dripped down the struts.

'Fuckin' hell! Now look what you've done. You stupid old prick,' cursed Bumbag.

'Get fucked cunt.'

Bumbag stepped closer and punched the drunken old blackfella in the face. For all his size, Les was surprised at how weak Bumbag could punch. But it was hard enough to knock the old Aborigine to his knees with a groan and jerk his cigarettes and lighter out of his shirt pocket.

'You're nothing but a fuckin' pest,' Bumbag cursed again. He stepped back and kicked the blackfella in the ribs. He gave out another groan and Bumbag went to kick him in the head. Somehow, by the way he was swaying drunkenly around on all fours, the kicked missed and sailed past his forehead. Bumbag stepped back to kick him again. By now Les had zipped up and thought maybe he'd better put his head in. Bumbag couldn't punch. But you don't have to be mike Tyson to kick an old drunk in the head.

'Hey, righto mate. I think the old bloke's had enough,' said Les.

Bumbag spun angrily around. 'Who the fuck are you?'

'To be honest,' answered Les, 'I don't know myself, half the time. But I think your mate there's had enough.'

'Ohh bullshit!'

Bumbag went to kick the old timer again. Les stepped over and blocked the kick with his right leg.

'Come on pal. Give it a miss.'

'Hey! That fuckin' hurt,' growled Bumbag.

'No it fuckin' didn't,' said Les.

'Yeah? Well, this will.'

Bumbag threw another big right at Les. Les managed to move his head back, but most of it caught him above the left eye. Norton could hardly believe it; the Rainbow Princess would have punched harder. Bumbag went to follow up with a clumsy left. Les stepped inside it and slammed his right knee up into his balls. Bumbag's eyes jammed shut with pain as he doubled up and clutched at his throbbing groin. Les grabbed him behind the neck and brought his knee up again into Bumbag's face, mashing his nose across his cheekbone. One arm flew out in front of him and he slid down Norton's legs, landing face down at his feet, out like a light, bleeding quietly into the grass.

My hero, thought Les. He looked down at Bumbag and across at the old Aborigine then had a look around him. No one had seen anything and they were both snoring peacefully, so Les thought he might leave them to enjoy the rest of their evening. Les went to walk off and found his left foot was stuck on something. He looked down to see what it was. Bumbag was wearing a thick, shiny silver bracelet shaped like a snake coiled round his wrist and when he slid down Norton's legs it caught in one of Norton's shoelaces and managed to get twisted right around. With a look of mild annoyance on his face, Les slowly shook his head. This could only happen to bloody me he thought, then bent down to try and untangle himself.

Les had his finger hooked under the bracelet, trying to slide it around his shoelace when he got a strange and uneasy feeling someone or something was watching him. He turned his head to the right and sitting at the water's edge was the mother of all crocodiles. It was at least six metres long with a row of huge, jagged teeth along its jaw and part of its snout had either been bitten off or blown away with a shotgun. Besides the crocodile's monstrous size it looked mean, ugly and above all hungry, with its sights set firmly on Les. It opened its mouth and hissed as it slithered up from the mangroves getting ready to strike; the look in its evil, saturnine eyes said it wanted Les that bad it could already taste him.

Not quite paralysed with fear, more mesmerised with terror, Les stared at the crocodile as two thoughts crossed his mind. What Jimmy the mechanic had told him in the RSL — crocodiles were bad up here and the rain might flush a few out. And secondly — maybe Cooktown Shire Council actually put all those signs along the water's edge warning people about crocodiles for a purpose; not just something for the tourists to take photos of. A few beads of sweat began to form on Norton's forehead as he stared at the crocodile, then at his foot still tangled up and wondered what he was going to do. He couldn't just slip his trainers off because they were tightly done up, ankle length Nikes. He could jump in the front of the helicopter for protection, but he'd still have one leg hanging out. And it was no good shoving Bumbag in front of the crocodile because its eyes were fixed squarely on Les. Norton suddenly found himself in extremely deep shit.

Something yellow in the grass near his other foot caught his attention. It was the old Aborigine's cigarette lighter. Les snatched it up. Flicked it on and held the flame against the rum splashed on the helicopter. In barely seconds a crackling, blue flame had started near the plastic bubble. The crocodile saw it and stopped momentarily in its tracks. A few seconds later a brilliant rum flambeau was running from the plastic bubble down to the struts and along the side of Steelman's helicopter. The crocodile blinked its horrible eyes at the flames then turned around and slithered back into the water. A huge feeling of relief swept over Les. Ohh, thank Christ for that, he breathed. Then something else Jimmy the mechanic said at the RSL struck Norton. Ruptured fuel line.

'Ow shit!'

Les jammed his fingers under Bumbag's bracelet, wrenched it as hard as he could and finally tore it off his wrist along with half the skin. He grabbed both Bumbag and the old Aborigine by the scruff of the neck, dragged them behind the nearest trees, untangled the twisted bracelet from his shoelace then sprinted across the road. By the time Les went past the Texas Clothing Store, Steelman's helicopter was burning away nicely. When he got to the vacant lot opposite the resort, the fuel tanks blew with a deep, hollow explosion that rumbled across the harbour and lit up the bottom half of town. All the pilots staying at the resort stopped their partying and ran to the edge of the balcony, while Les sprinted across the road, through the parking area and straight into his room. He splashed some water on his face, tidied himself and fixed his shoelaces, then casually walked out to the dining room.

The bar and dining room had come to a complete stop, with everybody out on the balcony staring down the street at the ball of orange flame and billowing black smoke that had once been Roy Steelman's helicopter. Some of the more drunken New Guinea pilots were making ribald comments and urging the flames on; others were saying it might be an idea if they went down and offered assistance. Les spotted Arnie standing on the balcony with some of the staff and walked over.

'What's going on, Arnie?' he said. 'I was in my room watching TV and I thought I heard an explosion.'

'I'm not sure what happened, Les,' replied the manager. 'But it looks like Roy Steelman's helicopter just blew up.'

Les capped a hand over his eyes and peered towards the flames lighting up the park. 'Shit!'

'He was sitting in the dining room having a meal with some friends when it happened,' said Arnie. 'They all bolted down the stairs.'

'I hope he doesn't forget to pay his bill,' said Les.

'Yeah. That's a thought,' said the manager.

Next thing a red fire tender with its siren wailing and lights flashing came howling down the street from somewhere on the hill behind the resort. Les got a glimpse of some men in overalls as it roared past the balcony then swung a right into Charlotte Street towards the burning helicopter.

'I might get my camera and take some photos.'

Les walked back through the dining room and out the foyer into the street. He rounded the corner into Charlotte Street and at an even pace started walking towards Waldo's. He was going past the middle hotel when the local police in a white four by four with its blue light flashing also came howling down Charlotte Street towards the fire. Les strolled casually on. When he got to Waldo's, he found the front door was locked, so he went round the back as he was told. Parked under a tree in the drive, was a light green Holden Rodeo. There were two small stairs in front of the back door; Les stepped up and knocked.

Sherry answered the door a few seconds later. 'Come in,' she said, and quickly closed the door behind him.

'Thanks.'

Les stepped into some kind of storeroom. The one light left on in a room behind the shop allowed Les a quick look around at the cartons of stock and tins of detergent sitting on the shelves; he then followed Sherry into the next room. She had a plastic bag full of fish fillets she'd taken out of a deep freeze sitting on a table and next to that was a white money bag containing the day's takings.

'What's all the commotion down the road?' she asked. 'I just saw the police truck go past like a bat out of hell.'

'There was an explosion down near the wharves,' answered Les. 'I think a helicopter blew up.'

'Not Roy Steelman's?'

'That's probably who it belonged to,' Les replied.

'Some of his film crew were in here earlier and bought some fish pies from me. Well, I'll be . . .'

'Yeah, like the man said. Shit happens.' Les gave Sherry a half-smile. 'So how was business today? All right?'

'Not too bad actually,' she replied. 'I've had worse.'

'As long as you're getting a quid. That's the main thing.' Les nodded to the bag of frozen fillets. 'Where do you buy your fish? Down the wharves?'

Sherry shook her head. 'I catch them myself.'

'Fair dinkum?'

'You don't have to be Rex Hunt to catch a fish up here, Les.'

Les reflected on the big cod he saw flopping around under the wharf. 'No. I don't suppose you would.'

'I got fish traps the other side of the harbour. They get me all the fish I need.'

'Fair enough.' Les watched Sherry put the bag of fillets into an old fridge and close the door. She turned around and looked at him. 'So where are we going for a cup of coffee?' he asked her.

'Well ...' Sherry stopped in mid-sentence and ran a finger across her bottom lip. 'I was thinking we may as well just go back to my place. It's not far from here. And I can run you home after. I have to come back to the shop and check the fridges. I've been having trouble with the thermostats.'

'Okay. If that suits you,' answered Les.

'I've got plenty of beer at home. Or Bourbon and whatever if you prefer.'

Les shook his head. 'Just a cup of coffee'll do me thanks.'

'Okay. You're easily pleased.' Sherry clapped her hands lightly and smiled. 'Then let's go.'

'Righto. Can I help you with anything?'

'No. I've got everything under control thanks.'

Sherry picked up the money bag and turned off the light. Les followed her out to the Holden Rodeo and got in, clicking his seatbelt while Sherry started the engine. She reversed around then nosed the Holden down the driveway into the side street running towards the hotel on the opposite corner. The pub appeared to have emptied out and they were across Charlotte Street and half-way up the street from the hotel corner when Les decided he had to mention something.

'What about your lights?'

'Oh. Tch, tch. Silly me.' Sherry flicked the lights on and the beam opened up the road ahead. She turned to Les and smiled. 'Just like a woman.'

Les was going to say something, or make a bit of a joke, but didn't bother. Instead he started to get a strange queasiness in the pit of his stomach. Maybe his nerves were still on edge after what had just happened in the park or his adrenalin was still up; Les couldn't tell. But for some reason he suddenly felt uncomfortable in Sherry's presence. They continued on in silence, turning right at one street, then left into another. Les noticed a church among the houses they went past and some trees; the houses thinned out and they slowed down next to a vacant block on another corner. Les remembered which way back to the resort and guessed it to be about a fifteen, maybe twenty minute walk.

Sherry's house was next to the vacant block of land and backed onto more vacant land. It was one-storey, white, with a grey galvanised iron roof and a row of windows facing the street over a small, fenced off front yard. There was a fenced off driveway on the left leading to an old wooden shed or garage at the rear and a door on the side of the house. Sherry stopped the car level with the side door, killed the lights and turned off the motor.

'So. Here we are,' she said, opening her door.

'Does the house belong to you?' asked Les, opening his car door at the same time.

'I'm paying it off. Come on in.'

A small flight of steps and a single bannister led up to the side door. Sherry opened it and Les followed her inside where she switched on a light. Les found himself in a small alcove facing onto the loungeroom. An opening in the wall on the right led to the kitchen then the enclosed verandah, a corridor on the left led to a bathroom and the rest of the house. The loungeroom had a very noticeable Indonesian influence. Wooden carvings, wooden bowls, brass bells and candle holders, batik paintings on the wall. A solid wooden coffee table sat in front of a bamboo lounge with batik covers over it; this faced a TV set and a small stereo set among several rows of bookshelves on the wall behind.

Sherry walked into the kitchen, while Les followed her and watched as she switched on another light. The kitchen was plain but tidy: a cork tile floor, red laminex bench tops round a small, stainless steel sink, wooden stools and a wooden table with a smoked glass top. Wooden cabinets and batik curtains across the kitchen window and more batik prints on the wall plus a wall clock. A row of white coffee mugs were neatly arranged on wooden pegs above the sink and next to that was a laminated map of the Great Barrier Reef from Port Douglas to Cooktown, showing all the reefs and the bays along the coastline and the national parks.

'Nice place,' said Les, trying to cover his uneasiness with small talk. 'You live here on your own?'

'Yes.' Sherry dropped the money bag on the kitchen table and began filling an electric kettle. 'I've got a dog. But he's with a vet at the moment.'

Les gave Sherry an understanding kind of nod and examined the coloured map of the Great Barrier Reef. 'Hey, Sherry,' he said, tapping a finger against the plastic. 'There's a place on here called Cedar Bay. Did something happen there once?'

Sherry seemed to study Les for a moment before she answered. 'There was a big police raid there years ago. Bjelke-Petersen sent the cops and the navy in to kick all the hippies out. They came in by boat. Beat up the guys, gave the girls a hard time. Burnt down all the huts, arrested everyone for smoking pot. It was pretty heavy.'

'Yeah. Now I remember,' said Les. 'Warren, the bloke I live with, bought an old magazine in a flea market, *Nation Review*. It had an article in it about it. Plus some old folk song, "They Burnt Down The Hippies Huts." Or something like that.'

'That's the one, Les.' Sherry continued to study Les. 'I don't suppose you would remember much about the hippie era, Les?'

Les shook his head. 'No. Not really ... man.'

'I didn't think you would. Anyway!' Sherry clapped her hands together again. 'You still feel like a cup of coffee?'

'Yeah. That'd be nice. Thanks.'

'How would you like — a hot chocolate, with Tia Maria in it?'

'That sounds even nicer again.'

'Well go into the loungeroom and make yourself comfortable while I make them. I'll put some music on.'

Les went into the loungeroom and sat down facing the TV over the wooden coffee table. Sherry shuffled through a small stack of CDs then put one on. It was quite a nice ballad with a good, soft beat.

'I like this,' said Les. 'Who is it?' Sherry handed Les the CD cover. It had a woman's face in orange on a purple background. The Loving Time and the track playing was 'The Land Of Love'. 'Yeah. It's good.'

'Thanks. I'm glad you like it.'

Sherry put the CD cover back, then went to the bathroom. Les sat on the lounge listening to the music and a few minutes later exchanged smiles with Sherry as she walked past him to the kitchen. The music was pleasant, the scene in the loungeroom with all the batiks and various bric-a-brac was relaxing, and Sherry could hardly have been more polite or a better host so far. But Norton still felt apprehensive. In fact, the longer Sherry was making the hot drinks, the more apprehensive he got. Finally she returned and placed two mugs of hot chocolate on the coffee table. Norton's was in one of the white mugs he'd noticed hanging on the wooden pegs. Sherry's was in an identical mug only it was brown and red.

'There you go,' she said, sitting down on the lounge next to Les.

'Thanks, Sherry,' said Les. 'They smell delicious.'

'They are,' she assured him. 'Drink up.' Sherry raised her mug to her mouth. Les was about to do the same thing when the phone rang in the kitchen. Sherry put her mug back on the coffee table, shook her head and smiled. 'I know who this will be. I won't be a moment.'

Les watched Sherry go to the kitchen, heard her pick up the phone, say something and laugh. Then his eyes settled on the two different coloured mugs of hot chocolate sitting on the coffee table. Another squirt of adrenalin hit the pit of his stomach and his apprehension rose again. If Les had a guardian angel in the room, it wouldn't have been whispering in his ear telling him to switch the drinks. It would have been belting him over the head with a piece of four by two and kicking him in the backside. Les had to switch the drinks. But how? And it was no good knocking his over while she was out of the room. That might look suspicious and she'd only make him another one. He could be wrong of course. But if he didn't switch the drinks, how would he know if he was right or wrong? He could wake up in the morning dead, drugged or any bloody thing.

Sitting on the coffee table was a small, carved wooden bowl half full of books of matches from various clubs and restaurants. Les dumped the matches out on the table, took his hanky from his pocket and wiped the bowl. He tipped Sherry's hot chocolate into the bowl then tipped half of his into Sherry's empty mug, gave the remaining half of his a quick swirl around and poured it into Sherry's mug. Les then poured the hot chocolate from the bowl into his mug, wiped the bowl and put all the matches back. He gave the table a wipe, replacing everything exactly as it was, then put his hanky back in his pocket. When Sherry returned from the kitchen and sat down, Les was sipping away at his hot chocolate, and looking very much as if he was enjoying it.

'That was the woman from Texas Clothing,' said Sherry, picking up her mug of hot chocolate and taking a sip. 'Her shop's just across from where the helicopter blew up. And she had to fill me in on all the details. It was Roy Steelman's helicopter.'

Les nodded. 'I thought so. Was anybody hurt?'

'They found a couple of men near some trees. But they were okay. Evidently they'd been in a fight.'

'Oh well, just as long as no one got killed.' Les smiled and raised his mug. 'Hey! These hot chocolates are the absolute grouse, Sherry.'

Sherry's smile lit up her face and almost seemed to bathe Les in a warm, golden glow. 'Thanks,' she said. 'I'm glad you like it.'

Les took another healthy swallow. 'You want to drink yours before it gets too cold.'

Sherry made an offhanded gesture with one hand. 'Don't worry. I can soon make some more.'

Les smacked his lips. 'I'll see how I go.'

'Good on you, Les. I like a man who appreciates nice things.'

Another laid-back song played on the CD while Les sipped his hot chocolate under the steady gaze of Sherry Waldren. Sherry didn't appear nervous or anything else out of the ordinary; she was watching Les steadily, not carefully. A lot of women would possibly seem a little cautious or apprehensive having a strange man back at their house alone — and Les certainly didn't look like your average chartered accountant or local vicar. Not Sherry, however. She was sitting back getting into her hot chocolate, completely relaxed, not a worry in the world; giving Les the odd once up and down, everything totally under control.

'So how long have you lived in Cooktown, Sherry?' asked Les.

'About a year,' she replied.

'You like it?'

'I love it.'

'You'd never think of living in the city?'

Sherry gave her head a shake. 'Never.'

'Where do you come from originally?'

'Sydney.'

'Fair dinkum?'

Sherry nodded and drained the last of her hot chocolate. Les did the same. Sherry seemed to give him an appreciative kind of look.

'Would you like another one?' she asked.

Les shook his head and placed his empty mug on the coffee table. 'No. One'll be fine thanks. That was nice,' he said.

Sherry placed her empty mug on the coffee table next to Norton's and ran a finger delicately around the rim. 'So tell me a bit more about Jade's mother,' she said.

'How do you mean?' asked Les.

'How did you meet her? Did you take her out? You know.'

Les gave his shoulders a bit of a shrug. 'It was a fair while ago. But yeah, I took her out a few times. In fact she did me a couple of favours.'

'Favours, eh?' Sherry smiled at Les. 'Did you screw her?'

Les gave Sherry a double blink. Her question had come completely out of the blue. 'What was that?' he said.

The foxy smile on Sherry's face became a lecherous grin. 'I said did you screw her, Les. Did you get her old knickers off and give her one?'

'That's a bit of an odd question to ask someone, Sherry,' Les replied evenly.

'You just look like a stud Les,' replied Sherry. 'That's all.'

'Thanks. Does it show?'

Sherry gave a chuckle and lay back against her corner of the lounge. 'Would you like to screw me too?'

Norton's eyebrows knitted as if he wasn't quite

sure what he heard. 'What was that?' he asked.

'I said, would you like to screw me, Les,' repeated Sherry. She nodded her head towards the hallway. 'Would you like to drag me into the bedroom, rip all my clothes off, and fuck the arse off me?'

Les gave his shoulders another shrug. 'Sure, why not. I suppose there'd be something wrong with me if I didn't, wouldn't there?'

'Okay, so first why don't we just sit here and relax. Let another couple of tracks play. Then we'll go inside.'

'Sounds good to me,' said Les. Another track cut in and he nodded across to the CD cover. 'Hey, this could be our special CD, Sherry. The Loving Time. You and me in Cooktown. Having a loving time.'

'Yes. You and me Les. My big stud muffin in ... Cooktown. In Cook ... town. In ... Cooktown. In Cook ... Oh shit.'

Sherry's head rolled slightly as she looked around and gave the room a long, slow, double blink. She looked at the stereo playing then across at Les as if she didn't know where she was.

'Are you okay, Sherry?' asked Les.

Sherry looked at Les like he was miles away. She focused again then stared at the two mugs sitting on the coffee table. She went to move forward. But fell back against the lounge instead. She stared at Les and her face twisted up.

'Did you. Did ... you ... ?'

'What are you trying to say, Sherry?' said Les. 'I'm sorry. I can't quite understand you, pet. Speak up.'

'Did . . . did . . .'

Sherry was having trouble keeping her head up. Her eyes rolled, her mouth hung open and her hands flopped into her lap. The last time Les had seen a look like that, it was either some bloke he'd just punched in the head, or a footballer who'd taken a heavy knock on the field.

'What are you trying to say, Sherry?' repeated Les. 'Did I switch mugs? Yeah. Of course I did. You dopey heap of shit.'

'Oh God!' Sherry gave it her best, then looked again at Les, her eyes rolling round her face with fear. She made one last, pathetic attempt to grab at him then fell sideways onto the lounge, staring across the room.

Les stood up to get out of her way then knelt down alongside her. 'What did you put in the drink, Sherry?' he said. 'You better tell me and I'll get an ambulance.'

Sherry's eyes were flickering. 'Ro ... ro ... ro. Ohh.' And that was the end of her. Her eyes rolled shut, her head went down and she slumped into the lounge completely out of it.

'See you later, Waldo.'

Les placed a thumb at the side of her neck. I wonder what the fish pie queen stuck in my drink? I don't think it was poison, because I'm still getting a pulse. She made a quick trip to the bathroom before she made the hot chocolates. Maybe ... Les got back up and walked down the hallway.

The bathroom had a blue door and was also painted blue inside, with a blue floral shower screen round the bath. There were crystals and coloured glass beads and trinkets scattered round the sink, with an indoor plant on the window sill and a dolphin transfer on the cabinet mirror. Les opened the cabinet and looked amongst the packets of soap and toothpaste, tampons, cotton swabs and so on. Hidden in the corner behind a small first aid kit was a small, white, screw top bottle. Printed in capital letters on a a label across the front was one word: ROHYPNOL.

Les nodded sagely to himself. I reckon that's it. What was she trying to say on the lounge? Ro ro something? I'll guarantee she wasn't trying to sing row, row, row your boat. The bastard's slipped some rohys in my drink. He wondered how many? Being a fairly big bloke, she'd probably thrown plenty in to make sure he got knocked right out. Which might be enough to put her to sleep for good. Fuck! This could be a bit dicey.

He didn't bother to check the contents of the plastic bottle, he closed the cabinet, wiped the handle and did the same round the light switch and the door knob. The CD was still playing softly when Les walked back in the loungeroom and Sherry was completely comatose on the lounge. But at least she was still breathing. Les picked his mug up from the coffee table and took it out to the kitchen. The light was off and Les left it that way while he rinsed the mug, wiped it and hung it back up with the others above the sink. Not much more I can do here, he thought, walking back into the loungeroom. That's not a bad CD though. A bit laid-back. But there's a couple of good tracks there. Fuck her, I'll have that. Les hit the open and close button with his knuckle, put the CD in its cover and stuck it in the back pocket of his shorts, then carefully replaced it with another one from Sherry's collection. The soundtrack from *Pret a Porter*. He had another look at Sherry and his lip curled. A bloke ought to give her one, in case she doesn't croak, just to be a nark. I know what I would like to do. Pour a bottle of hot chilli sauce all over her snatch. That'd teach her to go putting Rohypnols in blokes' drinks. The slaggy, rotten moll. Les left the light on in the loungeroom and went back out the side door, closing it quietly behind him.

Les stood next to the Holden Rodeo for a moment then turned to the old, rickety wooden shed at the rear of the house. Between the light reflecting from the loungeroom and the faint moon above, it looked like something out of a Henry Lawson poem. Les walked over and peered through a gap in the boards. Amongst the other junk inside he could make out a definite shape. A black rubber ducky with a black outboard motor at the back sitting on an aluminium trailer. What did that hump in Port Douglas say, when I asked him how you'd pull a scam like Jade and Hordern did? Get someone to come out and pick you up in a rubber ducky. Les stared at the boat for a few seconds more then made his way back up the driveway.

Les knew that to get back to the resort you had to go up to the right and just keep heading in that direction. The streets looked quiet and deserted with the odd lamppost here and there to light the way. He had another instinctive look around and started walking. By the time he was past the vacant block on the corner Les wanted to break into a run. But he knew it would only look suspicious if a dog started barking and somebody happened to see him. Between that and Bumbag putting his report in he could get identified if Sherry Waldren didn't make it through the night. Nevertheless, a couple of streets further and Norton was striding along at a brisk pace deep in moody thought.

Bloody hell! What about Sherry baby ...? I was lucky to get out of that one. I don't know what it was made me a bit suss about her. It was just too easy — come back to my place, leave your car, I can drive you home. And the way she got me to come round the back of the shop and whipped me inside. Then drove away with her lights off just like she was sneaking me out of the place. Broken thermostats my arse. And those two separate mugs — if hers had had her name on it or a star sign or something, I probably wouldn't have twigged.

Yep, he was sure she was in cahoots with Jade and her boyfriend all right. They're all snookered away up here somewhere, most likely Cedar Bay, and now she was covering for them. Les looked up as several night birds flew overhead. But apart from a few lights in some of the houses, there was still no sign of any people. He crossed another street and kept going. That's why she enticed me back to her place. To drug me, tie me up and probably torture me to find out what Jade's mother had told me. Then when she'd finished I'd be out there keeping company with her fishpots. I'd probably be in one. Just another missing person in good old FNQ. Yeah, she knew why I was up here all right. Still, it's my own silly bloody fault for opening my mouth in the first place. I should have let things slide. But why murder me over a couple of faked deaths? Money I imagine. Christ! It'd want to be a lot to go to that extreme, he concluded. Les went past some more houses and a church. One old dog barked as he neared Grassy Hill. He hung a left at the next street and saw the resort and the lights of Charlotte Street at the bottom. A minute later he walked into the parking area past the familiar shape of the mud spattered Overlander and went straight to his room again.

The first thing Les did was shove the CD in his travel bag then fill the sink in the bathroom and dunk his face in it. He towelled off then tidied himself up and decided he might put his head in the bar for a while and tell the manager a few lies about what he'd been doing that night. Les got a clean hanky from his bag, picked up his keys and walked out to the bar.

As far as the helicopter explosion went, things had settled down a little in the dining room. The fire had been put out and now the New Guinea pilots were back to their boozing, singing and dancing around in native costumes, while they ran the bar staff off their feet. There were three more drunks at the bar; Les found a stool at the end and placed his room key in front of him. Before long the blonde woman from the reception appeared.

'Hello, Mr. Norton,' she said pleasantly, despite how busy she was. 'What can I get for you?'

'Just a bottle of Fourex Gold thanks,' replied Les.

'Coming right up.'

Within about a minute, Les had a cold beer in front of him and a third of it had gone down his throat. He saw Arnie standing in the middle of a group of several pilots; talking, having a beer and being everybody's friend. Les caught his eye and raised his bottle. The manager smiled and waved back. Les swallowed some more beer and began to reflect. Well, that was the night, that was. I got into another fight, almost got eaten by a fuckin' crocodile, blew up a helicopter and someone tried to murder me. He chuckled mirthlessly to himself. And I got offered a root, but had to knock it back. Not counting the rotten day I had driving round in the rain. He drank some more beer and shook his head. This is a nice place, but I'll be glad to be getting out of here tomorrow while I'm still in one piece ... He finished his beer and placed the empty bottle on the bar.

The blonde woman came over and took the empty away. 'Can I get you another one, Mr. Norton?' she asked.

'Yeah. Thankyou.'

The woman returned with another cold bottle of Fourex and placed it on a coaster in front of Les.

'I'll be checking out in the morning too,' said Les.

'Oh. All right then Mr. Norton,' said the woman. 'What time do you think you'll be leaving?'

Les shrugged a reply. 'About nine.'

'Okay. Thanks.' Les didn't seem like a bad type of customer so the woman gave him one of her better service industry smiles. 'That was just a short stay in Cooktown Mr. Norton. I don't suppose you would have got to see much?'

Les shrugged another reply. 'I got to see Roy Steelman's helicopter blow up.'

'Yes. I suppose that's something you don't see often,' replied the woman. 'Did you get a chance to visit the Barrier Reef?'

Les had a drink of beer and shook his head. 'No. Maybe next time.'

'What about our famous Tigers Lair Hotel. Did you get to see that?'

Les reflected on the old pub he passed in the rain. 'No, looks like I missed out there, too.'

'Oh. That's a shame. Then you wouldn't have got to see all the writing on the wall.'

Les stared at the woman for a moment. 'See the what?' he said.

'The writing on the wall,' repeated the woman.

'Writing on the wall?'

'Yes. It's everywhere. It's well worth a look.' One of the young waitresses came over and said something to the blonde woman. She listened for a moment, nodded her head then looked over at Les and smiled. 'Thankyou Mr. Norton,' she said, and followed the waitress into the dining room.

Les watched her walk away then took another mouthful of beer and stared down the neck of the bottle again. Writing on the wall? Didn't that kooky sheila in Cairns say something about 'the writing's on the wall'? Now this one. What sort of a coincidence is that? He took another thoughtful sip of beer. Woody said some other strange things too. Les tapped his bottle against the coaster and stared across at the partying New Guinea pilots. They were having the time of their lives. But to Norton they were boring and noisy and he'd seen more than enough. Les decided to finish his beer in his room. He signed the tab and left.

He switched on the light, placed the bottle on the table near the TV set, then stripped down to his jocks and T-shirt and went to his travel bag. He'd put the piece of paper Woody had given him at the resort in Cairns in there with his plane ticket, his Avis insurance and some other papers. He took it out, opened it, then lay back on the bed with his bottle of beer and had another read. There it was again, all in that nice, neat print. Wolf. Tumbling Water. Danger. The Third Jewel Is Danger. The

Writing Is On The Wall. Les had a swallow of beer, stared at the piece of paper and gave it another very contemplative read.

This has to be more than a coincidence. It has to be. Okay, wolf — that was me on the radio station. Tumbling water though ... Maybe that wasn't whitewater rafting. Maybe that was all that bloody rain I saw yesterday. That was certainly tumbling out of the sky. And the third jewel is danger. Third jewel? Beryl. Jade ... And amethyst! The Amethyst Reading Room. That was part of Sherry Waldren's shop. And I couldn't have found anything much more dangerous than that. Hang on. What about the bloke with the silver bracelet and the crocodile? No, silver's a metal. Now right out of the blue that woman tells me the writing's on the wall. It's a funny one all right.

Les finished his beer, got up off the bed and dumped the bottle in the room tidy, then placed Woody's piece of paper back in his bag. If I wasn't going straight home tomorrow, I'd have a look in that old pub just for curiosity's sake he told himself. But no thanks. Or as Jim the mechanic might say — they can shove it up their arse. After laying down for a few minutes, the hotel bed suddenly never felt so good. Les adjusted the air-conditioning, turned off the lights and lay back down again. He stared up at the darkened ceiling for a few moments then closed his eyes. If there was anything worth worrying about, it could be worried about tomorrow. Before long the big, red-headed Queenslander was snoring soundly.

Les was out of bed and feeling pretty good around seven-thirty the following morning. He cleaned his teeth and decided to have one last wallow in the pool before he had breakfast and checked out; he climbed into his Speedos, threw a towel over his shoulders and walked round to the garden area. Outside, the weather had cleared up considerably compared to the day before. A bit of a nor'easter was flicking at the palm trees and apart from a few fat, grey and white clouds drifting languidly in the breeze, above the sky was sparkling blue. It was still hot, however, and still punishingly humid. Les draped his towel over the nearest banana lounge and dived straight in.

Like the day before, the water was gloriously refreshing with the slightest brace to it from having lain there all night. Les flopped under and swam aound, quite happy to have it all to himself. The way those pilots were sucking piss down their aviation throats last night, mused Les, they'll be lucky if they're out of bed by this afternoon. A bit like my girlfriend Waldo. I wonder how she is today? Not that I give a rat's arse in particular. She can lay on the lounge till the smell gives her away, for all I care. Les kicked a few strokes on his back and winked a silent thanks up at the sky, grateful that between Sherry Waldren and the crocodile by the harbour, he'd managed to squeak through again. Les flopped round a little longer. He could have stayed in the pool for ages enjoying the beautiful, cool water and the luxury of having it to himself. But somewhere between his stomach moaning and having to get on the road, Les reluctantly dragged himself out. He towelled off and went back to his room.

Les decided to wear his blue cotton tracksuit pants and give his 99FM T-shirt another serve. It was going to be hot and sweaty behind the wheel of the Overlander for almost half the day and he could get cleaned up and put on some fresh clothes when he found a motel in Cairns. He finished packing his bags, had a last look around the room then took them out and locked them in the back of the Overlander. With his keys jangling in his pocket and his sunglasses hooked on the collar of his T-shirt, Les strolled round to the dining room.

There were about a dozen or so people having breakfast. A small, bleary-eyed group sitting on the balcony, coughing cigarette smoke into cups of black coffee looked like they could have been some of the New Guinea pilots. Behind them in the distance was the charred husk of Roy Steelman's helicopter sitting on a patch of blackened grass amongst some flame-scorched trees. Les never gave it a second look. Instead, he got a table facing the opposite way and gave the food servery pretty much the same hiding he gave it the morning before; only with extra toast and strawberry jam. Satisfied Beryl's company had got its money's worth for breakfast, Les signed the tab and walked round to the front desk.

'Just as long as you enjoyed yourself while you were in Cooktown, Mr. Norton. That's the main thing,' smiled the blonde woman in the white dress, as she waited for the machine to punch out Norton's receipt.

'It was very enjoyable indeed,' answered Les, carrying on with the friendly chit chat. 'And I reckon I'll be back for another look.'

'That's good. And you might like to stay with us at Endeavour Resort again.'

'I probably will. Even if it's just for the food.'

'Thank you, Mr. Norton,' beamed the woman. 'I told you it was good.'

Les signed the bill and said goodbye, then walked back out to the Overlander and got behind the wheel. Well. That's that, he mused. Now I suppose I'd better get some petrol, make that diesel. He fired up the engine and drove off in search of a garage.

Les found one on a corner just round from the resort. It was your usual bush garage, with two rows of bowsers out the front, an office with a window full of dust-covered junk and a mechanics' bay alongside it. There was also a wet fishing boat out the front next to a gurney. Les pulled up at a vacant bowser opposite two tourists, a man and a woman in a four-wheel drive much like the one he was driving. They were wearing baseball caps and T-shirts with their fat backsides jammed into baggy, check shorts loud enough to deafen you. They were standing at the driver's side for a moment before getting back in the car and the woman was holding a video camera. Les got out to put the nozzle in the tank and couldn't help but overhear their conversation while he waited for the pump to start. It wasn't hard. They were

Americans, and their voices were set at about the same volume as their shorts.

'Are you sure we have enough film?' said the woman.

'Yes. I'm sure we do, Lori,' replied the man.

'Remember, you shot almost a complete roll in that old hotel yesterday.'

'Yeah, I know,' agreed the man. 'But all that writing on the wall. It was kinda neat.'

'Kinda neat?' said the woman. 'Kinda kooky if you ask me.'

'I'd really like to go back there and take some more,' said the man. 'And this time, let's get a texta colour and write something on the wall ourselves.'

'If that's what you want, Morey. But we'd better get more film and I need blockout.'

'Okay. If you say so. Let's go find a store.'

They drove off and Les blankly watched the numbers on the bowser tick over. When the tank was full, he washed the front and rear windscreens, gave the tyres a quick boot then went into the office with his VISA card. The proprietor was on the phone; in his old shirt and battered Akubra he looked like the bloke in the Yellow Pages ad on TV where the ute comes crashing backwards through the garage window. He gave Norton's VISA card the business, they grunted thanks to each other and the proprietor continued his conversation on the phone. Five minutes later Les was heading out of Cooktown on his way to Cairns, staring at the road ahead thinking what a nice day it was and how lucky he was to be living in Australia and trying hard not to let anything deter him from that train of thought or cloud his better judgment.

He reached the Annan River where he found that Jimmy the mechanic was right about the water running away quick. The flow was back to like it was when he drove in on Friday and the people were again sitting on the sides of the old wooden bridge fishing for barramundi. He rattled by them and onto the unsealed road. It too was nothing like the sea of red mud it was the day before. There were plenty of big puddles that were easy enough to avoid and a few loose edges. But compared to yesterday it was a breeze. Apart from a couple of cars coming the other way there was very little traffic and before long Les was cruising past the Black Mountains, jutting up as mysterious and eerie as ever in the bright sunshine. Soon the road made a slight curve and Les was fast approaching the turnoff to Cedar Bay. Les slowed for the curve then shook his head and dropped the Overlander back to second.

'No, fuck it,' he said, to no one in particular. 'I've got to see this old pub. What'll it take me? Twenty minutes? Half an hour at the most.'

The road into the old hotel had improved noticeably too since yesterday. Les went past the same farmhouses on the side of the road and over Mungumby Creek which was now running smoothly. He came to where the land went off into a wide plateau on the left-hand side of the road, then stopped at a range of mountains tapering away to the right. A little further along on the right was the old hotel. Les swung the Overlander into a U-turn and pulled up next to the phone box out the front. He switched off the motor, found his camera and got out without bothering to wind up the window.

On the left-hand side of the phone box was a sun-bleached wooden sign saying Tigers Lair Hotel, in front of two big trees, fenced in by gardens, with a pathway in the middle leading up to the hotel. Pinned to a pole next to the pathway was another sign saying Keep Your Dogs Outta The Bar And I'll Keep My Bullets Outta Your Dog. Signed God. When he'd gone past in the rain previously, all Les had got a glimpse of was a green single storey hotel with a grey galvanised iron roof. On closer inspection Les could see it was built mostly from roughly hewn wooden slabs on thick, wooden poles and had probably been there since before the turn of the century. Running along the front was a rough concrete verandah, furnished with chunky wooden tables, and chairs made from old dried logs. Five doors faced outside with a single step in front leading into the hotel. Inside it looked gloomy, there was no one around and the place didn't appear to be open yet. Les was about to go inside when an old bloke came out carrying a yard broom. He wore a battered Akubra and a black singlet tucked into baggy shorts which flapped round two skinny legs; he could have been the older brother of the bloke at the garage in Cooktown.

'All right if I go inside and have a look around, me old?' asked Les.

The old bloke gave Les the same indifferent look he'd probably given a million tourists who had asked him the same thing. 'Go for your life, mate,' he muttered.

'Thanks,' replied Les, and stepped through the door.

Inside were whitewashed walls of galvanised iron and concrete, a solid, wooden floor and a bar in the right-hand corner. Jammed against the far wall was a piano covered with jars, a door to another room behind and beyond that were gardens. There were more solidly built wooden benches and tables and covering a wall on the left was a painting of a tiger's head next to a pool table. Other than that, every square foot of the place was a storehouse of bric-a-brac and memorabilia. Old bottles, saw blades, snake skins, turtle shells, rabbit traps, dingo traps and bridles. Swordfish bills, crocodile skins, python skins, buffalo horns, saddles, old lanterns, axes, road signs, poles pinned with coasters and business cards from all over Australia. The standout feature was the walls — every square inch had something written on it. No graffiti, but cryptic messages or thoughts left in black texta colour, along with the date.

'Joe From Cascade Bay. Froggy from Bowen. Frank and Debbie from Murrarundi. The HD Holden Boys from Bendigo. Slippery was here, and had a cold beer, Christ it was dear. Squinter the legend. Gazza and Mazza. Two eyes, two hands, two swollen glands. Beneath the southern cross we stand. Drink more piss. Snowy, Johnno, Podge and Roo from Adelaide. The HG boys from Broken Hill. An HG is better than FA. Laziness is never any good unless carried out properly. Poor little bird, sad little thing, broken beak, broken wing, cannot fly, cannot sing, may as well kill the bloody thing. Go outside and look at the stars, they're amazing. Alice and Brian, fruit salad city. Dom from Italy. Frank McNeil, Tokoroa New Zealand.' There was even a Beverley and Steve Norton from Grenfell.

Les roamed around the walls of the old pub slowly shaking his head. It was as if everybody stopping or drinking at the hotel since the day it opened had left something on one of the walls. Christ, thought Les, what did Woody and those other people say? The writing's on the wall? They weren't kidding. You couldn't fit a game of noughts and crosses on there now. And if you were looking for something on one of those walls, you wouldn't find it in a hundred bloody years — not even if you were Indiana Jones. Les laughed to himself. Oh well, I suppose I may as well take a few photos while I'm here, he thought. It certainly was different. He took his camera out, wondering where to start first.

Les took a couple of shots next to one of the doors and another of the snarling tiger's head. He wandered across to the old piano and had a closer look at the dozen or so different sized jars sitting along the top. Each was half filled with preservative and floating or coiled up inside were dead spiders, snakes, scorpions and other horrible-looking nasties. Pinned amongst the countless messages on the wall behind them were several old tin drink trays. Carlton Draught, Fourex, Old Grandad; in the middle was a rusty, black, Grafton Lager one. The jars of spiders and snakes looked absolutely repulsive. But sitting the way they were with all the writing in the background, Les thought they'd make a good, if slightly macabre, photo. He was leaning on the piano with one hand trying to figure out the best angle when he heard the old cleaner walk back inside the hotel.

'You're not thinking of playing that, are you mate?' said the old cleaner.

'No. I was just going to take a photo,' replied Les. 'That's all.'

'You wouldn't get much of a tune anyway,' said the old cleaner. 'It's got no keys. It's been sitting against that wall for about a hundred years.'

'Yeah, right,' answered Les.

Les peered through the viewer and waited for the automatic flash to come on, while the old cleaner went back to whatever he was doing. Les was just about to press the button when suddenly his fingers seemed to freeze. He lowered the camera and gave the ancient piano a slow, ponderous stare. Hold on a minute. Hold on a bloody minute ... Les put the camera back in its case for the moment and walked out to the car. He opened the back doors, dragged his overnight bag over and unzipped it. Inside, and still in the envelope amongst the other papers and travel documents, was the photo Beryl gave him at Redwoods. Les picked up the envelope, plus a pen, then walked back inside the hotel and opened it in front of the piano. He turned the photo over and read what was written on the back.

'Where there's no tune,
through spiders and snakes,
in the big cat.'

Jade Biscayne the poet, eh? All right. What's a tiger? A fuckin' big cat, ain't it? The Tiger's Lair. And whereabouts in here wouldn't there be any tune? No tune. In that old piano. And through spiders and snakes. Those glass jars. I reckon amongst all the other messages behind those glass jars she's left some sort of message herself.

Les put the photo back in its envelope, walked over to the piano and beginning in the middle started searching through the messages behind the jars. Because he had a rough idea what he was looking for, it didn't take him all that long to find it. It was faded, but there it was, in between Carol and Lennie, Hobart Tasmania and Macca, Archie, Lorraine and Sharon, Sale Victoria. The blue beast got us here, so we all got pissed. The same neat script. The same circles over the i's.

Everything is nothing. And nothing is everything.
Beneath that in the same neat script was a poem.
'Bjelke kicked the hippies out of Cedar Bay,
yet some of us he missed.
Bjelke might have had his day,
but we had Amethyst.'

Beneath the 'but' was printed AB, and under that a tiny arrow pointed to the black Grafton Lager beer tray. Les looked around for the cleaner. He couldn't see him, so he shoved his fingers under the edge of the beer tray and prised it back. Well there you go, Les smiled to himself. On the wall, but written in a different script, was 'A lazy seven going back. A lazy five driving in. A lazy three walking down. Amethyst Bay.' Next to the writing was what appeared to be a small map of a road and a walking trail. An uneven line went up, then a shorter line with a zig-zag at the start went off to the left, then another line went diagonally right from that, ending at a long, squashed letter C in reverse, something like a hairpin. Les wrote everything down on the back of the envelope, and drew a copy of the map, then took a couple of photos and pushed the tray back against the wall again.

Norton stepped back from the piano, stared at the wall for a moment then turned around to find the cleaner had appeared from somewhere and was sweeping around the stools in front of the bar.

'Hey, mate,' said Les. 'Would you know if there's a place around here called Amethyst Bay?'

The old cleaner shrugged indifferently and continued with his sweeping. 'Buggered if I know, mate,' he answered. 'It could be any one of a hundred bloody bays running along the coast out there. I never heard of it.'

'Okay. Thanks anyway.' Les took another couple of photos of inside the hotel interior, then walked back out to the car.

He placed the envelope on the bonnet, rested a foot on the bumper bar and studied what was on the back of the envelope, turning away now and again to stare down the road towards Cedar Bay. A couple of cars went by in the sunshine; a white Holden utility and an old yellow Land Rover. Les watched them disappear out of sight then got his road map from the front passenger seat. He laid it out alongside the envelope, had another look along the road towards Cedar Bay and thoughtfully stroked his chin. If that way's going back, then I'd say around seven kilometres along the road, a lazy seven, there's a turnoff to the left and some off-road trail goes into the bush for another five kilometres. Then there's a walking trail for another lazy three kilometres and this brings you out at Amethyst Bay.

Norton checked the scale on his roadmap and compared it to what he'd sketched on the back of the envelope. Yes, he nodded to himself. If that's an inlet, it'd be roughly eight kilometres to the coast down there. A lazy eight. And that's where they're holed up. And you don't have to be Sherlock Holmes to know what they're up to — they've pulled an insurance scam. Sherry Waldren's in on the rort too. And Beryl's probably looking for some reward money as well as her granddaughter. All I've got to do is find them and I'm twenty-five grand in front. He picked at his chin for a moment then a lightbulb surrounded by neon dollar signs suddenly lit up over his head. But fuck Beryl and her twenty-five grand, he schemed. What about the papers? The tabloids?

Their disappearance was worldwide. If I was to sneak in there and get a few photos of them drinking piss and smoking a few hot ones, the tabloids'd pay a fortune for them. Plus TV. A movie deal. Even the women's magazines'd want some of it. Les Norton. My secret agony. I've got a few shots left in the camera and there's another roll of film in my bag. Shit! I could clean up here.

Norton kept plotting and scheming while he picked at his chin. Okay. Say I'm wrong. What would it take me to get in there and back? Four? Five hours tops. And the weather and conditions are nothing like yesterday. Plus this time, if the car should get bogged, I'm not stranded out in the middle of nowhere. I could walk or jog back to the hotel. Ring for a taxi, stay the night in Cooktown and catch a plane back to Cairns. Leave the car where it is. It's insured up to the hilt anyway. All right, I'm giving someone up to the press and ultimately the cops for money. But fuck them. That sheila trying to poison me last night. That made it personal. He drummed his fingers on the bonnet of the car and his scheming brown eyes narrowed. Five hours of my time, another day at the most, against a punt on making a bundle of chops. A big bundle ... Yeah, fuck it, why not? He gathered up the map and the envelope, climbed back in the car, then clicked the small odometer back to zero and started driving south.

The road towards Cedar Bay was still rough, but firm. The ribbons of water flowing across it the day before were now either gone or mere trickles and the torrent below on his left was back to a swiftly flowing creek. Soon the mountains on the left started to close in, the jungle on the right got thicker and Les had gone six kilometres. He slowed down almost to a crawl, keeping an eye out for the start of a trail on the left. A little past seven kilometres he spotted it. Not quite a trail. Two indentations in the side of the road, just wide enough for the wheels of a car. Les swung the Overlander up off the road, drove in a few metres then got out and engaged the front wheel hubs. The trail ahead was uneven and a little soft. But definitely driveable. He got back in and proceeded along slowly.

Jungle now closed in on either side; it was filtering out the sun and slapping against the doors and mudguards. However, Les was confident as he bumped along, until a point about a kilometre further on where the trail stopped at the edge of a river. He pulled the handbrake on and stared through the windscreen. The river was almost fifty metres wide; not only that, it was fast-flowing and looked to be at least two metres deep in the middle. Shit, he cursed to himself. This is it and the water's still too high to get across. Yet on the opposite side there was no sign of a trail going into the bush. Nothing but trees and boulders right up to the riverbank. Then Les remembered that the second line on the map he'd sketched had a little zig-zag going off to the right on it. He had a quick look at the envelope to make sure, then slipped off the handbrake, and reversed the Overlander back up the trail. Sure enough. Twenty-five metres back from the riverbank were another two small indentations at the side of the trail, and just like the other two, if you weren't looking for them, you'd never know they were there. More confident than ever, Les spun the steering wheel to the right and pushed the Overlander along the new trail through the jungle.

Five hundred metres further, the trail circled to the left stopping at the riverbank again and Les found his confidence suddenly taking another nose dive. In front of him now the river might have slowed down, but it had formed itself into a deep, wide billabong. Les couldn't believe it. There was absolutely no way of getting across to the other side unless you were in a boat. Yet to tantalise him, on the opposite side of the river there appeared to be the start of another trail. Les left the motor running and got out for a closer look. The water was fairly clear and just below the surface two huge old cedar logs, roughly a metre apart, had jammed themselves into both riverbanks, forming a crude bridge about the width of a wheelbase. The current flowing over the two old logs wasn't fast and it was less than half a metre deep. However, the water beneath them went into a dark, green nothingness that could have been any depth. But there were rocks piled round the front of the two logs and if you were game enough you could get a car up onto them all right. Les had a good look at the two, big logs, wondering if they were rotten in the middle or slippery on the top.

Probably a bit of both. He stroked his chin again and slowly shook his head. He'd come this far and with a bit of luck vast sums of money lay beyond the mountain in front. He got back in the Overlander, put it in low and momentarily holding his breath, bumped the front wheels up onto the two logs.

Les inched his way across the makeshift bridge, his eyes glued on the two logs submerged beneath the flowing water in front of the cabin. He reached a third of the way over and started to think it wasn't all that bad; the logs were wide enough and if you kept your concentration there was nothing to worry about. Only problem being if the logs broke, or you slipped on a big knot in one and went over the side, you either drowned or it was a long, wet walk back to the hotel. Half-way across, the log on the right started to shudder and gave a little. Les held his breath, gripped the steering wheel tighter and kept going. The big log gave another shudder as he passed the half-way mark, then it felt okay, and before long Les had made it safely to the other side and bumped down onto solid ground again.

Les jerked the handbrake on, closed his eyes for a moment and sucked in a deep lungful of air. That was just a little hairy. He got the bottle of mineral water from his overnight bag, gulped some down and noticed his T-shirt was soaked with sweat. He got out of the car and took it off, then rinsed it in the river, rung it out and put it back on again. He had another look at the two logs he'd just crossed and momentarily took in the serenity and beauty of the deep billabong they forded and the surrounding trees and boulders. After making a mental note to take a couple of photos when he returned, Les climbed back behind the wheel of the Overlander and started off again.

The trail rose slightly, then seemed to level off between a rocky gorge, thick with overhanging trees and creepers. He checked the odometer and found he'd gone two kilometres. A 'lazy' three to go and the trail wasn't all that bad. A bit muddy and with rocks everywhere, but it looked like it could have been part of an old, dried-up river bed. In some parts the smooth rocks were jammed together almost like cobblestones. Les kept bouncing along, slowly but steadily, keeping the Overlander in low and his eyes on the job ahead. Outside the car, huge, exotic ferns spidered against the windows and clinging to the surrounding trees were some of the biggest staghorns Les had ever seen. He began to get a feeling he was driving through part of an untouched rainforest; there were even cedar trees amongst the brushbox and red gums. After just on four and a half kilometres of bumping, lurching, apprehensive driving the trail came to a small clearing in the scrub, barely big enough for a Vee-dub to turn round in, let alone a larger vehicle like the Overlander. Les nosed the big four by four into the middle and had a look around. Oh well, he thought, what do they make these things for? Bush bashing. He shoved it back into first, then reverse, and kept grinding backwards and forwards bashing his way round again. Two more solid dents in the front mudguards and several in the rear and he was back facing the way he came again. Les edged the Overlander a few metres back down the trail, then turned off the motor and climbed out the back doors to have a look around.

The first thing he noticed were some very faint, single tyre marks in the hard clay at the start of the trail. Someone's been here, that's for sure, he thought. He stepped into the middle of the clearing. In the bushes on the right-hand side was a sheet of waterproof camouflaging. Les walked over and pulled it back, underneath was an unregistered black Honda XR 600 trail bike, complete with saddle bags and a pillion. Alongside it was a blue metal tool box and two drums of petrol. Well, what about that, Les smiled to himself. The plot definitely thickens. He replaced the camouflage sheet and walked over to where the edge of the clearing faced the Overlander. The start of a narrow walking trail led off into the jungle. I'd say that's it, Norton nodded to himself. Only a 'lazy' three kilometre walk now and I should be in Amethyst Bay. He had another quick look around and decided to make a move.

Les went back to the car, changed into his black gym boots and put his tracksuit top on. He had another swig of mineral water, then grabbed his overnight bag with the shoulder straps and placed the bottle inside it next to his camera, along with the car keys, the envelope and a couple of other essentials. He tied a hanky round his forehead, slung the overnight bag across his shoulders, then checked his watch. Happy to see he was making better time than he thought, he set off for the coast.

The narrow trail rose gradually through a jungle of moss-covered trees, hung with long twists of vine, thick as rope. Birds sang to each other from somewhere above and the cracks of sunlight coming through the canopy of leaves flickered across the bush orchids, wattle and the other exotic native plants and flowers. A bit further on Les noticed paw marks amongst the rocks in the trail. At first he thought they must have been dingo tracks. But they were too big and obviously a friendly old wombat had been using the trail at some time. Then the trail levelled out before starting a steady descent.

Norton strode along, not thinking about much, except all the money he was going to make when he got his pictures and story to the tabloids. He'd been keeping an eye on his watch however and figured at the pace he was going, especially downhill, he'd covered around two and a half kilometres.

He avoided a Lawyer Vine hanging by the trail then a little further on he heard a roaring sound that seemed to be getting closer and he was certain he could smell the sea. The trail went between two Moreton Bay figtrees then seemed to stop at a long, narrow freshwater inlet leading out to the ocean.

On the left was rocky bush and overhanging trees. On the right was a smooth cliff face about ten metres high covered by a thick hilltop of trees. The roaring sound Les heard was an underground stream tumbling out in a thick jet of freshwater into a deep, green pool. As well as being long and narrow, the inlet looked quite deep. Further along was an isthmus of sand between the freshwater and the sea; on his left a thin strip of white sand led to that isthmus. Les rinsed his hanky out, wiped his face and had a drink of water, then put the hanky back round his head and followed the strip of sand along the water's edge to the ocean. Half-way along he reached behind and took out his camera. Running along the cliff face on the left side of the underground waterfall was a cluster of Aboriginal cave paintings in red, brown and white ochre: kangaroos, emus, handprints and figures in strange headdresses. Les snapped off two quick photos, put his camera back and kept crunching along the water's edge.

The sand stopped at the start of the headland, then the isthmus cut across to a small, picturesque beach on the right. At the end, a small river ran into the beach at the start of another rugged little headland running out to sea. Both headlands pinched themselves close together as they formed an inlet to the ocean and in between the sea swirled over treacherous, oyster-encrusted reefs, lying not far below the surface. The beach backed on to palm trees and boulders and the whole area was lush with old growth forest, rich green foliage and colourful native flowers. Les could hardly believe what he was looking at. It was one of the most beautiful places he'd ever seen, and it was virtually inaccessible. The trail in was bad enough, if you could find it in the first place, and then there were the two logs across the river. The way it was so long and narrow and overhung with trees and jungle, a helicopter would fly straight over it — you might be able to land on the beach, but you could bet the wind sheers coming up from along that skinny inlet would make it almost impossible. And the only way in by sea over those reefs would be by canoe or maybe a rubber ducky. Sherry Waldren's rubber ducky. Even then you'd have to be extremely careful you didn't rip it to pieces on the oyster shells.

Norton stood there for a while, shaking his head in admiration. No wonder they holed up in here after they went missing. It was like something out of *Jurassic Park* or a James Bond movie. Even their little girl would love it. And it wouldn't be forever — once they got the insurance money they'd assume new identities and all live happily ever after. Sorry, me and my trusty little camera are going to put the stoppers on that though. He crossed over the isthmus of sand and started crunching along the beach. Apart from the waterfall, it was very quiet and there was no sign of any people. Maybe they knew he was coming and had run off into the jungle? Les had a strange feeling for a moment that someone could have been watching him when he stopped to take those photos of the cave paintings.

Half-way along the beach was a roughly-built log hut covered in flowering vines, hidden back from view beneath some palm trees. A door with two small flyscreen-covered windows on either side faced a short path to the sand and on the other side of the hut was a small vegetable patch fenced with sticks and broken branches. Near the front a sun-bleached, wooden bench table sat next to a tyre hanging from a tree by a length of chain. Les walked over and gave the tyre a light push with the toe of his shoe. I'd say the kid's about due for a new swing, he thought. This one's almost shredded down to the canvas. Smooth, granite boulders stuck out from the sand around the hut and a mango tree grew above the wooden table offering a little shade. Everything remained quiet and Les still couldn't see anybody.

Norton took his camera from his overnight bag and was about to take a photo of the hut when he noticed a movement at the end of the beach. A woman, carrying an empty flower pot and a garden fork, had come round from the river and started walking towards him. She was wearing sunglasses and a black sarong covered in yellow and white flowers with a plain, white cotton scarf tied across her breasts. A tousle of brunette hair topped an attractive face and she could have been any pretty young woman in her early twenties. But there was no mistaking that sixpack stomach, strong neck and square shoulders. She didn't appear nervous or surprised at seeing Les. It was as if she either knew he was there or was somehow expecting him and just kept walking confidently towards him. Because of the sunglasses, Les couldn't see the look in her eyes. But by the way her jaw was set, the expression on her face bordered somewhere between hostile indifference and bored contempt. Les waited till she was almost in front of him.

'Hello,' he said, politely. 'Are you Jade Biscayne?'

The woman gave Les a scorching once up and down. 'No. I'm fuckin' Elvis Presley. Have you got any cheeseburgers? Of course I'm fuckin' Jade Biscayne. Who did you think it was, you dopey-looking big cunt.'

'Shit. Sorry,' said Les. 'I was only asking.' Christ, he thought, has this sheila got attitude or what?

The woman continued to glare at Norton. 'So, who the fuck are you anyway?'

'Les. Les Norton.'

'Ohh yeah,' humphed the woman. 'I think I've heard of you.' She gave Les another withering once up and down. 'All right. I'm Jade Biscayne. So what the fuck do you want?'

Les made a gesture with both hands. 'Your mother sent me.'

'My fuckin' mother sent you!!?'

'Yeah, Beryl. She's worried about you and her granddaughter Amy.'

'She's fuckin' what?' Jade looked at Les like he was a fresh pile of dog shit she'd just found on her private beach. 'I don't fuckin' believe this.'

'It's the truth,' said Les.

Jade shook her head and looked away for a moment. 'Jesus Christ! All right. How the fuck did you find me? Hardly anyone knows where I am. Especially stinking bloody Beryl.'

'It was easy,' shrugged Les. 'I just read the writing on the wall.'

'You what?'

'I just read that message you left on the wall in the pub, that's all. After I'd compared it to this.' Les took the envelope from his overnight bag, opened it and handed Jade the photo.

Jade put the flower pot and garden fork down, snatched the photo from Les and turned it over. Next thing her face blackened and the veins in her neck stood out like they were ready to burst. 'Where the fuck did you get this? You cunt!' she roared.

'Off Beryl. Your mother gave it to me before I left.'

'She gave it to you? That fuckin' fat moll. This was meant for a friend. She's intercepted my mail. The fuckin' bitch.'

'Shit, Jade,' said Les innocently. 'That's not a very nice way to talk about your mother.'

'Fuck her.'

'All right. Fair enough.'

Jade Biscayne glared at the photo in her hand then at Les.

'I still can't believe a dopey-looking big prick like you could find me through this. I mean, it's just too fuckin' amazing to even contemplate.'

'Maybe my dim sims aren't as dim as they sim, Jade,' replied Les.

Jade nodded slowly. 'Maybe not,' she conceded.

Les got the feeling he'd taken the wind slightly out of her sails. He looked around and decided to play it cool for the moment. 'So where is everybody? Where's your boyfriend?'

Jade looked evenly at Les. 'You want to meet Hordern Genting do you?'

'Yeah. I'd love to,' said Les.

'Fine. Follow me, shit for brains.'

'Okay if I bring my camera?'

'Bring what you like. I don't give a fuck.'

Jade turned on her heel and started walking back down the beach towards the river, with Les a step or two behind her. Les wasn't quite expecting the red carpet treatment when he arrived, but her attitude and the open hostility towards him so far was almost unbelievable. He made a mental note to keep a close eye on Jade in case she tried to knife him in the back or something. The river flowed down from a shadowy gorge covered with more overhanging trees and vines. From one aspect it was quite beautiful, yet it also had an air of menace and darkness about it. On a corner of sand above the beach and the river was a mound of black river stones. A single blue orchid lay on the top in front of a flat stone with just the initials H.S.G. carved into it.

'So that's Hordern Genting, eh?' said Les.

'Doctor Hordern Spencer Genting to you, arsehole,' snapped Jade. 'One of the greatest minds of our time.'

'It's not doing him much good now.'

Jade glared at Norton. 'What would you fuckin' know?'

'I know where his bones are,' replied Les, taking his camera out of his overnight bag.

'Not his bones, pal. His ashes.'

Les was a little incredulous. 'You had him cremated?'

'I built a funeral pyre. No cunt's ever going to dig my man's body up.'

'Yeah. Right,' said Les. He took two quick photos making sure he got the flower and the inscription.

'Come on,' said Jade. 'You've seen enough.'

'Righto,' nodded Les.

Jade abruptly turned away again and Les followed her back along the tiny beach to her hut, where she nodded to the wooden table out the front.

'Sit down.'

'Okay.' Les sat down facing the river with his back towards the little isthmus of sand. He placed his overnight bag on the table with his camera next to it. 'Are you going to offer me a beer or something, Jade?' he asked flippantly.

'Get fucked,' was Jade's blunt reply.

'I thought that's what you'd say.' Les took out his bottle of mineral water, had a drink then put it back in his overnight bag.

'Do you mind if I ask you a few questions, Jade?' he asked.

Jade studied him for a moment then half-smiled. 'All right,' she shrugged. 'You're here now, shithead. What do you want to fuckin' know?'

Jade's attitude seemed to change from open

hostility to smug self-confidence; she was showing absolutely no fear or signs of nervousness. Her style was almost cat and mouse. Very similar to Sherry Waldren's when she gave Les the cup of spiked hot chocolate.

Les looked at her evenly for a second or two.

'All right. Firstly, what does "Everything is nothing. And nothing is everything" mean?'

Jade stared back at him. 'It means exactly what it says, you fuckin' idiot. It's an old zen saying.'

'Fair enough,' replied Norton. 'I just wanted to get that out of the road. That's all. But why the little messages anyway? You almost got sprung in Port Douglas.'

Jade gestured with one hand. 'Oh, for the fuckin' buzz, Les. That's all. For fun. I just liked playing "spot Elvis" with some of the locals. I probably shouldn't have done it. But it was a hoot. And it wouldn't make any difference in the end.'

'Whatever turns you on, I suppose.' Les stroked his chin and a smug half-smile formed on his face also. 'Well, it's pretty obvious what you're up to — you pulled an insurance scam, didn't you?'

'Oh, you fuckin' genius, Les,' said Jade. 'Go straight to the head of the class. But don't bother taking your books, because you won't be there long.'

'So how did you do it?'

'How did we do it?'

'Yeah.'

'We just jumped off the back of the boat after they took the head count. We'd been planning it for a while. We'd been out diving on *Sea Trek* a few times before and we knew the deckhand that took the head count was the dumbest, most miserable arse God ever put breath into. Even stupider than you. If that's possible.'

'His name wasn't Bill, was it?'

'That's right. How did you know?' said Jade.

Les shook his head. 'It doesn't matter.'

'The thing is, the day we did it we got a bloke that was even dumber than him. We couldn't believe our luck. So over the side we went. We'd planted a few things on the bottom before that to be safe. Like spare tanks and power heads in case of tiger sharks. But we were only in the water thirty minutes before a friend came out and picked us up.'

Les had a good idea who the friend was. But thought he might let it slide for the moment. 'Very clever, Jade,' he conceded. 'You pulled off the scam of the decade.'

'We made headlines,' answered Jade, with a definite smirk. 'That's for fuckin' sure.'

'Did you what.' Despite Jade's attitude and the way she spoke to him, Les still couldn't help admire her. Or their, audacity. He looked over at the hut then up at the mangos in the tree above where they were sitting and was almost tempted to pick one. He would in a minute. 'And you've been holed up here in Amethyst Bay ever since.'

'Yeah,' nodded Jade. 'Something like that.'

Les absently poked at his camera. 'Look, ripping

off an insurance company, and fooling the press, there's nothing wrong with that Jade. But what about your poor mother? Beryl's worried sick about you, you know. Expecially her granddaughter.'

Jade looked evenly at Les for a moment and shook her head. 'Les, Beryl's not my mother, you fuckin' idiot.'

Les stared at her and blinked. 'She's not? Well then who is she?'

'She's my fuckin' young sister.'

'Your what? Your sister? I don't believe it.'

'Les. How old do you think I am, you fuckin' moron?' Jade lifted her sunglasses for a moment.

Les stared at her face. She had the same beautiful violet eyes as Beryl. Maybe a little harder. But her face hardly had a line on it. 'I don't know,' answered Les. 'Twenty. Twenty-two.'

'Try fifty.'

'Fifty? You got to be kidding.'

Jade shook her head. 'You've been conned, dummy. Not that it'd be hard.' She looked down at the table for a moment then back up again. 'Okay Norton, what do you know about Hordern Genting?'

Les didn't quite know what to say or where to start. Jade had just pulled the rug from under him. He'd been conned all right. 'Mostly what I read in the papers. He was a geneticist or something. And I also heard he'd found a cure for baldness.'

'Hey! You have done your homework, brightboy,' said Jade.

'That's about all,' shrugged Les.

'Righto. I'll give you the whole story.' The look on Jade's face was one of total disdain and the tone of her voice was equally condescending. 'I suppose you've earnt it. You poor, silly cunt,' she added.

'Thanks.' Les undid his tracksuit top and had another drink of water.

'Yonks ago, there was a big police raid up here at a place called Cedar Bay.'

'I read about in an old magazine,' nodded Les.

'That's where I met Hordern. We were hippies and also doing our university degrees. The day of the raid, we'd just eaten a stack of peyote that Hordern had got hold of. There were six of us. We were out in the bush, tripping off our heads and wandered back just after the cops arrived. So we split and just kept walking and we came across this place. It's called Goodoo Goodoo, because of all the big cod in the bay. And an old bushranger, called Cow Manning, once used it for a hideout. No one knows about it. We all fell in love with the place. Hordern and I used to come here every chance we could get. The place is very special to us.'

'Could I hazard a guess and say your daughter was born here?' said Les.

'That's right, sunshine. She sure was,' answered Jade.

'And does your sister call her Amy for short?'

'Oh Les, you're just so cool,' said Jade. 'That little poem I put on the wall at the hotel, where it says, "And we had Amethyst", it means we had the place and our daughter too. We named it after her.'

'Why the little map under the old drink tray?'

'Hordern put it there. It was just a secret between the six of us who found the place. And a quirky way of leaving directions for anyone we wanted to come here.' Jade shook her head. 'I still can't figure out how a moron like you got onto it. Even with my fat fuckin' sister intercepting my mail.'

'Let's just say I had extraterrestrial help, Jade,' said Les.

'All right. Then if you're so extraterrestrial fuckin' smart, you'd know all about the Human Genome Project and super sequencers. The DNA double helix and decoding genetic material. You'd know a human being has 110,000 genes spread among three billion DNA segments. As well as mutating nucleotides, genetically engineered enzymes. Adenine, guanine, cystine, and thymine. You'd know all about that, wouldn't you?'

'Sure,' said Les. 'I got a draw full of them at home.'

'Yeah, like I said — you wouldn't know shit. That's Genomic Research, smart arse.'

'I thought that's what it was,' smiled Les.

Jade looked at Les as if he was beneath contempt. 'Hordern discovered a way to reverse ageing. That's why I look like this. Bit of exercise, natural food, you stay young forever.'

'Well if it's so good, what happened to Hordern?'

'That, unfortunately, is the downside. Which we found out too late. It gives you advanced osteoporosis. It destroys your bones. It's gradual for a while, then it hits your brain stem and bingo.'

'Bloody hell!' said Les.

'Hordern was still trying to figure it out when he died. Four months ago. Another three months and I'll be lying there next to him.'

'Shit!'

'Yeah Les. Shit. But by God it was good while it lasted. You're fifty and you feel and look twenty.'

'Live fast, die fairly young, and have a good looking corpse, eh?' said Les.

'Something like that,' nodded Jade. 'Hordern took out a life insurance policy back in America. Looking so young and fit, he was able to get a huge premium. But if they found out he died from an incurable disease it'd be worth nothing. So that's why we staged the disappearance.'

'And your daughter, Amy. I mean Amethyst. She's the beneficiary.'

'Someone else. A good friend who helped us. She'll take care of her when the time comes.'

Les had a good idea who the friend was, but decided not to say anything. Instead, he began to see things in a different light. Jade was dying. And all the poor woman wanted to do was live out her last days in her own private paradise with the man she loved, before joining him. Then when she was gone, she'd taken steps to make sure her daughter was taken care of. All Sherry Waldren was trying to do was protect their interests. Now if Sherry died, Jade's daughter could miss out. Aunty Beryl might take care of her, but it wouldn't be the same thing. And for a lousy twenty-five grand, it wasn't worth telling

Beryl anyway. As for the papers? He could come back in a few months when it was all over if he wanted to and give them the story then. He didn't need money that bad.

Les was beginning to hope Sherry was all right and wishing he'd left them all alone and minded his own business. Why not leave the poor bloody woman in peace? he thought. She's going through enough as it is.

'Well, Jade,' said Les, getting ready to put his camera away and leave, 'that's a fantastic story. Even if it is a bit sad. But you needn't worry, your secret's safe with me. I won't tell anybody where you are. And I hope your daughter gets all her money.'

'Gee thanks, Les,' said Jade. 'That's mighty white of you.'

'What else can I do?' shrugged Les. I'm not that big a dropkick.'

Jade batted her violet eyes at him. 'Oh Les,' she cooed. 'You wonderful, beautiful man.'

'Thanks.' After all the filthy language and abuse earlier, Les thought he might have been hearing things. But maybe Jade had simply calmed down and started to realise he was a decent, fairly honest bloke. 'Hey, talking about your daughter, Jade,' said Les. 'Where is she?'

Jade gave Les a lovely smile. 'You'd like to meet my daughter Amethyst would you Les?'

'Yeah, sure. Is she around?'

'She's sitting right behind you.'

'Behind me? I never heard ...'

Les turned around and his blood ran cold. Sitting across a smooth boulder, licking its arm was some kind of wolf — only it had long, reddish-brown fur. Its face was black with an elongated jaw, but it had small ears and a woman's eyes. Beautiful violet eyes just like Jade's. The creature had a tail and hind legs, but its arms were human with powerful, leathery hands that curled into razor sharp claws. Round its neck was a thick, studded leather collar with a large precious stone in the front that matched its eyes. An Amethyst. The creature was about seven feet tall. Powerful and graceful, beautiful yet hideous. It was also very, very frightening. The creature gave Les a disinterested look for a moment, in the way a cat might, then went back to licking its fur.

'Jesus Christ!' gasped Les. 'What the fuckin' hell's that?'

'Hey.' Jade reached across the table and slapped the back of her hand against Norton's chest. 'Show a bit of respect. That's my daughter you're talking about.'

'Your daughter?' Les could hardly believe his eyes. 'Good lord! What happened to her?'

'That's the second half of the story,' said Jade. 'You're now looking at Hordern's cure for baldness.'

'Shit a brick!'

'Yeah. Unfortunately, Hordern fucked up with the needles. And instead of getting my anti-ageing shots, I got the DNA nucleotides from some wolves he'd been working on at the University of Montana. The day I fell pregnant. And Amethyst was born like that. That's why I had her here and why we keep coming back to Goodoo Goodoo. She's safe here.'

'Bloody hell!' Les watched in fascinated horror as Jade's hybrid daughter continued to lick her fur.

'She's only got a couple of years left in her, too.' Jade's jaw set a little firmly. 'Then the whole sorry saga will be over. And no one will be any the wiser.'

Les continued to stare at Amethyst. 'God! I don't know what to say, Jade. I've never seen anything like it.'

'Now you know why Beryl keeps trying to find us. I've destroyed all Hordern's papers. But Beryl's got half an idea what's going on. If she could get her fat hands on my daughter, she'd sell her to a pharmaceutical company. They'd get her DNA, along with everything else, and treat her like a freak. Then when they were finished — get rid of her. And Beryl and the company would wind up with millions.'

'Nice sister you've got,' said Les.

'Yeah, I just love her,' said Jade. 'She knows Hordern and I come up here somewhere, but she doesn't know where. Luckily the lazy, fat bitch never leaves Sydney. But she keeps hiring people hoping one of them might find us.' Jade smiled at Les. 'And one finally did. Lucky you, Les.'

'Yeah,' gulped Les. 'Lucky me.'

Jade kept her smile on Les for a moment then turned to her daughter. 'Come over here to mummy, darling.'

The creature stopped licking its fur for the moment and rose effortlessly from where it was seated then walked over and stood by its mother's side. The natural, underlying power and liquidity of the creature's movements had a beauty about it that left Norton speechless. It also sent chills up and down his spine.

'Say hello to the nice man, Amethyst,' said Jade. 'Give him a smile. Shake hands with Amethyst, Les.'

The creature's beautiful violet eyes shone for a moment then its mouth drew back and two rows of razor-sharp teeth running back from two huge fangs gleamed moist and white in the sunlight. Its hand was twice the size of Norton's and felt hard as leather when it pressed over his.

'Hello Amethyst,' said Les, giving the creature's hand a quick, nervous squeeze. 'Nice to ... meet you.'

The creature made a funny, purring sound, took its hand away and turned to its mother.

'Show the nice man how you play with your swing, Amethyst,' said Jade.

The creature walked across to the tyre hanging on the chain, sat on its haunches for a second then slashed at the tyre with one hand. The creature's claws tore into the hard rubber like it was wet bread, making the tyre spin round and rock on the end of the chain.

'Good girl,' said Jade. 'Now show the nice man what you can do with a stone.'

The creature picked up a heavy stone from the sand about the same size as a half a house brick and looked up at a small flock of seagulls circling around above the inlet. The creature chose one of the seagulls and hurled the stone with its right arm. The piece of granite hit the seagull in the chest like a cannonball, killing it instantly in a quick flurry of feathers. The remaining seagulls screeched in panic then flew off, while the dead seagull and the rock plummeted down and splashed amongst the oyster-covered reefs in the swirling waters of the narrow inlet.

'Very good,' said Jade. 'Oh she's a clever girl, isn't she?' The creature smiled at her mother and again the gleaming rows of teeth and fangs caught the sunlight. 'Now come back over here and sit down next to mummy.' Smiling happily at what had just happened the creature did as it was told and sat down on its mother's left opposite Les. Jade scrabbled the thick, coarse hair on her daughter's head. 'She's my baby. Aren't you darling?' The creature made the same purring sound and placed its head on its mother's shoulder. Jade smiled over at Norton. 'Well. What do you think of Amethyst, Les?' she said.

'She's ... really something,' replied Les, staring mesmerised at the creature's face from a metre away. 'What do you feed her?'

'Oh ... Fish. Cassowaries, wallabies.' Jade smiled at Les. 'People now and again.'

'Well, a young girl like that, I imagine she needs a balanced diet.' Les started to casually do up his tracksuit top. 'Anyway, like I said before Jade — your secret's safe with me. You and your daughter can just go on living happily ever after, as far as I'm concerned. Or as ... long as ever after is, that is.'

Jade gave her head a slow shake. 'Uh uh. Sorry Les. But it doesn't quite work that way.'

'It doesn't?' said Les.

'No. I can't let you leave here, Les. I think you understand.'

'No, not really. What's the problem?'

'There's no problem for me,' shrugged Jade.

Les looked at the creature for a second. 'You don't mean ...?'

Jade nodded. 'I do mean,' she said simply. 'But don't worry, Les. You'll hardly feel a thing. When I give her the word, she'll just come up behind you, sink her fangs into your neck, break it, and ...' Jade snapped her fingers. 'Bingo! Lights out.'

'You're kidding?' said Les, futilely.

Jade ignored him. 'You can fight her if you like. But it won't do you any good. All it'll do is prolong the agony. And make a lot of mess.'

'Oh shit!' exclaimed Les.

'Hey! I might even take some photos!' Jade smiled happily at Les. 'You don't mind if I use your camera, do you?'

Norton's voice sounded like it was coming from far away. 'No, go for your life.'

Les watched Jade put the camera strap round her neck and began to realise he wasn't just in deep shit; he was gone. What could he do? He couldn't outrun the creature. Even if it didn't want to chase him, all it had to do was pick up a rock. Les wasn't just going to sit there and let the creature sink its fangs in his neck; he was going to go down kicking and fighting. But after what Amethyst did to the tyre, clearly one slash from those claws and he'd lose half his arm. Another slash and he'd be disembowelled. His only chance would be to throw some sand in its face and make a sprint for the sea. But how far would he get? The inlet was full of reefs covered in razor-sharp oyster shells. And they wouldn't worry baby Amethyst. About the only thing he could do, Les thought, was maybe buy a little time.

Jade looked across at Les with a smug smile on her face and his camera round her neck. 'Well, Les, I guess it's just about photo time. Anything you'd like to say before I give Amethyst the word?'

Les shook his head. 'No. Not really. I just hope you can trust Sherry Waldren with all that money. That's all.'

The smile vanished from Jade's face. 'What are you talking about?'

'Well, she is the beneficiary, isn't she?'

Jade's face went back to its normal, black scowl and the veins started to rise on her neck. 'What do you know about Sherry Waldren?'

Les shrugged. 'I know she makes great fish pies with coconut.'

'You've been round the cafe,' shouted Jade. 'You're lucky she didn't know who you were, you cunt. Or you wouldn't be here now.'

I knew it, thought Les. I've hit a nerve. But how long can I string this out before I think of something? Shit! I've got to try. 'I also know where the old shed is, where she keeps the rubber ducky. The one with the black motor on the back she used to pick you and Hordern up at Wine Glass Cay.'

Jade glared furiously at Norton for a moment. 'Okay, smart arse. You got a pie at the cafe and drove past her house. Big fuckin' deal.'

'Big deal,' shrugged Les. 'Big kitchen'd be more like it. I like all the batik furnishings in the loungeroom too. I imagine she brought them back from Indonesia. Especially that big, laughing Buddha near the stereo.'

'You were in her house? What were you doing in her fuckin' house?'

'Having a hot chocolate.'

The veins in Jade's neck stood out like battery cables. 'Hot fuckin' chocolate!' she roared.

The creature sitting next to her must have detected something in the tone of her mother's voice. Her eyes narrowed and the hair around her neck bristled. She moved slightly towards Les and snarled. Not very loud, but enough to bare those two frightening fangs. Les had certainly managed to buy some time. But unless he could come up with something pretty good and pretty bloody fast it was soon going to run out.

'Yeah,' continued Les, as casually as he could. 'With Tia Maria in it. It was beautiful.'

'You fuckin' cunt!' howled Jade.

'I like her CDs too. Especially one she had there. Land Of Love. I ended up borrowing it off her.'

'You fuckin' what!' Jade looked like she was ready to explode.

'Yeah, I like Sherry,' continued Les. 'She's got a good attitude. We had a real ...' Norton's voice trailed off and his eyes suddenly stuck out like a giant squid's. Something like the Swiss bloke's when they dragged him back in the boat going down the Tully River. 'Jade,' he said, desperately, 'I wouldn't worry about Sherry Waldren right now. Take a look behind you.'

'What ...' Jade turned around a little suspiciously. 'Oh Jesus!' she screamed. 'Amethyst, quick!'

Slithering up the beach, and getting closer all the time, was the mother of all crocodiles. More than that — it was the same six metre monster that tried to eat Les in Cooktown the night before. There was no mistaking its size, its colouring, its horrible, cruel eyes and the piece blown out of its snout. It had come down from the other end of the beach. How it had got there Les didn't have a clue. Maybe the explosion scared it that much it just kept going into the river system. But it had seen Les and recognised him as the red-headed meal that had got away the night before. It headed straight towards him, determined it wasn't going to miss out this time. Les wasn't sure whether the cavalry had arrived or it was just something else to add to his woes.

Amethyst let out a bloodcurdling snarl then jumped up from the table, sprinted across the beach and leapt straight on the crocodile's head slashing at it with her powerful claws. The crocodile rolled over, snapped its jaws and came up with Amethyst's leg in its mouth. The crocodile was big and mean and keen for a meal. And if it couldn't eat Norton, the thing with the hair all over it would do.

Jade leapt up from the table. 'Don't worry Amethyst! Mummy's coming! Mummy's coming!' she screamed, and ran over to join in the fight.

Amethyst was leaping round in front of the crocodile slashing at its face, while the monster reptile snapped back at her. Jade wrapped Norton's camera round her wrist and started beating the crocodile about the eyes with it. The crocodile moved back slightly from the new assailant then swung its mighty tail around and caught Jade a sickening blow right across the ribs. She screamed and went flying out into the water along with Norton's camera. Amethyst hissed out an angry snarl and leapt back on the crocodile, biting and slashing at its tough, leathery hide. The crocodile hissed too, snapped its jaws then rolled over and came up in a whirl of flying sand with its teeth around Amethyst's foot. Les thought this might be as good a time as any to blast off. He threw his overnight bag round his shoulders and sprinted for the other end of the beach. He had one quick look back as he ran across the isthmus. Jade was still floating among the oysters, and Amethyst and the crocodile were still going for it. Les couldn't tell who was winning, but he wasn't sticking around to find out.

Norton took to the trail like he was in the Stawell Gift. Even though it was uphill, whatever time it had taken him to come down, Les caned it going back. Les hated to admit it, but he was scared shitless. Another five minutes and he was gone, Sherry Waldren or not. Jade would have still put Amethyst onto him then gone and sorted Sherry out for herself. Even now Les could picture the creature beating off the crocodile or leaving it to come running up the track and sink its fangs into his neck. Les sprinted along the trail as fast as he could, glad he was fit and thankful that all that training he did was worth the effort.

When he reached the clearing, Les was in a lather of sweat and gasping for air. He tore open the front door of the Overlander, flung his overnight bag onto the passenger seat and slammed the door shut leaving the window up. He gunned the engine into life, all the time picturing Amethyst smashing a rock through the window and dragging him out. Les shoved the big car into first and started bumping back along the trail. He drove as fast as he could. But it was just a rough bush track and he could only do a certain speed or he'd crack the chassis. Les could imagine Amethyst running alongside the car slashing at the tyres then smashing the window no trouble at all.

Norton's face was drenched with sweat; his adrenalin was still pumping and so was his heart when he made it to the billabong. Without any caution, he bumped the Overlander straight up onto the two logs and drove on. Half-way across he skidded on a knot then bounced over it. There was a groaning crack and Les felt the log start to give. He gunned the Overlander and with water spraying up from under the car, bounced down on the other side just as the log on the right broke in half. The force of the water flowing against it started to dislodge the other. Les could see Amethyst swimming across the billabong or leaping over the broken logs and gunned the Overlander back up the first trail. He got to the end, took four seconds to disengage the wheel hubs, had a quick look either side of the road, then swung a bouncing right and drove straight past the hotel and back over Mungumby Creek. He swung left at Black Mountain National Park, gunned the Overlander along the bitumen, and was flicking mud and dust along the dirt road, and almost at Mount McDonald before he started to calm down. He wiped his face with a hanky, got the bottle of mineral water from his bag and drank what was left in one long swallow.

Jesus Christ, thought Les. What about that. That was just too scary and too diabolical for words. Forget the whole fuckin' thing. I ain't telling nobody nothing, as they say in that book I'm reading. Who'd believe me anyway? I can brush selling the story to the papers. My camera's back there with the fishes. And if I took anybody in there, what would they find? A pile of rocks with a few ashes under them. And I think I'd put my money on the crocodile — it would have eaten both of them by now. And you can bet there'd be no incriminating evidence in that old hut. She would have kept it clean, just in case she had to do a bunk herself. Besides, you can't drive in there now. I stuffed up the bridge. Somebody might stumble across that motorbike one day, they'd only think it belonged to some dope growers, Les smiled mirthlessly.

The only incriminating evidence Norton could think of was Sherry Waldren. If she's dead and I do say anything, he thought, I'm an accessory to her death for leaving her on the lounge with an OD and not reporting it. As for that greasy, fuckin' Beryl, I think I've figured out the rest of her angle. If I go looking for Jade and don't come back, I've found her. If I do come back, she still could be anywhere. So fuck Beryl. I'll tell her nothing either. The fat turd can still keep looking. All she'll get out of me is my hotel bill. No. That's it for Uncle Les. Cairns tonight. Sydney first thing tomorrow morning. But what about that old crocodile showing up again. I either entered the Twilight Zone there, or I've got a guardian angel. The big, red-headed Queenslander looked out the window and winked up at the sky. Thanks for that one, boss.

At the next bend, Norton slowed down for an old black utility full of wooden boxes tied with rope. Then another thought struck him. Hey! What about Woody? What about her? The writing's on the wall. She saw the whole thing. A wolf. That was the bloody creature — not me playing silly, bloody disc jockies. And tumbling water. The underground stream falling into the lagoon. And the third jewel. The danger. That was both Amethyst and the jewel round her neck. It's all written down on that piece of paper. Les shook his head. That little Rainbow Princess and all her mumbo jumbo. He dropped the Overlander back into second and went round the old black ute. You know, I wonder if we do all originally come from Mars ...? Les pulled in front of the ute and shoved the Overlander into third. After what I just saw today, I don't think anything'd surprise me from now on.

Available now

MUD CRAB BOOGIE
Robert G. Barrett

Les caught the DJ's eye. 'Hey mate,' he said.

'If I give you ten bucks, will you play two songs for me?'

'Mate,' replied the DJ. 'For ten bucks, I'll play you Tiny Tim singing *A Pub With No Beer* in Vietnamese.'

Look out Wagga Wagga.

Les Norton's in town and he feels like dancing.

Extreme Polo. The wildest game on water. That's what it said on TV. All Les had to do was drive down to Wagga Wagga for an old mate who owed him a favour, Neville (Nizegy) Nixon, and pick up the Murrumbidgee Mud Crabs. Then keep them at Coogee till they played the Sydney Sea Snakes in the grand final at Homebush Aquatic Centre. And naturally there would be a giant earn in it for him. Why not? thought Les, he had the week off from work. Next thing, Norton was on his way to the Riverina to meet the locals, the lovelies and oogie, oogie, oogie.

Do the Mud Crab Boogie.

ISBN: 0 7322 5843 X

Available now

SO WHAT DO YOU RECKON?
Robert G. Barrett

There was a time when Robert G. Barrett was 'in his forties, out of gaol, out of work, had three books published, but was stone motherless broke'. Political correctness had him confused and he had no desire to be more literary, even if he was the author of books that had been described as 'the scatological nadir of the pile' and 'insidiously revolting ... pray God they don't get published overseas'.

Then, through a twist of fate and good fortune, along came *People* magazine, who signed Barrett to produce a weekly column focusing on Australian life and its heroes and villains. *So What Do You Reckon?* is a collection of the best of these columns. Many are outrageous and all are written in Barrett's highly popular and immediately recognisable style. Together they represent an often funny, always entertaining and uniquely telling assessment of modern-day Australia.

ISBN: 0 7322 5961 4